I0788778

FORGED MAGIC

FATED TO THE WOLF – BOOK THREE

HEATHER RENEE

ISBN: 979-8352357132

Development Editing: Amy McNulty

Line Editing and Proofing: Jamie from Holmes Edits

Cover: Covers by Juan

Character Art Images: Samaiya Art

CONTENTS

atrix's Coven
l House
s Angeles
arlock
Holden's Pack
Vampire House
FATED
TO THE
WOLF

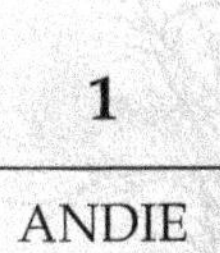

1

ANDIE

Burning fury. Icy-hot rage. Wrath unlike I'd ever experienced. That had been my constant mood since nearly a month ago when I'd been forced to walk away from *my* mate. From the man I could no longer feel inside my heart.

A fact that infuriated me to no end, because I only had myself to blame.

I was the one who'd used my syphon power. The one who'd taken on dark energy, allowing that magic to break the protective barrier between Foster and me, which had nearly killed him.

Me. I was the poison. I was the problem.

Yet, I was also the solution.

Though, I'd yet to convince the stubborn alpha Holden of that.

He'd learn soon enough. My willingness to be patient would only last for so long. The more my skin itched, the more I craved what I couldn't have, the less I was able to control myself.

A witch descended from two powerful founding families, one who couldn't keep herself in check, wasn't what the supernatural community needed, but I had no qualms about unleashing my power if it meant getting Foster back.

Once I had him, I knew our work wasn't even close to over. There were others who needed saving, too.

Charlie, for one. I'd been lost without her the last few weeks. I didn't know how I'd survived living so many years without her before, but I wasn't letting that happen again.

Moira would pay severely for taking the people I cared about away from me. She had taken my magic, my soulmate, my best friend, and my peace.

Though, I did have her to thank for pushing me to my limits. For forcing me to prove what I was capable of.

That was the only thing to bring a smile to my face in the past few weeks.

As I walked through the forest behind the main area of the coven, my magic ebbed and flowed freely from my hands, swirling around me in a comforting cocoon of power. The air warmed from my energy, and the surrounding animals quieted before scurrying away.

I took a deep inhale and grinned while closing my eyes and turning my face up toward the dark sky. "I'm coming for you soon, Moira. You can't hide forever."

She had run after the battle and hadn't stopped since—at least, from what we could tell. Beatrix had trackers working around the clock to track the dark witch's energy signature, but it was never in the same place for very long, something I was beginning to find more and more curious.

Moira might have been running, but she wasn't done. I knew that much for sure. She hadn't gotten what she wanted from me and, by now, I was certain she had figured out that I'd taken most of my power back.

The magic had been mine the day I'd been born and then taken from me when my mother worried that the energy would be more of a curse than a blessing. I didn't fault her for her choices, but I wished I'd had a say in things back then.

"Andie," Beatrix's voice called from several yards away.

I opened my eyes to find her staring at me with flat lips and narrowed eyes. "Beatrix."

"What are you doing out here?" she asked, even though I knew she was already well aware of what I did in the forest every day.

"Communing with the Earth," I said, my voice saccharine.

The old witch narrowed her wrinkled, green eyes on me, then tossed her silver hair behind her shoulder before stepping closer. "You know you're not supposed to be using your powers out here, Andie. You're making the coven uneasy."

An eerie laugh escaped from between my lips. *"I'm making the coven uneasy? What about me, Beatrix? What about all of the shitty things that have happened to me? Do I not get to be angry that I lost my parents, my aunt, my best friend, and even my soulmate?"*

A darkness pulsed within me. I gladly pulled on it, allowing that energy to keep pushing me forward. It wasn't Moira's dark magic, but it wasn't mine, either. It was like the emptiness where my bond with Foster had been.

Beatrix had tried to poke around and figure things out, but I'd yet to let her fully in. I wasn't ready to feel the anguish I knew was there. I couldn't break yet. I had to be strong. Not just for myself, but for all the people we still needed to save.

"Enough," Beatrix snapped. Her tone and the power that rolled off her shocked me.

So much so that I took a few steps back and drew my magic inward.

She pinched the bridge of her nose and sighed heavily. "You are going to be the death of me, child." Then, her gaze bored into mine. "You have every right to be angry, but the time for dwelling on that and moping has passed. You are a valued part of this coven, but you are too powerful right now. You've yet to learn how to properly harness the new energy inside you. That is something we all have a right to be concerned about, but it doesn't mean we don't care about you or sympathize with what's happened. Even so, it's time for you to stop this nonsense."

Ire rose within me, tinged with agony. My chest heaved with emotions I didn't want to feel, didn't want to process. "Stop what? This?" I sneered just as tendrils of midnight magic expanded from my hands, wrapping around my body before they began spinning rapidly.

"Don't say I didn't warn you," Beatrix tittered before she thrust her arms out in front of her.

In the next second, my back slammed into the tree behind me, snapping it in half. I screamed my frustrations as the top part of the oak fell behind me.

Without stopping to consider my injuries, I charged forward with my hands out. My power lashed out at the witch who was supposed to be part of my family, leaving red welts along her arms and neck where her green cotton shirt didn't cover her.

But she wasn't easily defeated. I relished the challenge just then.

Beatrix pushed back, sending lighter but just as powerful magic back at me. Though, hers wasn't trying to harm me. The energy was wrapping around me, encasing me in a bubble that only continued to grow smaller by the passing second.

I was forced to bring my arms closer and couldn't unleash my energy on her any longer. Her power tightened around my body until I could hardly breathe and certainly couldn't move.

She walked closer, a smirk on her wrinkled face. "Are you done now?"

"Screw you, Beatrix. You have no idea what I'm going through," I yelled at her through clenched teeth.

She made a clicking noise with her tongue and stepped

right into my personal space. "You're right. When I lost my parents over a century ago, I didn't grieve for them. Or when my sisters died in a battle unlike anything I hope you ever see in your lifetime. I hardly shed a tear. Or when my best friend died in my arms while we fought for someone else's freedom, and there was nothing I could do to save her. Of course, how would I know anything about what you're feeling? And I may have never found my soulmate, but that doesn't mean I haven't known sorrow thanks to never knowing him, Andie."

Unwanted tears fell down my cheeks, but my gaze remained hardened. I couldn't take on her pain. I had enough of my own. I needed to stay focused on the issues right in front of us. "You need to let me go."

"Not until you stop acting like a child," she countered.

"You're being ridiculous. The coven will be fine. I won't hurt them," I said with as even a tone as I could muster, given my trapped position.

She scoffed and smirked. "Trust, Andie. It's such a fickle thing. You've yet to realize there are dozens of witches here who would die for you, and you still don't see the bigger picture. We are all trying to help you. They're not afraid of you hurting them, but they do care if they don't feel as if your intentions are aligned with theirs. None of us want to fight for someone who only cares about what *they* need."

Her sharply spoken words penetrated the hard shell I'd kept around myself. I shook my head, trying to not care that I'd been selfish, that I'd failed to check in with Charlie's parents after she'd been taken, or that I hadn't attended any of the funerals that had been held for those who'd died the day Moira had attacked.

I'd avoided everything that could make me feel anything other than the wrath that kept me growing stronger. Hell, I could have bulldozed the pack by now, but even that task required me to open myself to emotions I wasn't ready for.

Except now, the longer Beatrix stared me down and kept

my body trapped, the harder the shield around my heart had to work to keep everything else at bay.

I'd done nothing other than give up pieces of my heart since I'd been a child. My dad, my aunt, my mom, my magic... the list went on. I just wanted to be selfish for this moment, however long it lasted. I didn't want to care about anyone else until I finally got what I wanted.

I didn't want to believe that was too much to ask for. Then again, I hadn't allowed myself to think about anything other than my soulmate and the vengeance I sought in weeks.

Vengeance that I'd yet to really do anything about except to grow stronger while hiding behind not only my own walls, but those of the coven.

Beatrix reached forward and flicked my forehead. "What you've failed to get through that thick skull of yours over the last few weeks is that while we may need you, Andie, you need the coven just as much. You can't get what you want on your own. I've let you throw your tantrum for long enough, but that time is over. Tonight is the new moon, and it's time for you to get your shit together."

The barrier around me began to crack from my efforts to break free. I couldn't let her tear through my protections with her words.

"The pack isn't running tonight," I said through gritted teeth.

Gemma, one of the few shifters from Holden's pack who'd befriended me, had been texting me daily with updates, even though I'd never once responded. She was a big reason I hadn't attacked the pack. I couldn't stand the thought of hurting her mate or putting their pup in danger if I showed up in their territory.

As furious as I'd been all these weeks, my rational mind hadn't completely left me. I was stronger after my weeks of training, but as the old witch had said previously, I was too powerful for my own good. By myself, I'd hurt people who might not deserve my wrath.

Beatrix smirked at me, the spark I used to hate bright in her eyes. "The pack run being canceled doesn't mean you're not seeing Foster tonight."

With one last effort, I broke the cocoon around me, then stepped into Beatrix's personal space. "Are you finally ready to go against Holden?"

I tried to keep the glee out of my voice, but I couldn't stop my grin when she nodded. "The alpha had his time, and if Foster isn't awake tonight when we get there, then there's no reason why you can't try to heal Foster on your own. *But* first, you have to agree to my terms or this whole thing is off."

My skin was humming with energy and my heart raced in anticipation. "I will do anything to see my mate."

Beatrix grabbed my hand and winked. "I thought you'd say that. Now, be still."

A fire pierced my palm where she was holding me. I tried to jerk away, but the old witch still had an iron grip.

"You will be bound to me until I release you, Andie Bishop. You will do as I say and nothing more. You will keep your power in check, and only then will you get to see Foster. Do you understand?" Beatrix asked, her voice full of authority.

Her magic pressed down on me. The silver of hers intermingling with my own energy, which was sometimes purple but now mostly midnight blue.

My first instinct was to tell her *no,* to jerk my hand out of her grip and figure out a way to get to Foster on my own, but Beatrix's earlier words echoed through my mind.

I needed her and the coven, whether I liked it or not. Even through my hurt and stubbornness, I could see the truth in that.

"Fine," I said with a growl that would have made Foster proud.

Beatrix *tsked.* "That won't do. Tell me you agree to my terms."

My blue eyes narrowed, and I blew pink strands of hair out of my face. "I agree to your terms, Beatrix Jacobs."

She released me as soon as I'd said her name then took a step back. "How do you feel?"

I shook my shoulders and closed my eyes. My power was still pulsing inside me, but it wasn't pushing for a release like it had been for the last several weeks.

"I'm good," I replied, purposely keeping the details to myself.

She rolled her eyes at me. "Right. Well, let's get going then. We don't have all night."

With a heavy sigh, I hoped like hell whatever I'd just agreed to didn't hurt in more ways than one. I wasn't sure I could handle any other kinds of pain.

2

FOSTER

Complete awareness had remained elusive for what seemed like countless days. Time was no longer relevant, and I had no clue if I was dead or something else altogether. All I knew for sure was that the hole in my heart wasn't supposed to be there.

Andie was.

Where I'd once felt the pull of our bond, there was nothing more than a void that led to nowhere good. I tried not to focus on the darkness, because I knew I had to fight. I just didn't understand what I was fighting against.

Worse than that, my wolf was gone. He hadn't been in my mind since I'd found myself wherever I was currently stuck.

There was nothing left within me except darkness and emptiness.

Not even rage existed any longer.

I knew I should have been furious for whatever situation I was stuck in, but that took energy I no longer possessed.

My memory only allowed me brief glimpses of what had happened. I knew we'd been fighting Moira's witches, and I knew we hadn't been winning, but I hadn't given up. I never would have, because Andie had needed me.

Yet, I'd left her somehow.

One minute, we'd been connected, and the next...nothing.

The silence inside my mind was almost unbearable.

Not knowing how much time had passed since I'd last felt anything real was starting to wear on me. As much as I wanted to keep pushing myself, I didn't know the point of doing so.

I could see nothing. Feel nothing. Hear nothing.

How was I supposed to make my way back to where I belonged without having anything other than my own thoughts? Hell, those didn't make sense half the time.

I was fucked, and I didn't know how much longer I could prevent myself from succumbing to the darkness that lulled me further into nothingness.

Maybe it would be better for everyone if I floated away. I'd failed to save my pack ten years ago, and I'd failed to stay by Andie's side when I'd promised her that I'd always keep her safe.

If I was gone, I couldn't hurt anyone else.

Is that where you've gone, Foster Kline? To self-pity? I thought you were stronger than that, a woman's voice sounded within my mind.

Who are you? I demanded.

The person you owe your life to. Now, I need you to get your thoughts straight and find me. I might have put you here, but only you can pull yourself out.

I badly wanted to be furious, but I still couldn't muster the rage I wanted. All I felt was hollowness inside.

Come on, Foster. Do you want someone else taking care of your mate if you don't come back? the woman taunted.

A snarl built inside me. *Don't talk about Andie.*

Why not? Does that upset you? Or do you still feel nothing?

I couldn't see anything. I didn't even know if I had a human form where I was, but the heaviness pressing in around me was new. I drew on that, finally getting glimpses of the agony I knew I should have been feeling all along.

Where am I? I shouted.

Find me and you'll find out, she replied challengingly.

I'd find her and rip her throat out for putting me wherever I was.

Fury fueled my thoughts as I pictured Andie's light-pink hair and creamy skin. And her smile, which made me want to do anything in the world for her.

I had to get back to her. I couldn't leave her alone.

A light flickered in my thoughts, or maybe it was right in front of me. I had no clue, but it was something different for the first time in days.

I thought to reach for it, but I had no arms with which to do so. I pushed my energy forward like I was trying to shift, and the flicker appeared again.

That time, I felt something else. No, some*one* else.

Was that the woman who'd locked me away? Fuck, I hoped so.

I continued to fight against the pressure holding me back, and inch by miserable inch, I got closer and closer to the pink glow. Then, when I was nearly ready to grasp whatever it was, something tugged on me, yanking me down and away.

No! I bellowed, but it was too late.

The light was gone, along with any hope I'd had.

Don't give up so easily, Foster. You should have more faith in your creator. The woman's voice echoed around me.

Just when I was going to demand she tell me what the hell was happening, my form began falling. I tried calling for my wolf, but there was still no sign of him within me.

My speed increased, and I couldn't breathe or move from the ball I felt like I was tightly bound in. All I could do was picture Andie's face and apologize for failing her. Again.

Then I hit a surface so hard that I felt like all my bones should have shattered on impact.

My mouth opened, but no air came in. My lungs burned, my skin was on fire, and an ire unlike I'd ever known scorched through me.

"Andie!" I bellowed, finally hearing my own voice.

Water splashed over me, soothing the burning throughout my body, but not calming my wrath. In the next second, I was on my feet and shaking the water from my hair.

I searched around me and found I was in a meadow surrounded by a forest. The night was dark thanks to the new moon, but there were still plenty of stars out.

My eyes closed, and I searched for the presence of the woman who had been talking to me. I could sense something in the air, but I couldn't pinpoint exactly where.

"Are you going to calm down now?" she asked, her voice sounding close.

I looked around me but still didn't see anyone. "Sure, I can do that." My words were partially true. As soon as I got my hands on the woman responsible for taking me from my mate, I'd feel a lot better.

"I didn't take you from Andie. Do you still not remember?" She *tsked*. "You were dying, and I kept your soul safe until it was time to rejoin your body," she said, but her voice felt like it was moving all around me instead of staying in one place.

"Who are you?" I insisted.

She sighed. "You still don't understand. Just know if you attack me, you're never going back to Andie."

That was a threat I didn't want to believe, but something in my chest tightened as if I should.

"Fine. Show yourself," I said, flexing my hands at my sides and coiling my muscles.

There was a tap on my shoulder, and I whirled around, but instead of launching myself forward as I'd planned, I stood there stupefied.

Holy shit.

I didn't know how I knew, given she looked nothing like the woman who'd approached me all those months ago, telling me to find my mate, but still, somehow, I was absolutely certain this being before me was the Moon Goddess Luna.

A faint, pink glow emanated around her tall form, and her silver eyes seemed to sparkle like the stars in the sky. Her ebony hair was braided over her shoulder, the end reaching her waist.

As she stepped forward, the midnight-blue dress she wore billowed behind her. "Do you understand now, young one?"

I didn't know how to answer her question. I believed she'd saved me, but I had no idea why I was here and not with Andie.

"I brought you here because you would have died otherwise, and it would have been your mate's fault. That never should have happened, but once again, the darker side of our world has been playing dirtier than normal."

"What do you mean?" I asked, staring up at her now that she was closer.

Her hand waved nonchalantly. "Nothing. What's most important is explaining what you need to know before you get back to your body." She glanced up at the sky. "Come. We don't have much time."

Luna moved ahead of me, her form seeming to float just over the grassy ground. I hurried after her until she stopped at a pond filled with bright-blue water, but when I looked down, all I could see was my reflection and not her standing next to me.

"What is this?" I asked when I got the impression it wasn't a normal body of water.

She grinned over her shoulder. "One of my creations. Now, as I was saying, time is of the essence here. We need to get you back before it's too late."

I took a few steps back. "What about my wolf?"

"He's waiting for you in there." She pointed to the water.

Of course, he was.

"But that's not what we need to talk about," she said, pushing her braid behind her back. "Things are going to feel different for you when you return. I can't say how or why exactly, just know this was unavoidable. Once you're back with the pack and coven, you and Andie will need to convince the races to work together. Enough of them have seen hardships that this shouldn't be a problem, but if it is, find a solution. You will need the others to do what needs to be done."

Confusion coursed through me. "Which races and why?"

She smiled, but it wasn't comforting. It seemed more like she enjoyed not giving me all the answers. "Just as I didn't tell you who your mate was, I cannot tell you who or why, but I know you'll figure it out just the same."

"Like the vampires we already met and the pack in Texas people keep talking about?" I asked, even though she said she wouldn't tell me.

"As I said, you'll figure it out. Now, the other thing you'll do is go see the Supernatural Council. Beatrix will understand why. She's already been thinking about it. Tell her to trust her instincts." Luna glanced at the sky again and frowned. "Lastly, when Andie gets her necklace back, she must destroy it. It cannot exist in your world any longer."

My lips opened to ask why, but I didn't bother. "Anything else?"

"Yes. Hold your breath," she said with a wink.

"What? Why?" I asked, but she didn't answer me.

Instead, the Moon Goddess gripped my wrist and shoved me toward the water. I wanted to jerk back, but the moment her skin touched mine, energy shot through me, fueling a power inside my chest that I'd never known had existed before.

"Swim fast, Foster," I heard her say right before my head was sucked under the surface of the pond.

The cool liquid pulled me farther under, and I blinked several times before I could see anything. There was a funnel of water ahead of me, and I swam toward it with my renewed energy.

My legs kicked hard, and my arms cut through the water as fast as I could manage until the current was doing most of the work for me.

I glanced ahead and could see the funnel getting smaller. *Shit.* That must have been why Luna had been in a hurry to shove me in the water.

I worked hard and finally found myself inside the swirling tunnel, but before I could celebrate the win, my vision faltered, and the air was pulled from my lungs.

Fuck.

This didn't seem good.

3

ANDIE

Beatrix took me back to my house and ordered me to go inside and change, stating she already had clothes laid out for me. Thanks to the little spell I'd agreed to, there was nothing I could do to object.

I opened my door and headed right for my bedroom. On my bed were black combat pants with lots of pockets on the sides, a thin, long-sleeved shirt of matching color, and black boots. Next to the clothes was a grey bag with a note on top that read, "Open me."

I changed first, and as soon as I had the boots laced, I dumped the contents of the bag onto my mattress.

Inside were potions and small knives that I'd worked with plenty over the last few weeks, but I wasn't sure why I needed them now unless the crazy witch thought to attack the pack in order for me to see Foster.

I grabbed the paper that had been on top and flipped it over. "Put as many of these in your pockets as you can fit. — B"

Well, okay, then.

Just as I was shoving knives into the sides of my boots, Beatrix appeared in my doorway. "Done?"

She was dressed identically to me, and her silver hair was pulled into a tight bun at the base of her head.

I nodded. "Now I am. What's all this for?"

She grinned, and it wasn't just any grin, but the evil one I used to hate. "None of it is lethal, but they're just in case we run into more trouble than we expect."

I plucked one of the knives from my boot. "With the right amount of force, I'd say this is plenty lethal."

"Well, then don't use the right amount," she stated, as if that was the most obvious thing ever.

My chest ached at the thought of seeing Foster again. He'd been kept from me for too long now. I hated that I hadn't fought harder for this moment, but with Beatrix's spell giving me a semblance of clarity and control over the worst of my emotions, I could see now that I'd only been afraid.

Afraid of what would happen if Holden had been right all along and I couldn't save Foster. Afraid of starting a war with the wolves that had been kind to me up until the battle with Moira. Though, even understanding all of that now, I could push those thoughts aside and focus on the task at hand.

I considered thanking Beatrix for doing whatever she'd done but then shrugged the thought away. I'd thank her properly if all of this worked as she seemed to think it would.

She walked out of my bedroom, and I followed her down the short hallway, then out the door. "We're going to teleport as close to the pack house as the trees will get us. Once we're there, we might have to fight our way in. Are you ready for that?"

"I'm ready to do whatever it takes to see my mate." I didn't need my rage to stay motivated about that.

She grabbed my hand. "Good. Let's go before someone tries to change my mind."

I tried to ask what she'd meant by that, but everything around us disappeared. The time for questions was over.

We reappeared behind a line of trees, and I could see the

pack house from where we stood. Wolves were roaming outside in small groups, and howls sounded through the air.

"They know something is going on," I whispered to Beatrix.

She nodded, keeping her eyes forward. "Yes, but it's not just us they need to worry about."

"What does that mean?" My eyes cut toward her, but she still didn't look at me.

"It means there is always something bigger at play than what we think. Now, we can do this one of two ways. We could cause a diversion that won't soon be forgotten around here, or we can try to sneak in, likely get caught, and fight until we find Foster."

Diversion and Beatrix seemed like a bad idea, but I didn't want to fight the wolves, either. It hadn't been the pack that had forbidden me from returning. It had been their alpha.

"Option one. What's the diversion?" I asked quietly.

She smirked. "I was really hoping you'd say that." She pulled a phone from her back pocket and sent a message to an unknown number.

"What did you do?" My eyes searched the open field in front of us, but I couldn't see anything happening.

"I called in a favor from a friend," Beatrix said, looking up at the sky while she answered.

My eyes followed hers until I finally saw something big flying toward us. "What is that?"

"Not what. *Who.* And that would be Lucinda Morrow. A fae who used to live around here. You'll like her. Maybe," Beatrix said just as the winged woman landed in the middle of the grassy area about fifty yards ahead of us.

"Hello, puppies," she called out to the wolves with a ball of magic bouncing in her hand. "Does anyone want to play fetch?"

Beatrix shoved me hard. "Go."

Instead of getting to watch what this Lucinda had

planned, we ran toward the pack house as soon as the wolves who had been blocking our path started moving toward the fae.

I could hear snarls and yelps behind us, but I didn't turn around. We had to get inside. We had to find Foster.

As soon as I stepped on the back porch, feeling like success was within reach, Holden opened the back door. The wrinkles around his light green eyes intensified as he glowered at both of us with his arms crossed. "You're not coming in this house, Beatrix."

She feigned a sweet smile. "I know." Then she sent a stream of silver magic toward the alpha's chest.

He dodged her first hit and glanced at me. "Don't do this to Foster, Andie. He needs more time."

"I gave you time. And you're wrong. He needs *me*," I said, sending one of the potions from my pockets toward his feet.

Mack came out behind Holden just as blue energy wrapped around his legs. The beta met my hardened gaze and shook his head. "You shouldn't be here."

"I should have been here the whole time and you know it."

Other wolves joined us on the porch, and there was no easy way past them. I dodged teeth that tried nipping at my legs and threw more potions of varying colors.

A set of claws ripped the back of my shirt, and I spun around before the second attempt could cut through my skin. Blue eyes bored into me, and snapping teeth dripped with saliva. I didn't know who this was, but they clearly weren't happy to see me.

Too damn bad.

I tossed another potion, but the wolf dodged the throw and pounced on me. My head slammed into the wooden surface of the deck, but I kicked my feet up and out, forcing the shifter off me.

I couldn't decide if I was thankful Beatrix had forbidden

me from using my overly powerful energy or annoyed, because if I could just unleash a fraction of what I'd been practicing with, this could be over already.

Given I also knew the latter was the exact reason I hadn't shown up at the pack on my own, I did my best to be more grateful while I threw more tiny bottles and shoved more foaming-at-the-mouth wolves out of my way before finally making it inside the pack house.

I slammed and magically sealed the door shut behind me. I wasn't sure how much time that would buy me, but every extra second counted.

With a deep inhale, I quieted my thoughts, closed my eyes, and did my best to concentrate on locating Foster within the big pack house.

Even though I hadn't been able to feel my connection to him, I hoped being physically closer to his body would help. Unfortunately, that wasn't the case. At least, not enough to know which of the three people I could sense still inside was my mate.

While frustrated with that fact, I didn't sit around and pout. Instead, I followed the first and weakest bit of energy to the second floor. When I shoved open the door, I cursed and bowed my head. "I'm sorry."

Before the bedridden old man could respond, I closed the door and quickly turned for the other end of the hallway. Entering the other room more gracefully, I scanned the dark corners, but I saw nothing.

Weird. I'd sworn there'd been something there before, but apparently, I was wrong. I backed out and took three steps forward until Holden leapt from the first floor and propelled himself over the railing.

"Andie, you need to stop this." He growled.

"Stop what?" I demanded. "Stop trying to get to my mate, whom I have every right to see? You can't keep him from me, Holden. I saved Benjamin and James from dark magic. Why don't you understand that I'm what Foster needs? I gave you time to do things your way, but that time is up. Where is he?"

Holden stepped forward with his hands partially shifted to claws. "It was agreed by pack leadership that the best thing for everyone was to keep you away and, if you can't even sense when he's near you, maybe you're not his real mate."

The alpha's words were harsh, unexpected, and felt like a slap across my face. "How dare you? I thought I knew who you were, but clearly, Foster and I were wrong, and I never should have left him here this long."

Holden had Beatrix to thank for keeping his life, because if he'd said that to me without her spell dampening my magic, I wouldn't have thought twice about striking him down for that comment.

He sneered, and his green eyes flicked in the direction of the room I'd just looked in. "He's right behind you, Andie. If you were his mate, you shouldn't have missed him."

A stabbing pain struck my heart. He didn't seem to be lying, and I hated more than anything that I briefly wondered if maybe the wolf was right.

Still, I tried to refute what he was saying. "The room is empty. I didn't miss him. Unless you have a witch concealing his body, you're full of shit and trying to play games that I don't appreciate."

A frown pulled down on his face, and he took another step closer, but his stance was no longer defensive. "You had to have missed him. He was there before you showed up."

Holden's voice changed from wrathful to confused as he spoke, then he shoved past me and headed right for the door I'd just come out of. He turned on the lights and I followed in behind him.

The covers to the bed were thrown onto the floor, something I hadn't noticed before, and the window was open. I hadn't thought much of it before, but now with Holden's confusion? What if someone had come to take Foster?

What if Moira had gotten my mate?

"Fuck!" I pointed a finger at the alpha. "This is your fault. If he dies, I will hold you solely responsible."

I didn't bother to let him respond. Instead, I raced for the balcony and jumped over, landing on my feet with an echoing thud.

Beatrix was there, a grim expression on her aging face. "Where is he?"

"I don't know, but we're going to fucking find out. Right now," I snarled just as the fae woman came waltzing into the pack house as if she lived here herself.

She flicked long, iridescent, teal hair behind her and smirked. "That was fun." She picked a chunk of fur off her black jeans and straightened the white tank top she wore. "What's next?"

Beatrix glanced over, offering Lucinda a tight smile. "Nothing. Thanks for helping while you were in town."

She pouted. "Nothing? You're telling me that I ditched Finn for nothing more than a game of fetch? You've gotten boring in your old age, Beatrix."

I nodded at the fae. "How good are you at tracking?"

Maybe we could still use her assistance. I didn't know this woman, but if Beatrix had brought her in to help, then that was good enough for me now.

Her bright-blue eyes sparked with mischief. "The sky gives me an advantage. What do you need?"

"My mate was taken tonight. I don't know by whom, but it likely just happened when we arrived." I pointed to the room upstairs. "He was staying up there and taken out the window."

Lucinda grinned and sharp, feathered wings expanded from her shoulder blades. "Be right back."

Holden's hard voice sounded from behind me. "You can't just invite anyone you want into my territory."

I wasn't sure if he was talking to me or Beatrix since I

hadn't actually invited the fae woman in, but I didn't care.

I took three steps toward him and poked him roughly in the chest, making him stumble. "We can do whatever we want. If you think you can stop me right now, then I welcome you to try."

As much as I'd admired and respected Holden before all of this, I was furious and heartbroken and hellbent on revenge. If he wanted a fight with me, no longer would I hesitate to give him one.

Before he could respond, Lucinda reappeared. "I didn't sense anyone in that room besides wolf shifters and you. Could one of the dogs have taken him?"

Holden snarled at her comment, but I didn't dismiss it so easily, given everything that had happened in the past. "Possibly. The witch we're dealing with has a tendency to control other supernaturals with her dark magic."

The fae smirked. "Then let's hope the trail leads us to her so we can teach her a few lessons. I'm happy to help if I get to kick some ass."

Oh, I really did like this woman.

I looked over at Beatrix, and she didn't seem thrilled with the idea of a chase. "We need to go to the coven first."

My head shook sharply. "No, you need to go there. *I* need to find my mate. He needs me, Beatrix. I won't wait any longer. Too much time has already been wasted."

She pinched the bridge of her nose and breathed deeply. "Fine. If you find him, you call me first. Do you understand?"

"Sure, Beatrix," I said, because that was the only way to get out of here quickly, thanks to the agreement I'd made with her earlier.

The old witch rolled her eyes, then turned to Lucinda. "Don't let her do anything stupid. We need her."

The fae saluted Beatrix. "Yes, ma'am."

"This is a terrible idea," Beatrix muttered, but I was done

talking. She and Holden could finish whatever they needed to do. I had somewhere to be.

I headed toward the door and Lucinda followed, folding her wings back to fit through the door. When we were outside, the wolves were scattered about. Some were shifted still, and some were back in their human forms.

None of them looked at us with kindness, but I snarled back just as equally. "Because of your stubborn alpha, Foster is missing. Before you decide to be angry with me, just remember this all could have been avoided if I'd been able to see him."

A hand grabbed my wrist, and I spun around with a glowing fist raised to find Mack, the pack beta, standing next to me. His normally shaved hair had grown out, and his normally wide-set shoulders were hunched. "I'm sorry, Andie."

Lucinda nudged me with her foot and nodded behind us. "I can sense big energy that way."

My eyes moved in the direction she pointed. "That's where the coven is."

"Then, we better get going." Her wings extended, and she grabbed my upper arm before pushing us into the air.

I glanced back down at Mack before we got too far away. "If you're really sorry, follow us and help me get him back."

My affection for the wolves might not have been high at the moment, but I would take any help I could get if it meant I got Foster back alive.

Anything else, I wasn't sure I could survive.

4

FOSTER

Getting back to my body was an experience I hoped to never repeat again. As soon as my soul had been sucked inside my physical form, a painful howl had echoed through my mind. *Wolf.*

Our connection stitched itself back together slowly and painfully while I lay in bed. I couldn't move or hardly breathe as I adjusted to the sensations and fought to feel my wolf's presence again.

Minutes or maybe even hours later, I finally heard his voice.

Andie.

We have to find her, I replied.

He was already clawing at my mind to shift and search for her. It had been too long since we'd seen her. Yet, there was a hesitation inside me.

The tether I normally felt to our mate wasn't there. It hadn't returned like my connection to my wolf had and that had my rage intensifying.

Once my thought registered with the wolf, he asked, *Do you think she isn't ours?*

I don't know, but we still need to find her.

He growled in agreement, and I glanced around the room I'd woken up in. There were no lights on, and the door was closed. I could hear voices downstairs, but whatever the wolves were up to wasn't something I cared to involve myself in until I found Andie. I needed to know what was going on with our bond and if she was okay.

Let's go, my wolf said, urging me toward the window.

I yanked the glass open and looked around. I couldn't see the front of the pack house, but I could sense there were even more wolves out there.

It's the new moon. They're supposed to be on the pack run, my wolf reminded me.

Maybe they were just getting ready to leave. I didn't know and wasn't going to wait around to find out.

I crawled out the window, sticking close to the siding until I got to the side of the house farthest from the noise. We were maybe twenty feet up, and I jumped without a second thought. As soon as I landed on two feet, I searched around us.

Nobody was coming closer. It was time to shift.

Calling my wolf forward was painful, as if we were transforming for the first time. Bones cracked slower, and my muscles ached from being pulled taut, then ripped apart before being stitched back into a new form. I ignored the rising nausea and pushed harder to bring my wolf energy to the surface.

When I was finally on four paws, my breathing was rough and everything ached, but it wasn't enough pain to distract us from where we wanted to be: with our mate.

My wolf trotted forward, taking it easy to start. The longer our strides became, the less pain we felt. He headed toward the coven. Given Andie hadn't been at my side when I'd awoken, that was where I assumed she'd be. If she wasn't...I wasn't sure what we would do.

It took nearly twenty minutes to get to the barrier of the

coven, but as we crossed the road, I breathed a little easier. We were almost there, almost back to Andie.

After spending days or weeks or maybe even months suspended in a nothingness with my emotions suppressed, I wasn't sure how to feel, but focusing on Andie was helping.

Let me shift back, I said to my wolf.

He easily relinquished control, but this transformation to my human form was just as painful as the prior had been.

I stretched side to side and groaned. *This shit better not last long.*

My wolf grunted in reply.

I glanced down at myself. I was wearing grey sweatpants and a white T-shirt. I didn't have on shoes or socks, and I probably looked like death, but that didn't stop me from continuing forward. Andie wouldn't care what I looked like.

When my bare foot touched the barrier to the coven, a shock blasted through me and sent me back a solid ten feet. I landed on my ass in the dirt road and glared.

"Beatrix!" I shouted. She would have been the only one to remove my access. I didn't know why she would have done that, but she was going to find out how I felt about it just as soon as I saw her.

I got up and walked back to the shield, glaring hard at the opaque magic. As much as I wanted to see inside, all I could spot in front of me were trees that didn't actually exist.

"Beatrix!" I yelled again. "Let me see Andie right fucking now."

We can shift and I'll howl until someone comes out like we used to do, my wolf suggested.

I considered that, but something wasn't right, and I didn't want to be quick to act without knowing what I was doing.

My eyes closed, and I listened to the sounds around us. There were animals in the forest we'd just walked out from. Birds in the sky. And nothing else.

That wasn't normal. Not around here, anyway.

My fist raised, and I was tempted to slam it against the shield, but I knew that would only result in more pain for me.

"Ava, Evelyn, Benjamin!" I bellowed, hoping someone would respond if Beatrix wasn't going to.

I flexed my hands at my sides and gritted my teeth as I waited and paced in front of the barrier. If someone didn't let me in soon, I was going to lose my shit.

Do you hear that? my wolf asked.

I paused my movements and calmed my racing heart. When I focused, the sound of beating wings too big to belong to any normal animal sounded above us.

My wolf pushed to shift again, but I stopped him, focusing on the incoming…fae? I was pretty sure that was what I was seeing, even though their kind didn't come around often. More interesting was that this one wasn't alone. She was holding another woman and…holy shit…

Andie.

I didn't know if it was me or my wolf who'd thought her name, but what was more important was the fact that the moment I laid eyes on her, the bond I'd let myself consider might have been gone for good reignited.

I fell to my knees and nearly cried from the joy coursing through me. My hands shook, and energy exploded inside my chest, making my heart race so wildly, I was sure I was going to have a heart attack.

It was *her*. Our mate. And she was safe.

At least, I assumed that last part based on the smile beaming from her perfect face.

The fae stopped right in front of me, and Andie stumbled into my arms. I tried to stand and catch her, but we ended up tumbling to the ground with the force she used to wrap her arms around my neck.

"Foster," she cried into my neck.

My hands rubbed over her back, and I held her close to me. "I missed you so fucking much."

She pulled back just enough to kiss me, and I thought my heart was going to explode from the power of our bond. The invisible tether that had pulled us together before had been nothing like this one. My connection to Andie this time was strong and sure and unbreakable.

I had so many questions I wanted to ask, but holding her and touching her as I was…that was everything. I couldn't stop from stroking her creamy skin, running my fingers through her pink hair, kissing her as if my life depended on it.

My heartbeat thundered so loudly in my chest that the sound echoed inside my head and my body trembled from so many emotions.

"I can't believe you're really here," Andie whispered against my lips when our kisses began to slow.

I pressed my forehead to hers. "I'm sorry I couldn't get back to you sooner."

A throat cleared behind us. "Um, as uncomfortable as this is, maybe the two of you could get off the ground and tell me why there are no asses here for me to kick as previously promised?"

As much as I'd missed Andie and needed time alone with her, clarifying a few things first would probably be the smarter choice, given I had no idea how long I'd been gone.

I was on my feet first, then helped Andie up. She dusted herself off, and I wrapped an arm around her waist, holding her close to me.

The fae pointed at me. "How did you get here when you were supposed to be unconscious in that pup house back there?"

A growl built in my chest. "That's *my* pack house and the rest isn't your business, Fae."

Andie's palm covered my chest. "Foster, this is Lucinda. She's a friend of Beatrix's and was going to help me hunt down the person or people I thought took you. Why weren't you in the room when I finally got there?"

Lucinda smiled smugly at me, but I ignored her and gave Andie my full attention. "I woke up and knew I had to find you. I didn't want to deal with the wolves on a new moon, so I went out the window. I didn't know you were at the pack house."

"It's fine." Her hand pressed over my chest again, then she frowned. "But are *you* okay? I can sense something different about you that's hard to describe."

I flicked my gaze to the fae, who was still standing close with her arms crossed and too much interest in her bright eyes.

"Maybe we can talk about this later," I said quieter to Andie.

My mate glanced back and nodded. "Sure. Let's get you inside the coven and checked out."

Lucinda grabbed Andie's other arm and spun her around. "Uh, nope. I didn't bring you over here to get left in the dark. What's going on? Beatrix only told me you needed help breaking into that house. Now I know there's something else happening, and I want to know what."

My fingers shifted into very sharp claws, but before I could swipe at the fae's hand still holding on to my mate, Andie blasted her with midnight-colored magic, forcing Lucinda to let go and sending her back a few feet.

Andie met her steely gaze with a hardened one of her own. "While I appreciate your help, you have no idea what we've been through the last six weeks. If my mate doesn't want to talk about what he went through right now, then he doesn't have to."

Lucinda arched a brow at both of us, then turned around. "Beatrix, you've been hiding more things from me than usual."

The witch, Holden, and Mack walked out of the tree line, none of them looking happy to see me standing next to Andie.

"I've been a little too busy to call," Beatrix replied before casting her eyes between Andie and me.

I expected her to say something else, but she stayed quiet.

Lucinda extended her impressive six-foot-wide wings. "As fun as this has been, if I'm not kicking anyone's ass, I need to get back to Finn." She turned to Beatrix. "Come see me at the penthouse. I'll be in town for a little while. We should catch up."

Beatrix gave her a curt nod. "I'll do that soon."

With one last glance around, Lucinda launched herself back into the sky.

"How did you get here, Foster?" Holden asked first.

"I shifted and ran." My hold on Andie tightened, not liking the tone in his voice or the way he glared at Andie next to me. "Is that a problem?"

He shared a look with Mack that I didn't like, but Beatrix walked between them and spoke first. "How about we discuss anything more inside?"

Andie tried to pull me along, but I stopped and looked at the old witch. "Why did you take away my ability to get through the shield?"

Her brows furrowed. "I didn't." Then she reached out to grab my arm and energy pooled beneath where she touched. "Interesting. We'll get you access again after we're done talking."

Interesting was right. The Moon Goddess had said she'd saved me and that things would be different when I returned, but I was beginning to realize that I should have demanded more details about what "different" was going to entail.

5

ANDIE

Seeing Foster standing outside the coven gutted me in the best way possible. I couldn't believe he was finally here with me. That I could touch him and feel the connection to him again. Only when the thrill of knowing he was okay began to settle, I realized nothing was quite the same as it had been before.

Beatrix let the shifters inside the coven, and we followed her to the meeting building, where she quickly sealed the walls so that no one could overhear our conversation who wasn't supposed to.

"How about we start at the beginning," Beatrix said once we were all seated in the chairs still out from the last gathering in here. "Six weeks ago, Moira attacked the pack. Dozens were killed or taken to God knows where and Foster fell into a coma. Foster, do you care to fill in the blanks for us there?"

He glanced down at me and squeezed our combined hands. "I don't know much. I was aware for a lot of it, but not to what was happening around my body. I was stuck somewhere in the dark and had no awareness of time. Most of my senses were gone and it wasn't until today that I finally spoke with the Moon Goddess."

All eyes, including mine, widened at that last bit.

"What does *she* have to do with this?" Holden asked first.

Foster still kept his gaze on mine. "She said that she'd saved me and that I couldn't come back until the new moon. That I needed to be with Andie again in order to help the supernatural races, that we needed to all work together."

Beatrix stepped forward and held her hands up toward Foster. "Did she say why?

Foster shook his head. "Just that things would be different and—"

"That's an understatement." Beatrix scoffed and I agreed with her.

His chest rumbled, likely from being interrupted. "*And* she said that what happened was unavoidable. We're supposed to work with the other races—I'm assuming to beat Moira—and Luna also said that we need to go see the Supernatural Council." Foster gave Beatrix his full attention this time, and they had some weird stare-down I didn't quite understand.

"What does the council have to do with this?" Mack asked.

Beatrix looked over at the beta. "Enough that it deserves our attention sooner rather than later."

Foster brought his attention back to me. "She also said that when we find your necklace, we have to destroy it."

Now, *that* I wasn't happy to hear. The necklace in question had been a gift from Aunt Junie. Even if I hadn't known what it meant back then, the stone was still important to me.

"I don't know that I can do that," I said softly.

"If you can't, then I will," Beatrix said. "Given how dark your energy has been, I can presume it's because Moira tainted your magic with every attempt she made to steal it from the moonstone. Foster will help balance things out for you now that he's back. Maybe if you're done acting like an out-of-control teenager, I can even help with a few things I've seen you doing wrong."

Foster snarled at her, but I shook my head. "She's not wrong. Holden wouldn't let me see you and I didn't take it well."

Foster turned slowly in his seat to face his alpha. "You wouldn't let her see me?"

His tone was calm yet deadly, sending goosebumps along my arms.

I nearly opened my mouth to defend the alpha but decided Holden had dug that grave for himself. He could find his own way out.

"Listen, Foster," Holden pleaded. "You might not remember, but I do. Andie nearly killed her coven and half of our pack. She'd lost control, and I had no way to prove that she wouldn't do the same thing again if I allowed her into the pack house. We lost more than you can understand that day."

He wasn't completely wrong. We all had lost too much in the fight against Moira, but keeping Foster from me hadn't been the way to make things right.

"She's my mate. You didn't have the right to make that decision," Foster said, still sounding calm, but his grip on my hand was nearly painful.

"I'm your alpha. I have every right," he countered.

Foster released me and shot out of his chair. His heavy strides closed the distance between the two alphas until Foster was towering over him. "Then maybe we should fix that."

Mack stood and put his hand on Foster's chest. "Why don't we save that conversation for a later time? What's important now is that you're awake, Andie seems more in control than ever before, and we have information we didn't before."

"The beta is right," Beatrix said. "What the Moon Goddess

said is intriguing, given my previous thoughts about wanting the races to find a way to live together instead of separately. If she says we should gather the other races and see the Supernatural Council, then I already have thoughts about why that might be."

"Care to share those thoughts?" I asked since Holden and Foster were still having their standoff.

"I heard a rumor that the wolf council was disbanded without many people knowing. I also know that the fae have no interest in obeying the Supernatural Council after they were compromised last year. Based on the direction I've been led by our ancestral magic lately, I think it's time for the council to cease to exist and for us to start a new world."

That had everyone's attention again. "What do you mean?" Holden asked as Foster came back to sit with me.

"I'm sorry," he whispered in my ear.

I leaned my head against his shoulder and listened to Beatrix's response as she paced in front of us, talking with her hands.

"The council hasn't properly governed our races in years. They used to be a mixture of different supernaturals, and the roles were supposed to change hands every year to prevent any corruption, but given their identities are kept secret and memories of what they did and learned during their time there are supposedly wiped once members left their seats...how are we to know that's even been happening?"

She made a damn good point. Those were all things I hadn't known but probably should have.

Beatrix continued. "They don't even enforce their own rules anymore. Instead, they send out hunters to handle the dirty work. Ones who don't always uphold the rules that are supposed to protect supernaturals, then pretend nothing went wrong. It's time someone told the council that enough is enough. I'm tired of wondering if they're going to step in when they shouldn't or do something stupid to get us all exposed."

"You've given this a lot of thought," I said, "but what about those who don't like rules? I may not understand the workings of this world as well as most, but it doesn't sound like a good idea to remove what some may consider a big enough threat to make them think twice before acting with evil intent. If there is no one to impose laws, people could do whatever they want."

She smiled widely and stopped pacing. "It won't be easy, but there will still be law and plenty to fear. No worries there."

Something about her response didn't make me feel better.

"But we're getting ahead of ourselves here." Beatrix pointed at Foster. "You have new energy inside you. How was your wolf when you shifted?"

Foster grimaced. "It was painful, but after a few minutes, he was fine. Not stronger, but not weaker, either."

Beatrix tapped her chin and hummed. "Maybe it's the bond between the two of you that's causing things to seem different."

Holden scoffed. "What bond? It was broken the day Andie nearly killed everyone. It wasn't just the risk of letting her into the pack, it was their lack of connection that reaffirmed my decision to keep her out."

I rubbed a hand over my chest, feeling Foster now but remembering all those days that I'd felt lost without him. Could Holden have possibly been right to do what he had?

"How did you know our bond was broken?" Foster asked with a growl in his voice.

"Because I'm your alpha," he answered cockily. "At least for now."

Clearly, the two of them were going to need to have words, but at a much later time. I needed Foster to myself once we were done catching up here.

Beatrix came over to me and placed her palm on my forehead. Shivers raced through my body and magic wanted to escape from my hands, but I was able to keep control more easily than usual.

"The wolf might be right." She bent down and briefly grabbed both of my hands. "The two of you need to finalize your bond again. It shouldn't have been possible for it to break that easily in the first place, but we can just be grateful that you have a second chance. I need you to have your shit together for what's next."

Now that I had Foster with me and I was taking Holden's words into consideration, a thought I'd considered before yet had refused to accept circled through my mind. I hadn't wanted to believe it could be true, because then I would have had to accept that my mate was never coming back to me.

"I think Foster died that day. At least for a short time. That's why our bond ceased," I said quietly when Beatrix was done examining me.

Foster met my tear-filled gaze. "No, I didn't. The Moon Goddess saved me."

I shook my head and placed a hand over my heart. "I killed you, Foster. A part of me knew it then, and I know it now. She brought you back and gave *me* another chance to make things right."

Damn it, that was painful to admit, but with the words spoken out loud, I knew I wasn't wrong.

Foster let go of my hand and wrapped an arm around me, pulling us closer together. "Whatever happened then doesn't matter any longer."

In that, I badly wanted to believe he was right.

"So, what's the plan now?" Mack asked, breaking the tense quietness and still standing next to Holden.

"Now, we need Andie and Foster to go have some alone time." Beatrix smirked, and my cheeks reddened.

Then, I remembered I wasn't the same witch I had been

when we'd bonded last time. I had the ability to make sure the coven had no clue what was happening within the walls of our house. They weren't ever going to get another chance to know when I had sex again.

Then my heart constricted. There was one person who was still supposed to remember the first time. One who wasn't here. My best friend.

Foster held me tighter when I tensed against him, and I prayed we'd get Charlie back soon. I missed her too damn much.

"Once their bond is complete, I'll make sure Andie isn't going to kill his wolf with her syphon energy," said Beatrix. "After that, we need to gather the other supernaturals and deal with the council."

"And have you pinpointed Moira's location yet?" Holden asked. He had just as much of a reason to find that witch as I did.

She'd not only taken my best friend, but the alpha's daughter as well.

Beatrix frowned. "Not for any length of time that we can do anything with, but we're working on it night and day. I assure you of that."

Holden snarled. "As are we."

Of that, I had no doubt.

Moira had messed with the wrong pack and coven when she'd come for us. No matter how long it took, we'd find her. She'd pay for everything she'd done.

6

FOSTER

Once the meeting was over, I gladly took Andie back to her house. The bond between us was burning inside me, and I'd missed her so fucking much that I could hardly breathe, even though I was constantly touching her.

When we were inside, Andie surprised me by pushing me against the wall before the door was even all the way closed. "I don't know how I survived without you all these weeks, but I'm glad I managed," she murmured, pushing up onto her toes and pressing her lips to mine.

My left hand tangled into her hair and the right wrapped around her waist, holding her tightly to me. "I'm sorry I wasn't here," I said quietly between kisses.

Her breath came out in heavy puffs. "That wasn't your fault. It was mine."

I shook my head before she even finished speaking. "No, it wasn't, but I didn't come back to argue with you."

She grinned up at me. "What *did* you come back for?"

My fingers brushed over her cheek. "To keep you safe. To love you. To be the mate I should have been before. The one you deserve."

Her eyes filled with emotion, shining under the light that was leaking in from the porch through the window. "You already were, and you still are."

I gathered her into my arms and pressed her head against my chest. The need to apologize was still strong, but I knew that wasn't what she wanted to hear. Plus, if I didn't focus on my love for Andie, then I was going to remember what Moira had done and how Holden had kept us apart.

Andie's hand skimmed over my grumbling chest. "It's okay, Foster. We're together now, and that's all that matters. We'll get the rest of them back soon."

I jerked back, still holding on to her arms but needing to see her face. "The rest of who back?"

A tear fell down her cheek. "Charlie, Piper, and so many others. They were taken by Moira's witches when they retreated. We haven't been able to find them since."

Fuck. Andie had been all alone *and* Holden had banished her from the pack? I wanted to fucking kill him for that, or at least tear him a new one, but that was a conversation to worry about later.

"I'm so sorry, Andie. I'm sure Charlie is fine. Moira should know better than to kill her," I said, then I realized that probably wasn't the right thing to say to make my mate feel better.

Andie's frown turned into a sneer. "But there's so much that witch can do without taking their lives, and that's what pisses me off most."

Her fury ignited like gasoline to a match. It was the first glimpse I'd had of what the others had been talking about before, but how could they have faulted Andie for her rage after what had happened?

I didn't blame her. I couldn't wait to burn that bitch of a witch to ash.

"What can I do for you?" I asked her, softening my voice

as best I could. She didn't need my wrath along with her own.

Andie chuckled darkly. "You're the one who just got out of a coma, and I mauled you as soon as we stepped inside. I should be asking *you* that."

My lips pressed to her forehead, and I squeezed her shoulders tightly. "Your love is something I will never deny."

Her breath came out harshly as she took my hand, leading us away from the entryway. "The bond feels so different now."

"It's what I suspect it should have always been." I grinned, thinking about how things might have been before if Andie's magic hadn't been taken from her.

She glanced back at me before turning down the hallway, her lips twitching upward. "I wonder what else might be different."

As much as I wanted to love all of Andie, I wasn't going to rush her into completing the bond just because Beatrix said we should. "We have a chance to do this all over. I don't want you to feel pressured to do anything just because we accepted the connection before."

The hurt on her face had me stepping back a step.

She closed the distance between us easily and rested her hand over my chest. "I have no doubts in my heart or mind when it comes to who and what you are to me, Foster Kline. *I* don't need time, but if *you* do, then that's okay. You were gone for weeks. I'd understand…"

My mouth covered hers before she could finish. I didn't need time, and I didn't ever want to be the cause of pain on her face again.

I pressed my tongue against her soft lips, and she opened for me. My hands moved down and over her ass so that I could lift her up. She wrapped her legs around my waist, kissing me back with fervor.

"I love you, Andie. All of you. Now and forever," I murmured into her mouth.

Her nails dug into my shoulder and neck. "Then take me to our room and show me."

Her wish was my command—and only mine.

I walked us to the bedroom and kicked the door closed behind us in case anyone decided to walk into the house uninvited. I laid Andie on the bed, and my hands began to tug at her pants, but she sat up, giving me pause.

"Watch this," she said proudly.

Her hands pressed together, and she closed her eyes. My gaze roamed over her body, then finally landed back on her joined hands when a midnight-colored light pulsed from them.

She muttered words under her breath that I didn't understand, then separated her fingers. Energy rose up and around us until the tendrils touched the ceiling, spreading out until they disappeared from sight.

"What was that?" I asked.

She winked. "A privacy shield."

Ah. So, the coven *wouldn't* know we had sex this time, which was probably good because I had a feeling Beatrix wouldn't have saved Andie from that embarrassment twice.

"You've been busy," I whispered against her cheek while my hands slid under her shirt.

She nodded against my lips. "I had a lot of free time on my hands."

I didn't want to talk about the time I'd been gone. More than anything else, I just wanted to feel Andie and know she was mine in every way, like she should have been all along.

I lifted her shirt up and over her head before throwing it behind us. Her pants weren't as easy to discard, but she lay back on the mattress and kicked off her boots before I helped her wiggle out of the thick material.

She propped herself up on her elbows and pointed at my chest. "You're wearing too many clothes."

My lips twitched into a grin while I removed my shirt. "Is this better?" She shook her head. "The pants, too?"

Her head shook again. "Everything. It all has to go."

I leaned forward, slowly dragging my mouth over her stomach, then up to her mouth, before whispering, "Then, so do all of yours."

She shivered beneath me, and her hand wrapped around my neck when I tried to pull back and finish undressing.

Andie's tongue parted my lips, and I gladly let her in. Her legs wrapped around my waist, and my straining cock pressed against her center. I could smell her arousal. The need to drive into her was stronger than ever as the bond pulsed inside my chest.

The connection between us was tangible. We clawed at each other, needing to be closer, to feel every inch of the other.

"Clothes. Off. Now," Andie demanded between breaths.

I stood up, only long enough to shove my sweatpants and boxer briefs off, then I had Andie back in my arms and moved us farther onto the bed.

Her underwear was still on, so while she unhooked her bra, I ripped the black cotton at her hips and flung the material behind us.

She grinned at me as the bra finally disappeared. "I love you so damn much."

I growled into her ear, nipping at the lobe. "Never as much as I love you."

I was tempted to ask if she was ready for the bond to be complete again, but she grabbed a hold of my throbbing dick and guided me where she wanted. "Prove it."

Fuck. I hated that Andie had been in pain all these weeks while I'd been gone, but I couldn't deny this new version of her—one that seemed more confident in who she was—was sexy as sin.

I thrusted inside her, trying to be slow, but my mate wasn't having any of that. She lifted her hips and begged for everything I had to give. As soon as I was fully seated, energy exploded from my chest and wrapped around us.

It was bright blue like my wolf's eyes, but then it turned darker until it was a deep blue like the depths of the ocean, a few shades lighter than Andie's magic had been.

Her eyes widened, and her mouth opened, but no words came out. Though, they weren't necessary. I could hear the rapid beating of her heart as if it were my own. I could taste the sweetness of her euphoria. I could feel her love and awe for me just as I could her body beneath mine.

"How?" she finally whispered, holding on to my arms so tightly that I was certain there'd be bruises when we were done.

"The how doesn't matter, love. Only that it is," I replied, leaning my head forward until our noses were touching.

A few errant tears leaked from the corners of her eyes, and I wiped them away with my thumb. She smiled up at me, beaming brightly even in the darkness of our bedroom.

As the tether between us strengthened, there was no extra burst of energy like before. Only a slow build, like bricks being stacked one by one, ensuring that the bond we shared this time wouldn't be broken.

We wouldn't be broken.

Not again.

My eyes locked with Andie's while I moved above her. There was no rush in our movements, just the pure enjoyment of being together again.

Her hands roamed over my back, and she tightened around me, urging me to go harder. I lifted one of her legs, angling her higher and thrusting forward. She sucked in a breath, then moaned.

My wolf howled inside my head, thriving from the bond

finally being whole and being able to truly connect with our mate.

His excitement had me picking up speed. I knew the moment Andie felt what I did, because she grinned at me, grabbing my arms again. "Give me everything you have."

And that I did.

I kissed her hard, pinning her arms above her head, and loved her fiercely until my balls began to ache.

Reaching a hand between us, I pressed my thumb over her clit. Her back arched up, and she tightened hard around my dick. I kept up the pressure and continued pounding inside her, hard yet slowly, until her moans grew louder and she was breaking skin on my hand that still had hers pinned.

I leaned forward and kissed along her neck, trailing my lips down her chest until I pulled a taut nipple into my mouth.

She cried out and came apart beneath me. Energy exploded around us again, the same dark blue as before. I couldn't tell if it was from her, me, or both of us.

Though, that didn't matter. What did was that I had Andie again, and this time, I had all of her. There was nothing holding back our bond.

Nothing to pull us apart ever again.

7

ANDIE

Never before had I felt such a deep-rooted love as when the bond between Foster and me had reformed into something I hadn't even known could exist.

Everything inside me had changed the moment our connection had exploded. The anger I'd held on to, the fear I hadn't been able to shake, the weaknesses I hated about myself—all of it had evaporated into thin air.

In their place was a security I hadn't had since my mom passed away and a love that knew no boundaries.

Foster's joy and hurt and worry became mine as well.

We'd both suffered while he'd been unconscious or gone or whatever it was that he'd been. I really wanted to know more about exactly what had happened to him later, but for now, loving him was exactly what both of our souls needed.

"That was how it always should have been," he murmured against my cheek, still keeping his body weight pressed over me.

"I don't know what I would have done if we were never able to have this moment," I said softly. "Being without you was one of the most painful things I've had to live through."

His rough hands brushed strands of my hair away and his brows pushed together. "I'm going to talk with Holden about what he did. He had no right to keep you away when you might have been able to fix things sooner, like you did with Benjamin and James."

I'd have agreed with him even just a day ago, but with our bond reaffirmed and having Foster in my arms again, my fury was waning, allowing more room for clarity. "As much as I hate what Holden did, I think he might have made the right choice. I wasn't okay. I had more control than I realized, but I was still acting on my emotions instead of rationally. A part of me wanted to burn the world down to get you back, but something held me back. I kept telling myself that I needed to be strong and better before I acted, but that was just an excuse to keep training instead of unleashing my wrath on everyone else."

His brows furrowed. "What do you mean?"

"I was acting out of fear and hate over having you and Charlie taken from me when I'd already lost so much. It wasn't fair in my eyes, and there wasn't anyone who could make me think differently. If Beatrix hadn't forced my magic down before we went to the pack, I'd have hurt people who didn't deserve it. I was being drawn to the darker side of my energy, and I enjoyed every moment there, because that was when the suffering hurt the least."

Foster rolled us until he was on the bottom, then wrapped his arms tightly around me. "I'm so fucking sorry you went through that alone."

I pressed a palm over his chest, trying to physically push the joy I felt now into him, while hoping he could read the sincerity not only on my face, but in my tone. "There's no reason to be sorry. Even if my intentions were wrong, I learned a lot in a short time. I'm ready to face Moira again. She won't get away a second time. We just need to find her."

Foster's frustration seeped into me. "How could she have disappeared so easily?"

"She hasn't, but she moves quickly. We don't know what she's doing, but she's been bouncing all around the world. Her energy signature pops up for a short time, but it's never anywhere long enough to get a team together to go after her. Even when we have them on standby."

There was a twitch in his cheek, and his chest rumbled. "She needs to die."

For the first time since meeting Moira, my initial instinct was to disagree with Foster. The thought shocked me to my core, but as my thoughts continued to deepen, I began relating to her. The feeling not only confused the hell out of me, but disturbed a part of me as well.

Foster's cobalt eyes turned stormy, and his lips thinned. "Why don't you seem to agree with my statement?"

While I appreciated being as close to Foster as I felt, him knowing my true emotions was going to take some getting used to.

"I'm just wondering if maybe Holden was right before. When he suggested that maybe, instead of killing her, Moira could be rehabilitated in a way that she'd no longer be a danger to anyone else."

"Why the hell would you wonder that?" He growled.

I pressed my palm over his heart, and our combined skin warmed. "Because of this. I wanted to burn the world down when I lost you, but something held me back. I got lucky, but if this new bond had been what we'd been sharing before… I don't think anything or anyone would have been able to hold me back from getting to you. If this is what Moira is missing, a part of me can relate to her."

He grimaced and squeezed hard around my waist. "I don't want to have sympathy for that woman."

"Neither do I, but I also don't want to consider myself a murderer. We have what we've wanted from the beginning:

my magic and each other. If Moira's soulmate can be saved, she might not be a threat to others any longer."

"Go back a second," he said, his eyes pinched at the sides. "How do you have your magic? I mean, I knew something was different with you, but I didn't think it was *your* magic."

I grinned proudly. "I syphoned it from the necklace when I was fighting Moira. She had no idea. I didn't get all of it, but apparently, I stole back enough. I first thought that was why our bond was stronger, but now I think it's because we're both different."

"No wonder Luna told me the necklace needed to be destroyed. You don't need it anymore," he said, stroking the sensitive skin over my spine.

I might not have needed the necklace anymore, but I'd have liked to keep it. There was very little I still had of Aunt Junie's. Though, that thought reminded me that I'd still yet to get the items she'd left for me at Spell House.

"Do you think you'd be up for helping with something?" I asked him.

He leaned up and kissed me before answering. "I'll do whatever you want, every day, for the rest of our *long* lives."

Hell, why did he have to be sweet? My chest filled with so much love, I wasn't sure what to do with it all after so many weeks of feeling alone.

"I'd like to finally get Junie's things from Spell House tomorrow morning before things get too crazy again. I have a feeling now that you're back and you've shared the information that the Moon Goddess told you, Beatrix is going to be working even harder to push for disbanding the council. She's been talking about how worthless they are for weeks now after they said they'd only send a few hunters out to help find Moira."

Foster tensed beneath me, and I frowned, taking on the stress that suddenly spiked with him. "What's wrong?" I asked.

"Luna told me that you and I specifically needed to help bring the other supernatural races together. I don't want to add any other risks into our lives when we still have Moira to contend with. If anything happened to you…"

I pressed my head against his chest and held him tightly. "I know. I feel the same way, but everything is going to be okay. I know that now."

His hands nearly crushed my ribs as they wrapped around me. "You'll have to believe that enough for the both of us."

And I would, because I couldn't lose him again. Not in this lifetime or any other.

THE NEXT MORNING, WE GOT UP EARLY AND HEADED TO SPELL House. The place was buzzing with witches who were working on various things to help either find or beat Moira.

There were new shield potions to combat the dark energy she and her followers used. New spells to protect the wolves should they keep helping us. Tracking spells and a containment one that might allow us to keep her in one place for longer than an hour or two.

Everyone was making progress, but still, we had no way to act even if we were ready without knowing when and where Moira would be.

Foster took my hand and led the way up the stairs. "Have there been any other attacks over the last six weeks?"

I shook my head. "That's what makes me most nervous. Moira had the upper hand after that last attack. The coven and pack were divided. We'd lost dozens of witches and wolves, but she didn't take the opening."

Knowing that witch could have been back at any moment had been part of my motivation to get my shit together while I hadn't had Foster. I couldn't fathom letting her get away again—or letting her hurt anyone else I cared about.

We got to the "pink room," as I'd been calling it, and I opened up a portal to my guest bedroom. I wouldn't be able to hold it for long, but it would allow us to get the bigger items like the bed and dresser back to the house quicker than teleporting with each item.

I could sense Foster's astonishment over my abilities, but he didn't say anything. Instead, we both got to work and within the hour, everything Aunt Junie had left for me was safely where it belonged inside our house.

I spent the next couple of hours with Foster rearranging everything until I was satisfied. Only then did I finally sit down for the first time that day.

"How about lunch?" he asked when I fell onto the bed.

Going through all of the items left behind was more emotionally exhausting than it was physically, so I wasn't really hungry. "Maybe in a bit, but there's plenty of food if you're hungry."

Before I even finished speaking, his stomach growled and he shrugged. "Shifter appetite."

I laughed and followed him out of the room. "You're probably starving. I should have cooked you breakfast or even dinner last night. Have you even eaten since waking up after six weeks in a coma?"

Saying that out loud made me feel like the world's worst mate.

He kissed me briefly. "I got up in the middle of the night and made a sandwich. That was enough until now, and helping you this morning was the priority for me." His lips pressed to mine once more, then he traced a finger down my cheek before walking away.

Damn, he really was perfect.

While he went into the kitchen, I lay on the couch after he turned down my offer to help make something. As I stared up at the ceiling, the smile on my face grew until it was almost painful. It hadn't even been a day since Foster had gotten back, but everything already felt right. Whatever anger I had been clinging to before was no longer the beacon that kept me moving forward.

I listened to Foster while he opened and closed the cabinets, then the fridge while I rested my eyes, but that peacefulness didn't last for long.

A knock sounded at the door, and I rolled over to answer it. Foster peeked out of the kitchen, but I was already up. "It's just Beatrix." He raised a brow, so I added, "I can sense her magic."

"Ah," was all he said as he went back to making food. He was hungrier than he'd let on. Stubborn shifter should have eaten again hours ago.

When I opened the door, Beatrix was glaring at me with her arms crossed. "Why didn't you bond last night?"

I smiled lightly and shook my head. "Good afternoon to you as well."

When I stepped aside, she let herself in. She paused when she got closer to me, then her eyes traveled over me accusingly. "You did bond. How did I not feel it?"

My hand patted her shoulder. "You weren't always watching me while I was working on using my magic."

She mumbled something unintelligible, then stomped her way toward the kitchen, where she pulled out a stool to sit on. "Well, now that the bond is settled, we have other business to discuss."

Foster was already mid-bite into the four-inch-tall sandwich he'd made, so I asked, "Like what?"

"Like meeting with the other supernaturals and going to the council," she said.

I leaned against the fridge and folded my hands in front of me. "And we're sure the council won't help us with Moira?"

She scoffed. "Those shady bastards aren't going to lift a

robe. After reaching out to them before, I'm rather certain they'd love to see us fail, and I'm going to enjoy making sure they regret turning their backs on this."

Foster set his sandwich down and wiped a napkin over his face. "Why is disbanding the council so important to you?"

"Because it is," Beatrix snapped. She drummed her fingers over the counter.

I stepped forward and reached for her fidgeting hand. "It's okay to show you have a heart every once in a while. We won't tell anyone."

She pulled out of my hold, ignoring my comment. "I've already been in touch with some of the people I trust, and they're all on board to head to the council within the week."

"Who would that be?" Foster asked with curiosity in his voice and eyes.

"What does it matter to you?" the old witch countered.

"Beatrix," I warned.

She huffed and pinched her lips together. "You're still not any fun now that he's back." She paused, then added, "I called Roman and Cait from East Texas. They'll be here within a few days. Maciah and Amersyn, the vampires you met before, will be here with Rachel and Zeke. And a coven leader you haven't met yet."

Foster set his nearly finished sandwich down once again. "What about that fae who was here last night?"

Beatrix grinned. "Oh, Lucinda? Yes, how could I forget about her? She'll be returning with her mate Finn."

"Great," Foster muttered, giving Beatrix even more joy.

"I need the two of you ready to show off your bond, though," she added.

"Excuse me?" I tilted my head in confusion. "How and why are we supposed to do that?"

She stood and wiped her hands over the sides of her black, flowy skirt. "How you'll do so is by making sure you don't let your magic get out of control, and why you'll do so is because we need everyone to see that there should be no concern regarding the two of you being bonded. In case you've already forgotten, the council *does* have an interest in that."

Shit. I *had* forgotten.

My gaze met Foster's hardened eyes. I didn't need his words to know that we were both thinking the same thing.

Beatrix had been right.

The council needed to go away, and everyone else who thought we shouldn't be together could fuck off.

Our bond was none of their damn business.

8

———

FOSTER

The next evening, I forced myself to leave Andie and go to the pack. Mack had brought my phone to the coven, and he'd been texting me non-stop to come back.

I still didn't have anything to say to Holden. I understood that Andie didn't hold any resentment toward the alpha, but I did.

He'd had no right to keep me from her, and he should have known that I would have rather been with the coven than the pack if that had been the choice.

But Mack's insistence was annoying me and I finally broke.

Ignoring Holden gives him power over us. We need to show him he's not the only alpha, my wolf said.

My inner beast had been rather cocky since the bond with Andie had reformed. There was a new sense of pride I sensed from him each time he spoke that hadn't been there before.

Would you rather I disappear like before? he countered, and I grimaced.

No, and I wasn't thinking your new attitude is bad. It's just different.

He didn't reply, and I didn't push.

Something was off with us, but this time, it had nothing to do with my mate. He knew something I didn't and wasn't sharing, though I knew he would eventually. Regardless of how much that frustrated me, I had too many other things to worry about to care about his secrets for long.

I arrived at the pack and reached out to Mack through our pack connection.

I'm here.

Where? I can be there in less than a minute, he replied almost immediately.

In the trees on the left of the pack house.

I heard a door open and slam closed at the back of the house and then paws digging into the earth as Mack's tan wolf made his way toward me.

He bowed his head in submission, even though he technically ranked higher than I did, then shifted back to two feet.

Mack's hand reached out. "It's good to see you, man."

I accepted the handshake. "Yeah, it's good to be awake. Something that might have happened sooner if I'd been with Andie."

He ran a hand over his shaved, dark hair. "I know. I tried to talk to Holden once things settled, but he said this was the way it had to be and wouldn't tell me why. He really was trying to help you. He even brought out this crazy shifter called Serene who's supposed to be good at healing wolves."

I stiffened at hearing that for the first time. "Did she do anything to me?"

"I wasn't there, but I heard her tell Holden that 'all would reveal itself in time' or something batty like that. Holden was even more convinced after she left that Andie had to be kept away."

As my anger rose, I could sense Andie's strength filling me. We couldn't mind-speak, but last night, we'd tested the distance our exchanged "feelings" could last. So far, we hadn't found a length in which I couldn't sense her.

Her steadfastness reminded me of what she'd said before I'd left.

"We can't change what has already happened. Just focus on what we can do to make sure it doesn't happen again."

She wasn't wrong, but I badly needed to be furious with *someone* over the time lost. That was what my mate couldn't understand.

Not that I was glad she'd had all that time to rage, but I hadn't had any. All of this was still fresh for me, and though our newly reformed bond quelled the worst of my ire, it didn't make everything okay.

Mack kicked a rock past me. "So, what do you think?"

I rubbed my hands over my face. "I'm sorry, man. About what?"

"About talking to Holden and remaining part of the pack. Do you think there's any way you'll stay with us?" He spoke with an uncertainty I'd yet to hear from the beta.

Tell him we're undecided. They don't need to know we're not going anywhere yet, my wolf said.

I didn't play games, so that thought was unappealing to me. Though his suggestion wasn't far from the truth, either.

"I'm staying in the area, but I don't know if I'll be remaining with the pack. I'm not going to fight with Holden, which he can thank Andie for, but I don't know if I can trust him again," I said earnestly.

Mack nodded, a tightness forming in his shoulders. "I think that's understandable, given the situation, but you should know Holden has thrown every resource into finding Moira. He's even called in favors I'd thought he'd never act on with other packs."

I knew he was trying to sway my choice to forgive Holden, but nothing he said could help. "Holden is only trying to find his daughter. He doesn't give a shit about ending Moira merely because it would be better for all of us as a whole."

The beta rubbed a hand over his chest. "Piper wasn't the only one taken whom we want back."

I cocked my head. "Charlie? Is she why you're different?"

"Maybe." He shrugged and looked off to the side. "Just know it hasn't been easy for any of us. There were nine wolves taken plus the eleven witches. Moira can do a lot of damage without alerting us, and it's been a long fucking six weeks since that battle."

He wasn't wrong about that. My weeks spent unconscious had felt like an eternity. "Have the trackers only been trying to find Moira or are they searching for each of the individuals as well?"

"All of the above, but none of those taken have emitted any kind of traceable signal. Not even a blip like we get of Moira. We don't know where she has them or how she's hiding them, but we need to figure it out soon."

His voice was coarse, and his hands flexed at his sides. I knew frustration like that, so I sympathized with him.

Holden strolled around the front of the pack house, and I realized I hadn't really seen him when I'd been standing outside the coven with Andie.

His face was pale, his shoulders were slumped, and the life that he normally held in his eyes was dim. He wasn't anything close to the alpha I'd first met all those months ago.

Mack's eyes followed my stare. "None of us is okay, man. We're all just trying to do the best we can."

I wanted to believe that, but how could Holden have thought keeping me from Andie was the best choice? I didn't care that her magic hadn't been working right or if he thought she was dangerous. She was still mine, and I was hers. We might have been able to help each other weeks ago if we hadn't been apart.

He walked back into the house with tense shoulders. I

wasn't sure if he'd seen me or had already sensed I was in the pack. Hell, maybe he didn't even want me as one of his wolves any longer.

I considered saying *goodbye* to Mack and leaving until I felt Andie's warmth rise inside me. Her strength and assurance matched her earlier words—that maybe this had all worked out as it was supposed to.

It was hard to accept that, but feeling her and knowing that she'd want me to make things less tense between all of us had me second-guessing my decision to leave.

Mack watched Holden disappear inside just like I had. "I know Holden fucked up, but you haven't been here. Like I said before, we did what we thought was best. If you ever cared about this pack, please talk to him."

Fuck.

I drew on my connection to Andie, using it to give me the fortitude I needed. "Fine, but I'm still not promising anything."

Mack nodded, then gave my shoulder a squeeze. "The fact that you're willing to talk to him and haven't issued a challenge for his position is more than most of us expected."

We could still do that and you know we'd win, my wolf said.

I agreed with him, but running a pack wasn't the right move for us. Not now and maybe not ever again. Keeping Andie safe was what I cared about most, and I couldn't do that with pack members to also consider.

I know you're just as pissed as I am about being gone for so long, but I wouldn't mind having my optimistic wolf back, I said. We'd balanced each other well and if he was constantly raging, then I wasn't sure how I was supposed to stop.

He didn't respond to me as I stepped toward the pack house.

Mack surprised me when he headed deeper into the forest instead of following me inside. My feet grew heavier when I went up the steps. A part of me hadn't forgotten the respect we had for Holden. That same part didn't want me to say anything to him that I couldn't take back.

Mack and Andie were right about one thing: my conversation with him couldn't wait any longer.

I navigated through the house until I reached his office. The door was cracked open, but still, I knocked.

His sharp intake of breath was loud enough for me to hear when I assumed he realized who was on the other side of the door. The fact that it had taken me knocking for him to figure out I was there, though, told me the alpha was truly in a bad way.

"Come on in, Foster," his rough voice said.

I stepped through, shutting the door behind me. The blinds were closed, and only a lamp on Holden's desk provided light into the shadowy room.

Without being invited, I took a seat in the chair directly in front of him. "I thought we should talk."

His hands folded over his lap. "Agreed. How are you and your wolf?"

"Better now that we're with our mate again," I bit out with narrowed eyes.

"That's good." His jaw tightened. "Listen, Foster. I'd apologize to you, but I haven't lied to you yet and I don't want to start now. I did what was best for you. I thought you were as good as dead. That your body was nothing more than a shell. Your wolf was gone. You gave no response to anything we tried. I honestly expected you to die the night of the new moon, given how slow your heart rate had become."

His words were sincere. His heart rate didn't change. The truth was there, but still, it was hard to accept.

"And you didn't think that my mate might have been able to help because...why?" I asked, my voice full of tension.

Holden sighed. "You didn't see her, Foster. She was different after that fight. The times I'd seen her, energy pulsed off her that wasn't necessarily dark, but it wasn't right, either.

Weighing the risks and listening to my wolf, we kept her away."

My hand slammed down on his desk. "Maybe she was only that way because she was hurting too fucking much to contain everything while you kept her from me."

Holden didn't even flinch from my outburst. "I thought about that, but even Beatrix wasn't sure what was going on with Andie. Moira had compromised Andie's necklace, and when Andie took her energy back, she wasn't the same witch we'd been getting to know. I know that's hard for you to believe, but it's the truth and I don't regret what I did. My only priority was to keep you and the rest of the pack safe. If that isn't good enough for you, then I don't think we have anything left to say to each other."

Damn it. This was why I respected Holden. He didn't waste time. He didn't pretend things weren't as they were.

I wanted to take my rage out on him. I needed someone to blame for the shit situation we were all in, but…

Maybe Andie was right, my wolf chimed in. *I didn't want to forgive Holden, either, but it's hard to ignore his sincerity. He's the same trustworthy alpha whom we knew before.*

And there was the wolf I'd always known.

At least something was beginning to feel normal again.

With a deep breath, I settled my hands back onto the arms of the chair and met Holden's stern stare. "I don't think I'll ever be able to understand why you did what you did, but I do understand the pressure you were under as an alpha. I'd like to put this behind us and continue to work together."

Holden leaned forward. "'Together' as part of the same pack or just as two people who have a common enemy?"

Shit. That was harder to answer than I wanted it to be.

The short time that I'd given in to the pack life again had been…enjoyable, but it had quickly turned into something that might have gotten me killed and left Andie unprotected.

The pack will still protect you and Andie. Holden wouldn't have shown up at the coven otherwise, my wolf said.

He was right, but did that make everything okay? Did I move forward with the pack and forget they'd kept my mate away from me when I believed we'd needed each other most?

I didn't know the right answer, but I did know what Andie would want me to do, so I looked Holden in the eye and answered confidently. "As part of the same pack, so long as my mate is still welcome here."

Holden's shoulders dropped ever-so-slightly. "Of course she is. We're going to need her to get the others back." Then his true fury finally seeped through his emotions. "That bitch took my daughter, and she's going to know hurt unlike she ever thought possible by the time I'm done with her."

There was the alpha I needed.

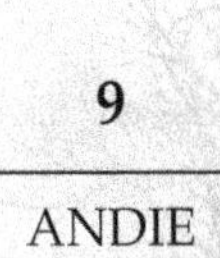

9

ANDIE

The last two days had been filled with constant meetings and playing catch-up with all the things I'd ignored while Foster had been gone. Like visiting Benjamin and Reah, my cousins and only remaining family, to whom I'd done a terrible job showing how grateful I was to have around.

Thankfully, they'd understood and didn't take my absence personally, but I still knew I needed to try harder. Not only with them, but with Charlie's parents, too. Though, I wasn't quite ready to face them yet.

Once Foster had gone to the pack, I spent my afternoon working with Beatrix, Ava, and Evelyn, watching and learning about their individual ways of using locator spells.

I was getting tired after a long afternoon of peopling and also making sure Foster could sense my support while he was off doing something I knew he didn't want to. Just when I was about to excuse myself and go back to the house to rest, I sensed Foster entering through the coven shield.

Warmth filled my chest, and I sighed with relief while renewed energy rose inside me. The relief was more for my benefit than Foster's, though. I hadn't been worried about him at the pack, but I'd worried about myself while he'd been gone. Something I didn't want to bother him with.

As Foster's presence grew nearer, I stood from the table inside Beatrix's house and nodded at her, Ava, and Evelyn. "Thank you for helping me today, but I need to go."

Beatrix winked. "Is your wolf back? Invite him over."

Ava and Evelyn shared matching grins as I shook my head.

"Not happening. You had your fun with me, and that will have to be enough for now. Foster still needs more time to adjust."

"I could help him like I did you." Beatrix's hand glowed silver when she held it up.

I stepped toward the door. "I don't think he'll go for that idea, but I'll talk to him. Do you need anything from me before I go?"

Evelyn's white hair floated around her while she shook the vial of blood that they'd already taken from me for some deeper testing. "This should be enough. If we find anything that shouldn't be there, I'm sure Beatrix will welcome herself inside your house."

A snort escaped me. "Please don't."

The old witch said nothing else as I made my way out of her house. She, Ava, and Evelyn had poked and prodded at me between showing me some of their skills. According to initial assessments, there wasn't any dark energy inside me, and my magic had merged perfectly with Junie's, taking precedence, as it should have all along.

Even better, I was no longer drawing on anyone's power without meaning to.

The bonding with Foster was the last thing I needed to feel whole again, but still…I couldn't help but wonder if we were missing something. After all that had gone wrong, Moira staying quiet while I grew stronger seemed too good to be true.

But none of the others had seemed to think the same, and I didn't want to further worry Foster, so I shoved those thoughts down and focused on the positives.

Having Foster again was like having my soul returned to me, giving me a clarity that I hadn't been able to grasp through the agony of missing not only him, but Charlie as well, while feeling guilty about all the others having been taken.

When I got back to my house, he was waiting on the porch for me, leaning against the siding with his arms hanging loosely at his sides while he watched my every step.

I took in his tattoos showing past the sleeves of his form-fitting black shirt, then his dark-wash jeans before refocusing on his face, which was half-hidden by hair that had grown a couple of inches since I'd met him. His jaw was covered by a beard that had come in while he'd been with the pack those six weeks, but it was his eyes that held my heart.

The cobalt blue called me forward and right into his now-open arms. My head pressed against his chest, and I held on tightly to him.

"I missed you," he murmured against the top of my head.

"Missed you, too, but hopefully it was a good visit?" I asked, staying happily wrapped in his arms.

He nodded above me. "Let's go inside and I'll tell you about it."

Before I could take a step back, he swept my legs out from under me, cradling me against his chest, and grinned when I looked up at him.

"I don't need to be carried," I said, but there was no conviction in my voice.

"But I need to hold you, so tonight you will be."

My heart cracked at his softly spoken words.

Foster had been through so much since losing his pack all those years ago. He'd punished himself by keeping others at a distance until he'd been told to find me. The fact that nothing had been easy for him since finding me added to the mounting guilt I held inside.

He carried me through the door, closing and locking it behind us before carrying me to the couch. He sat down, keeping me secure against him even once I was settled onto his lap.

I leaned my head against his shoulder. "Tell me what happened."

"Between you and Mack, I decided to talk to Holden. I don't know if I forgive him, but I trust him enough to stay with the pack." Foster paused to grab my hand, bringing it to his lips. "And you're welcome back with me anytime. I made sure that wouldn't be an issue."

Maybe it wouldn't be with Holden, but it might be with some of the other pack members, especially those who'd lost people the day of the battle. I was to blame for Moira showing up at their pack. It was an easier place to attack than the coven, but she would have never gone there if I hadn't had a connection to them.

I would gladly accept the blame if that made even the smallest bit of difference for some of them who had buried loved ones during the aftermath.

"I'm glad the visit went as good as could be expected," I finally said. "I tried to stay busy so that I didn't intrude on your feelings the whole time."

"You're never an intrusion." His thumb stroked my cheek. "What did you do?"

I briefly closed my eyes, soaking up his touch before I answered. "Visited with Benjamin and Reah first. I might have ignored them while you were gone." I winced saying the words out loud. "Then I met up with Beatrix, Ava, and Evelyn until you came back. They took some of my blood to test a few things. Beatrix doesn't like how 'normal' I've suddenly become, but what she doesn't realize is this is how I always was before I was teleported to the coven for the first time."

I was working overtime to hide my lingering guilt and uncertainty. Nobody needed to worry about me when there was so much else going on.

Foster's hold on me tightened. "I like this new, old you. It reminds me to not snarl so much at people who piss me off."

His words made me laugh, but there wasn't even a twitch on his face. "Foster, you can't let fury guide you. Even if something happened to me—"

A growl echoed from his throat. "Nothing will ever happen to you."

My head rested against his chest again. Maybe it was too soon for this conversation. Maybe never would be too soon and I just needed to hope for the rest of the world's sake that nothing happened to me like it had to him.

Foster stood, still keeping me in his arms. "Let's go to bed."

At the mention of bed, a yawn escaped me and I nodded. "Bed sounds nice."

He walked us to the bed and set me down but didn't remove his hands from my body. They roamed over my arms, then down my sides and to the button on my jeans. I said nothing as he unbuttoned them before pulling the zipper down.

My eyes watched his every move while his thumbs hooked into the belt loops of my pants, then wiggled them down my legs, taking my flip-flops with them.

His heated palms moved slowly up my exposed legs, sending shivers along my spine. He kissed my shins, knees, and thighs, making me quiver under his careful touch and forget all the tiredness I'd previously been feeling.

"I hope you don't still intend on going to bed," I

whispered when he kissed my stomach, lifting my shirt as he continued upward.

"We're already in bed, but I never said anything about sleeping," he murmured against my sensitive skin.

Thank fuck.

My shirt was gone before I knew it, and I reached for Foster's pants, trying to hurry things up. His movements' urgency matched mine, and we were both naked in seconds.

I wrapped my fingers around his biceps and hooked my ankles around the backs of his thighs. "I missed you so fucking much."

I didn't know how many times I'd said that to him, but it would never be enough.

The sexy grumble echoing from his chest had my core tightening and my need for his touch skyrocketing.

In one thrust, he was fully seated inside me, but instead of taking charge like I'd expected him to, he pushed us further onto the mattress and flipped our positions.

I adjusted to the new depth and spread my thighs farther apart while I leaned down and captured his mouth.

His widespread fingers gripped my hips and ass, moving me over him while my tongue nudged between his lips. He devoured my moans as they grew louder, and the vibrations from his still-rumbling chest had me ready to fall into oblivion within a matter of minutes.

I lifted up, digging my nails into his abs and rotating my hips forward, a hiss leaving my lips. "There is literally nothing in the world that feels better than this," I muttered while letting my head drop backward.

Foster could only manage a grunt while I grinded over him, finally hitting that magical precipice I was searching for.

Shudders tore through me, and I called out his name over and over again. My eyes squeezed shut, but I could still feel him moving beneath me while euphoria held me immobile.

When I was able to think properly again, I opened my

eyes and found Foster grinning below. "And there is nothing more beautiful than watching you come apart in my hands."

My body was spent. Foster knew it, but he wasn't done. He gently guided me off his hard cock and positioned me on my hands and knees in front of him.

I bent forward, resting my head and elbows on the pillows, then moaned loudly as his hands moved down my spine, over my ass, squeezing hard everywhere they touched.

"Do you have another one in you, love?" he asked, his voice husky and hot as hell.

I nodded. "Give me everything you have."

He didn't respond, but with our bond, I could feel his eagerness growing between us. Being with me, away from the stress of everything that had happened, was what my soulmate needed. I planned to give him as much of me as he needed for as long as he needed until he was ready for what came next.

We didn't have a lot of time before then, but I needed Foster at his best, and time together was the only way he was going to get there.

My thoughts were cut off when he thrusted hard inside me, stealing my breath and forcing my face further into the pillows.

Words left my mouth, but I didn't even know what I was saying as I held on for the ride.

Foster's fingers dug into my hips while he indeed gave me "everything" he had to give. I focused on my own feelings as best I could, sending him all the love I could. The return emotions from him had my breath coming in pants and my nails poking holes into the pillowcase.

A love like this wasn't anything I'd believed existed before. Not even the first time we'd bonded. There was something different here, something stronger and fiercer than any elements that existed in the world.

I knew then that there would be nothing that could ever

tear us apart again. Not Moira, not Holden, the Supernatural Council, or anyone else who might not agree with our bond.

Foster was mine and I was his.

End of discussion.

As those thoughts settled inside my heart, I trembled beneath him. He wrapped his arm around my waist, nipping at the skin on my back before flicking his tongue over the bites, soothing whatever aches they might have left.

"So close again," I muttered, turning my face away from the pillows.

Foster's weight pressed down on me, and my thighs touched the bed, but he kept my hips elevated just enough to keep thrusting harder and harder inside me.

His muscles tensed wherever they touched my body, and the rumble reverberating from deep within him told me he was close as well.

I pressed my hips back, sending him farther inside me. Without warning, his teeth sank into the top of my shoulder.

I cried out, but there was no sound of pain coming from me. Only unfiltered desire that had my pussy clenching hard around him and my screams getting louder by the second.

Somehow, I'd forgotten that for wolves, in order for the bond to be fully complete, there was an exchange of blood. I badly wished I had the urge to do the same to him.

Foster's tongue licked the blood from his canines, and he growled in my ear. "Mine. All mine."

His words hit deep inside me, and all it took was one more thrust from him before an orgasm ripped through me so fiercely that I couldn't hold my body up any longer. All I could do was succumb to pleasure and hope I didn't drown in the process.

Foster shuddered above me, pressing kisses all over my back and saying words I couldn't quite understand, but I felt his love for me all the same. His need to always keep me safe and his unyielding devotion.

It was more than I'd ever thought I'd have, and I planned on spending the rest of our lives showing him that I felt the same damn way.

10

FOSTER

Biting Andie hadn't been my intention when I'd taken her to bed the night before, but when I became overwhelmed with the amount of love she was pushing through our bond, I couldn't stop my wolf from breaking through, laying his part of our claim to our mate.

As I stared at the marks on her shoulder the next morning, I smiled and hoped she had no regrets.

My fingers traced over her porcelain skin, and she shivered in her sleep. I pressed my lips as close as I could get to the mark without moving her.

She moaned, but I couldn't tell if the sound was from pain or something else.

Her light-blue eyes fluttered open, and she shot me a lazy grin. "Good morning."

"Morning. I didn't mean to wake you up." My hand splayed over her stomach. "You can go back to sleep if you want."

She rolled onto her side and reached behind my head to tangle her fingers in my longer-than-normal strands. "What I want is…you."

My chest swelled, and I closed the distance between us.

My leg slid between hers just before I reached for her ribs to roll her on top of me, but mid-movement, loud banging sounded on the front door.

Andie sighed and gave me an apologetic look. "Beatrix."

"At least she didn't barge in." Witches didn't seem to have any boundaries.

She rolled out of bed, and I had to clench my hands to keep from following her to the bathroom. As much as I needed my mate, we still had things to do and people to save. We would have our evenings, but even I knew our days needed to be committed to finding Moira and those she'd taken.

When Andie got out of the bathroom, she was still naked, but her hair was brushed, and she was wide awake with a grin on her face. "All yours."

My wolf rumbled. *Yes, she is.*

We'll find some time for you to be with her today or tomorrow, I said as I grabbed pants and boxers on my way to the bathroom.

I'd appreciate that.

I knew he would. Plus, Andie would enjoy the time with my wolf as well.

I quickly took care of business. By the time I was dressed, I heard Andie's laughter floating back to me from the living room.

Following the sound, I found her on the couch with Beatrix across from her in the chair. Instead of sitting next to Andie, I picked her up and settled her over my lap like the possessive mate I was.

She didn't push me away. She merely laid her head against me and filled me in. "Beatrix confirmed that the vampires we met before, the wolves from East Texas, the fae who was here before, plus another coven leader who has history with the council will be joining us this week."

My brows furrowed. "Why?"

"We're going to approach the council before their next quarterly meeting," the silver-haired witch said. "Like I said before, it's time that they be disbanded once and for all. If they're not going to be helpful, then we need to make sure they're not a threat. With what William and Marlene said before about their interest in the bond between the two of you, we need to make sure we're not going to have any other problems."

That was something we could agree on.

"How do you plan to 'disband' the council?" I asked.

She grinned widely. "By asking nicely."

I chuckled. "And if that doesn't work?"

"I'm sure it will. Let's not worry about things that we don't have to." Beatrix's eyes bounced between the two of us. "Your bond grows stronger by the hour. I didn't expect that."

Andie pressed closer to me. "Nobody will tear us apart again."

A snarl ripped from my chest, and the hollowness I'd remembered from my time away momentarily resurfaced. "Never again."

"Okay, then." Beatrix stood up. "I've had enough alpha male for the day and I haven't even had my breakfast yet. I just wanted to make sure both of you were going to be around today to greet our guests. They'll want to see the two of you together."

Confusion rolled off Andie. "I still don't understand why that's important."

"Go look in the mirror and you'll have your answer." Then she was out the door without another word.

I stroked Andie's hair and kissed her temple. "Beatrix wants to show off the power from our bond. It will sell her idea of living in combined communities."

"I'm not sure I like that." My mate frowned. "What if we're giving people a false sense of hope? Even if the races have always lived separately, there should have been more cross bonds than just us over the last decade, right?"

"Maybe. Maybe not. As the crazy witch already said, let's not worry about things we don't have to right now." I grimaced. "I can't believe that I just agreed with her on something."

Andie laughed and pushed up to kiss me. "Neither can I. I should mark this on a calendar." She wiggled out of my grasp, then turned back when she was a few steps away. "What do you want for breakfast? We need to be feeding your wolf better."

I could feel my wolf's smugness. "Tofu is what he asked for."

Andie rolled her eyes. "Eggs and bacon it is."

She loves me more than you, he tittered.

I didn't bother to justify his thought with a response. Instead, I went to the kitchen and helped Andie with the breakfast so that we could both eat together.

Once everything was done, I quickly inhaled my food, grateful that Andie had thought to eat when I hadn't. It wasn't just my wolf who needed the sustenance.

After we were done and had cleaned up our mess, we went in search of Beatrix. She had called to tell us the vampires were already inside the coven.

I could scent the newcomers before we even came close to the building they were in. The smell of blood—even if it was donated—was strong and made my nose scrunch.

"What's wrong?" Andie asked with a crease between her brows.

"Nothing. Just takes a little adjusting to get used to the scent of Beatrix's guests."

She took a deep inhale. "I can't smell anything different, but I do sense something foreign in the air. It's not quite magic, but not human, either."

I nodded and pointed toward the meeting building up

ahead. "All supernaturals have a little magic inside them. It just manifests differently for each race."

Andie seemed to consider that fact harder than I'd expected as we walked up to the meeting room that was beginning to feel like a second home.

I opened the door first, sticking my head inside to make sure there wasn't a reason to be concerned for my mate's safety before letting her step inside.

The female I remembered from before with ebony hair—I think her name was Amersyn—waved at me and winked, then I moved to the side so Andie could enter.

She waved at the four vampires without an ounce of fear rolling off her. "Hello."

The leader Maciah stood. His broad shoulders filled out a pale blue dress shirt and his eyes seemed browner today than the previous muddy crimson they'd been before. He nodded at me, a piece of his dark hair falling over his forward. "Nice to see the two of you again."

"You as well." Then I realized that the second woman with them hadn't been here last time.

When my eyes cast her way, Maciah turned and introduced her. "This is Rachel. She couldn't join us before, but she's been with me for years now."

I didn't miss the inflection in Maciah's voice, and he must not have missed the distrust in my eyes. I wasn't a fan of doing business with new people, but I didn't need to voice my opinion out loud. This was Beatrix's show. For the time being.

Rachel brushed brunette hair out of her eyes and smiled at Andie and me. "Hi." She waved animatedly, seeming too excited about being here.

Zeke, the other member who had been here before, tugged her back and she went willingly into his arms.

"All right." Beatrix drew out the word, breaking the awkward moment. "Well, I heard from Roman and they won't be here until tomorrow, but Lucinda and Finn should be along shortly."

I turned toward the elder witch. "What do we need the fae for?"

Except it wasn't Beatrix who answered my question.

"Lucinda saved my life the day I officially became a vampire. She might lack a filter…or two, but she means well," Amersyn said confidently.

Andie nudged me. "She was also the first person to volunteer to help me find you once I realized you weren't in the pack house anymore."

With a heavy sigh, I conceded. "Fine. I won't complain about more help."

I grabbed Andie's hand and led us to some of the chairs several feet from the vampires. I might not have minded working with them, but I didn't need to smell them from so closely, either.

Thank you, my wolf added once we'd sat.

Ava and Evelyn entered the room from the back door. "Lucinda and Finn are here. Want me to show them in?" Ava asked, brushing her short ebony hair behind her ear.

Beatrix nodded, but before she could answer with words, Lucinda slammed the front door open and grinned widely. "Hello, Rebels."

Andie squeezed my hand as I ground my teeth. This fae was going to be a lot to handle.

"Lucinda. Finn." Beatrix addressed them and I finally saw the man standing behind her. He kept his hands shoved in his jean pockets and closed the door with his boot. His sharp eyes moved around the room before they stepped too far inside.

He was cautious and much quieter than his mate. I liked him more already.

Finn moved ahead of Lucinda, walking toward the seats, and sat down one seat from me. He tilted his head in my direction and reached out a hand. "Finn."

"Foster. Nice to meet you," I said stiffly.

Lucinda sat next to him and leaned forward to wink at either me or Andie. I couldn't tell which and didn't care.

"So, what did we miss?" the fae woman asked after turning to look over at the witches.

"Just some introductions, but I think you know everyone here," Beatrix replied as she moved to the center of the room, floating a chair behind her without touching it.

Ava and Evelyn flanked her, standing beside the elder witch even once she'd sat. "As I said on the phone when I spoke with you, I want to approach the council as soon as everyone has arrived. I want them to relinquish any control they have over the supernatural and allow our communities to govern and handle our own problems like we have been, but this time without worrying if they'll suddenly decide to step in."

Finn leaned forward in his chair. "What has the council ever even done? As far as I'm aware, they've never set foot on Fae Islands. If they don't do anything, why do we need to even bother disbanding them?"

He made a good point, but Beatrix was quick to counter. "Because there are still too many people who will live a life that's less than because of the council's hunters and the reputation they have made for themselves over the last couple of years. Because at any moment, they could come for us for any reason they want to make up. What if it's Lucinda next for her special wings? How would you feel then?"

His jaw tightened, and he cracked his knuckles. "I see your point. Proceed."

Beatrix continued. "The council has always operated in the background of our world. Roman and Cait can attest to what happens when they get involved. Even if the council was compromised back then, it doesn't matter. They left themselves open to that, and so many people needlessly died from their mistakes."

My arm wrapped around Andie and squeezed her shoulder. Her Aunt Junie had been one of those who'd died, and I knew how much her heart hurt having never gotten to truly know her aunt.

Maciah cleared his throat. "They've also stood by for decades while some of the vampires killed humans and have done nothing about it. If we're supposed to keep supernaturals a secret, it's going to be harder to do that when murders are happening every night."

I'd thought Beatrix only wanted to gather the others so that we would have more of a presence in front of the council, but now, I could see that everyone here had something to fight for and keep safe.

Just like I did.

Maybe the old witch wasn't so crazy after all.

Beatrix crossed her ankles and folded her hands over her lap. "We'll get into the details of everything tomorrow once the wolves and other coven leader arrives, but just know, it isn't my intention to start a battle with the council, but if they won't listen, I'm not walking away. I know this is the right path for us. I also know each of you has been trying to create something better for your races, and we can't quit now."

"You know I never back down from a fight," Lucinda said with a cocky grin.

"And we're in, too. We haven't come as far as we have to stop now," Amersyn added, her muddy-red eyes deepening in color.

Beatrix's eyes fell on me. "What about you? Do you believe the L.A. wolves will stand with us?"

I held her stare, curious as to why she was asking me instead of Holden. "As you're already well aware of, I will do whatever it takes to keep my mate safe. I can't speak on behalf of the others, but I can go back to the pack and mention your intentions to Holden if you haven't already done so yourself."

She raised a brow. "You'll tell the alpha that you agree with my plans?"

"I'll tell him that we all have a reason to do the things we do and that even the Moon Goddess guided us in this direction. Holden can do whatever he wants with that information," I said pointedly.

No one person ever needed to join a fight they didn't have a vested interest in. That only resulted in people getting killed, and the pack didn't need any other deaths.

Beatrix's shoulders relaxed some and she glanced back at Evelyn. "Please, call the alpha to invite him over for a drink and a chat tonight."

Evelyn nodded, then she quietly walked toward the back door.

"Well, I think that's all for today." Beatrix stood, glancing at each of her guests. "I know you all live locally, but you're welcome to stay within the coven. Consider it a vacation of sorts." Then she smirked at the vampires. "I assumed you'd want two separate spaces for the four of you unless you're all closer than I realized and would prefer to share one bed."

Zeke choked on a cough, Rachel's mouth dropped open, and Amersyn chuckled while Maciah sighed heavily. Interesting crowd.

"Two separate houses are preferred. Thanks, Beatrix," Amersyn finally responded with a matching grin.

Beatrix stood and left without another word, Ava on her heels.

Andie let out a sigh. "I know this is the right thing to do, but possibly fighting with two powerful groups doesn't sound like fun to me."

Lucinda laughed from her seat. "They're only as powerful as you allow them to be."

I was pretty sure that was the first thing the fae had said that didn't make me want to silence her with my own hands.

"Lucy is right," Finn added. "We've spent more than a

year rebuilding our islands, thanks to the destruction of one fae. For too long, our people allowed him to do whatever he wanted. If we hadn't let fear control us, we could have found happiness a lot sooner."

Lucinda, or "Lucy" as Finn had called her, smiled longingly at him and played with the ends of his hair as she spoke. "Beatrix might be old, but she's smart. I'm sure she won't get any of us killed."

Andie grabbed my hand, likely sensing my returning annoyance. "Or maybe there won't be a fight at all," my mate said.

Amersyn stood next, the rest of the vampires following her. "Maybe, but it never hurts to be prepared. If anyone wants to join us, we'll be practicing defensive and offensive moves behind the cabins."

I could sense Andie's interest as soon as the female vampire had mentioned "defensive."

Apparently, we weren't going to have much alone time for the foreseeable future, but I would find a way to be okay with that if it meant we were one step closer to keeping Andie safe and making people less interested in our bond.

11

ANDIE

About a half hour after leaving the meeting room, we'd all gathered in the field beyond the three power stones. I side-eyed the rocks, remembering my time spent locked between them. Having my essence torn to shreds hadn't been the highlight of my twenty-one years on this Earth.

Though, seeing my mother one last time had been. My chest warmed at the thought of her, and I stumbled.

Foster grabbed my arms, turning me toward him as his eyes inspected every inch of me. "What's wrong?"

I held my finger up and closed my eyes. I pictured my mother and the energy of hers that I could recall. I thought of the love we'd shared and how bright her light had always seemed to me.

The harder I concentrated, the more my chest bloomed. Tears pricked at my eyes, and if Foster hadn't still been holding me, I'd have dropped to my knees.

Mom.

I couldn't hear her response, but I could feel her there. Beatrix had said my parents and aunt would always be with me, and my mother had repeated the same sentiment when I'd seen her, but I had yet to *feel* her like this.

The hold that drew her to me loosened, and I reopened my eyes, grinning like a fool. "I felt my mom."

Foster's unease disappeared, and he pulled me into his arms. "That's so much better than the other scenarios I was coming up with in my mind."

His hands shook as he held me, and I murmured an apology against his chest.

"Can you do that with any of your family?" he asked when we moved apart. "Or only your mom because of the syphon thing?"

Lucinda was suddenly next to us. "What 'syphon thing'?"

Foster stepped between me and the fae. "Nothing that you need to worry about."

"On the contrary," the fae countered, meeting Foster's sneer with a raised brow, "I'm here and trying to keep the two of you alive. I believe anything unique with this little witch pertains to all of us."

Finn gently grabbed her arm. "How about we let them finish their conversation? If there's anything important that needs to be shared, then I'm sure they or Beatrix will do so."

Lucinda scoffed, but Finn tugged her closer to his chest. They shared a challenging look and she finally walked away, but not before turning her head and eyeballing both of us with a little too much interest.

Maybe I'd been too quick to like her.

Foster pressed his lips against the side of my head, whispering, "We'll talk more later."

And I'd have to focus on my family more later, because Maciah and Zeke were training together and I'd never seen two vampires brawl before.

They moved with unbelievable speed, which I assumed they purposely slowed down so we could actually see what they were doing.

With every jab Zeke made, Maciah ducked or dodged. They went in circles, getting in small hits every now and then as we observed, but then Zeke began to get sloppy. His punches slowed, and his feet didn't move as precisely as they had before.

Maciah shoved his arm and grabbed the other vampire by the throat, then tossed him a good ten feet in the opposite direction. He turned toward us, keeping his face neutral. "You can wait until your opponent gets tired or—"

"Or you can make them think they have the upper hand," Zeke said as he pounded on Maciah's back, punching him in the kidneys then jerking the both of them to the ground.

They became nothing more than a blur again. I glanced at Amersyn and Rachel. Neither seemed overly concerned, so I moved on.

Lucinda was standing farther away with her wings out. Within the blink of an eye, her feathers hardened into sharp weapons. She caught me watching and smirked at me before plucking one of the feathers from her wing and tossing it into the air without watching what she was doing.

Finn stepped into my line of sight and began addressing me and Foster. "We have other residents of our island who will be joining us later on. One of them is a sorcerer I think you might be intrigued to meet. He's been around for a long time and doesn't much like people, but he has a wealth of knowledge that our people have been grateful to have since he joined us."

"Why is a sorcerer living with the fae?" Foster asked, getting the attention of the vampires as well.

"That's a story for another time, but he's free to go whenever he feels the need, which he does every so often," Finn replied. "We don't keep him captive. He even has his own island, where he gets to ignore people to his heart's desire."

Lucinda snorted. "That man doesn't have a heart in his ogre body."

Finn sighed. "Lucinda and Yury haven't always gotten along."

"Yeah, because that bastard tried to kill me."

Foster grinned, but I cut a look his way, warning him with my eyes to stay quiet.

"I'm sure Yury will feel right at home here with Beatrix." Zeke whipped his head back and forth, likely making sure his words hadn't been heard.

Amersyn shoved his shoulder. "You didn't learn your lesson last time we were here not to talk bad about the old witch?"

He shrugged, but the conversation in front of me continued, so I gave Finn my attention again. Though, as he spoke, I didn't miss the way Lucinda kept casting long glances at me and Foster. I wasn't sure what her interest was with us, and the longer she stared, the more I didn't appreciate it.

Finn continued. "So, Yury will join us, along with some of the other fae who have proven themselves in battle before, but they won't be here until Moira has been found."

"After the way the last battle went, any help will be appreciated," Foster said. "Are they aware that these witches use dark magic that isn't easy to combat?"

Lucinda stepped forward, draping her hand over Finn's shoulder. "Our people are familiar with dark magic. No need to worry there, pup."

Foster growled at her. "I'll show you 'pup,' fairy."

Finn pulled Lucinda away just as I reached for Foster. "Now is not the time to be fighting with the people trying to help us," I said once we were a few paces back.

He scoffed. "Besides bringing you to the coven, how has she *helped*?"

I didn't answer him. Instead, I continued to lead him

toward our house. "How about we head to the pack to talk to Holden like you told Beatrix you would?"

The sigh that left him was nearly as conflicting as the emotions I felt warring inside him through our bond.

He stopped and glanced behind us, likely taking in the fighting I could hear resuming. "As much as I don't want to leave you, I should probably go alone and clear some more things up with Holden before we start showing up whenever we want like before."

I grabbed his shirt and pulled him closer until our lips were nearly touching. "Everything is going to be fine. You need to believe that."

He pressed his cheek against mine. "I'm trying."

"I love you. Go talk to Holden and remind Mack he's welcome here anytime. He didn't look so good last time I saw him," I said, wondering if the beta had lost anyone during the battle with Moira's witches.

Foster nodded stiffly. "I love you, too. I'll be back before dark."

He kissed me, and the tether that I considered to be our bond pulsed hard. My hands gripped his sides, and I suddenly didn't want to release him.

He pulled back, breathing heavily. "I should go before I drag you back to the house."

"Okay," I said, but I didn't loosen my hold on him.

His smile finally broke through my need. I hadn't seen him do that sincerely since getting him back. Abruptly, I hated everything about our situation a whole lot more.

"Hurry," I added before finally releasing him.

"Always." He turned away, then shifted midair as he launched himself forward.

His wolf trotted back to me and pressed his furry head against my chest. "Hey, there," I cooed.

The rumbling that came from his chest vibrated through my body, sending chills down my spine.

My heart stuttered, and I kissed his head. "Make sure nothing happens to him."

The wolf nodded and yipped, then turned slowly enough that I could rub my hand down his neck and over his back before he ran toward the forest that would lead to the pack.

When I turned back to the group behind me, they were all staring with mixed expressions. "What?" I asked.

"I've never seen a wolf that docile before," Amersyn said.

A howl cut through the air that sounded more like a warning than anything else.

"Not that that's a bad thing," the vampire added.

Lucinda's gaze was on me again. "Another interesting thing."

"Well, that's why Beatrix wants us to be here. So that a bonding between different races won't seem so different or *interesting*," I said defensively.

Zeke snorted. "At least until you start popping out supernatural babies, since nobody knows what they'll be capable of."

Rachel hissed and punched him. "Don't be rude."

"What? I'm just saying what everyone else is thinking," the dark-skinned vampire replied. "I'm not saying they shouldn't be together, but I won't lie and say I'm not curious what that actually means. Does anyone know if a kid has been born from a mixed-race bonding yet?"

Everyone shared looks, but nobody nodded or spoke up.

"See?" Zeke said. "Curiosity justified."

Lucinda smirked but glanced up at the sky instead of continuing to stare. "I'm going to fly around above and stretch my wings."

Before Finn could object, she was twenty feet in the air. He watched her until she became nothing more than a speck in the sky, then he glanced at Maciah. "What can you teach us that will help if any of the hunters or the council members are vampires and we need to defend ourselves?"

Maciah grinned. "Plenty."

I moved to stand with Amersyn and Rachel while the three men discussed offensive strategy.

"So, you and the wolf," Amersyn said. "Does that freak you out at all that he turns into a massive dog?"

"Oh my God. What is wrong with you and Zeke?" Rachel huffed. "You can't ask things like that."

Amersyn shrugged. "Pretty sure I can. That doesn't mean she has to answer, though."

"It's okay," I said. "It freaked me out at first since I didn't have any clue the supernatural world existed for nearly fifteen years, but it doesn't bother me anymore. The wolf is part of Foster, and I accept all of him."

Rachel made a soft "aw" sound. "That's super sweet. Most vampires don't have mates. Amersyn and Maciah are unique with their bond, but we sometimes still get lucky and find the one we're meant for anyway." Her gaze casted over to Zeke, and her stance softened.

"Maybe that will change once the races are living in the same communities," I said, but that was apparently the wrong thing to say, because her eyes widened and her lips downturned. "Or maybe not."

Amersyn grabbed Rachel's bicep and squeezed hard. "Breathe. If vampires were going to have mates, more of them would have bonded with each other. Being around the other supes won't change anything."

Rachel bit her lip and nodded but still didn't smile like she had been earlier.

So much for making new friends.

I could have used Charlie in that moment. She always knew what to say. Knowing she wasn't here to make the tension go away made my heart hurt for her more than it had since Foster had returned. He'd been a nice reprieve from the emptiness I'd been living in, but having everyone here and moving on to a new task was a stark reminder that we were still far from okay.

"Why do you look like you want to murder someone?" Amersyn asked me.

She apparently had no fucks to give about asking the invasive questions.

"My best friend was taken during our fight with the witches. Her and many others. Sometimes it hits me harder than others that she's gone. Especially since I don't know when I'll get her back or if she's okay," I answered honestly.

Some of the tension left Rachel. "I'm really sorry, Andie. We can relate."

"I'm sorry, too." I swiped angrily at the tear that escaped down my cheek. Today wasn't the day for a breakdown.

Amersyn grabbed me by the shoulders and turned me so I could see the three men fighting. "Watch them act like macho men. It will give you something to laugh at."

I chuckled. She wasn't wrong, and I gladly did just that until Lucinda returned and knocked each of them on their asses.

Maybe it wasn't going to be such a terrible day after all.

12

———————

FOSTER

I returned from the pack with good news and eager to see Andie. It was almost dinner time, and I followed the pull of our bond to find her at our house, in the kitchen, standing over a steaming tray of lasagna.

She grinned widely at me and jumped into my arms as I came around the corner. "I missed you."

"I missed you, too," I said, loving how that was the way she'd been greeting me lately. I kissed her quickly before taking a deep inhale. "That smells divine."

Andie slid out of my hold, and her face beamed. "It was my mother's recipe. I found a few of them with the things Aunt Junie left for me."

"What can I help with?" I asked, reaching for the pasta.

She smacked my hand away. "You can get plates and silverware, then wait at the table."

I sighed, but inside, my chest was ready to burst. This felt normal. For a moment, I could imagine we weren't planning to confront the Supernatural Council or plotting a war against a witch who wanted my mate's magic.

For a moment, everything was perfect. I held on to every second I could.

I did as Andie had asked while she pulled golden bread from the oven and cut the loaf into wide slices. She brought those to the table first, much to my dismay, then slowly walked back over with the main dish.

"You don't seem so worried about my appetite like you were just this morning," I said in jest.

She smirked. "Just testing your patience now. I think you're going to need quite a bit of it over the coming days."

Her comment brought reality crashing back in. "How did today go after I left?"

"Interesting, in a good way. Finn and Lucinda showed off their flying skills and the magic they're capable of producing from their hands. They're not as different from witches and warlocks as I expected them to be. The vampires were all friendly and almost human-like, which I didn't expect. Overall, I think Beatrix chose well. I'm excited to meet Roman and Cait tomorrow." She paused, serving lasagna onto our plates. "How did things go for you? What did Holden say?"

"Too much" was what I wanted to reply with, but she didn't need to hear about the hours we'd spent going back and forth on several things. He didn't agree about going to the council. He'd even turned down Evelyn's invitation to the coven, but he still wanted the help of the others when it came time to hopefully rescue those taken.

Something I doubted he'd get without going along with Beatrix's plan.

I reminded him many times that even the Moon Goddess had said we needed to trust Beatrix, but all he cared about was finding a way to locate his daughter and pack members.

I didn't blame him. I couldn't imagine how I'd be if that had been my kid taken, but I wasn't in his position, and he'd had to make a choice.

One that was finally what I wanted to hear.

"He'll go with us to the council and leave Mack at the pack to keep an eye on things as long as Beatrix will be ready at a moment's notice to open a portal to the pack should anything go wrong."

Andie nodded before I continued. "Of course she will, and if not her, then I can. Mine don't come as easily as they do for her yet, but I'm getting better."

I gave her hand a squeeze, and she sat next to me. "We need to spend some time together so you can show me more of the things you've learned."

I hated that I'd missed all of her growth with her magic, but I wouldn't deny that, selfishly, I was glad she'd cared enough about me to need the outlet of hardcore magic practice while I'd been gone.

Our bond hadn't been fully formed and, at the time, it had been severed once I'd fallen unconscious. She could have walked away and moved on when Holden had kept her out of the pack, but she hadn't. That proved to me that our relationship was more than just a connection fate had given us.

She smiled, holding a fork covered in steaming pasta in the air. "Maybe tomorrow while we wait for the wolves to get here, we can do that. Then we'll need to check in with the group dedicated to tracking Moira and the others. I usually do it once a day, but we've been so busy."

I inwardly cussed. I hadn't been considerate of how much she was likely still missing Charlie. I'd only considered the fact that she seemed better with me back. At least, based on how Holden and Mack had described how she'd been in my absence.

But now that I was paying more attention, I searched through our bond and could sense the worry, pain, and guilt she carried there. Emotions I was fairly certain she'd been hiding from me.

"I'm sorry. We've barely talked about Charlie, but I'll do whatever it takes to make sure we get her back safely," I said with conviction. Charlie was Andie's family, and that made her mine as well.

Her eyes shimmered, but she smiled. "Thank you. I'm trying to believe they're all okay. Can Holden sense the wolves at all through the pack connection? Beatrix said she couldn't with the witches, but I know things aren't quite the same for us as they are for you."

"Holden said he can tell they're still alive, but nothing more than that. He has his best trackers hunting for their scents, but nothing has come up yet and he's in contact with your witch group as well."

Andie shuddered next to me, never having taken the bite of food she'd put on her fork. "I don't know how he's still standing with Piper gone."

I pressed my lips to her temple. "You really are too kind for this world."

"I couldn't understand it then, but Holden made the right choice," she replied. "Even if it hurt, I can see now that everything worked out the way it was supposed to, or at least the way it needed to."

Maybe one day I'd have her optimism.

For now, I'd just count on my wolf to agree with her.

Always.

THE NEXT AFTERNOON, ANDIE AND I WERE OUT NEAR THE TREE line and as far from the cottages as we could get while still having open space. She'd been having a blast unleashing her magic and showing off. Was it really showing off if I was impressed, though?

Given she'd only started using magic a couple of months ago, the fact that she could easily call energy to her, open portals, and teleport wherever she wanted was remarkable.

"We could go get beignets and nobody would be the

wiser," she joked when she reappeared with a seashell in her hands.

I laughed, enjoying the peacefulness I felt when it was just the two of us. It was almost too easy to forget everything else was going to shit.

"We could, but I'm still rather full from the breakfast you made me eat," I said with a groan. She'd made enough French toast to feed an army, and I'd eaten every slice until she'd stopped hovering.

She winked. "Maybe for dessert then."

My good mood plummeted when I sensed others getting closer. I turned my head to see Beatrix walking toward us with two others I didn't know.

The man was just as tall as I was with wide shoulders and dark brown hair that fell over his forehead. He was dressed casually in jeans and a navy-colored T-shirt. His head was held high, and he had an arm wrapped protectively around the petite, brunette woman next to him.

She grinned at me as I appraised them, taking in her small frame but honed muscles and bright blue eyes.

"This is Roman and Cait," Beatrix said. "They wanted to meet the two of you before we gathered with the others." Then she pointed at me. "Play nice. I'll be back."

The old witch disappeared into thin air, and I sighed. I reached my hand out to Roman. "Foster. Nice to meet you."

He shook my hand, then tensed while glancing around. "I wish it were under better circumstances."

Before I could greet Cait, she left Roman's side and went to Andie. The alpha female wrapped her arms around my mate. "I'm really sorry for everything you've been through, but we're going to help and make sure you get your friends back."

Andie's eyes squeezed closed as she nodded against Cait's shoulder. "Thank you."

My chest tightened from Andie's unexpected onslaught of emotions, but I didn't step in.

"Cait didn't have the easiest entry into the supernatural world, either," Roman said. "She's been dying to meet Andie ever since we heard what happened."

I nodded and met his gaze straight on. "I appreciate that she cares so much. We can use all the help we can get."

Roman stared at me a beat longer. "You're not the alpha around here, right?"

Of course he'd pick up on that.

I shook my head. "No. Just a regular member of the pack. Holden is still alpha and will remain as such for as long as he chooses."

"But you are an alpha yourself," Roman said as a fact and not a question.

"I have alpha power, yes." I crossed my arms and kept his stare.

I wasn't sure if his wolf was challenging us or not, but either way, I didn't feel up for talking. Though, I wouldn't back down from him.

He finally conceded and glanced at Andie and Cait, who were still huddled close together. "They're going to be fast friends as long as Andie is open to that."

I couldn't sense any new panic from my mate, so I nodded. "I think she'll be more than okay with it."

"Good. Let's let them get to know each other then and you can tell me more about what we're dealing with." Roman laughed. "Beatrix is a formidable ally, but knowing what to believe out of her mouth isn't always easy."

I grinned right alongside him. "I can agree with that."

At least Beatrix had done something right calling these two for help.

Cait was the kind of person I hadn't known I'd been looking for in my life. Within the first five minutes of talking with her, I felt like I'd found a long-lost friend. She understood the struggles I'd experienced coming into the supernatural world as an adult. Knew what it was like to have a wolf shifter for a mate. Empathized with me over missing Charlie.

She was just amazing. I didn't know how else to describe her without crossing a line or two.

"So, can you transform yourself?" she asked as we walked arm-in-arm back toward the main section of the coven.

My face scrunched. "Huh?"

"You know. Like turn yourself into a wolf with your magic." Her tone made it seem like that should have been an obvious thought for me to consider before.

"Um, not that I'm aware of," I answered.

Her eyes roamed over me. "Interesting. I don't know if you heard, but my wolf isn't normal. We were Luna Marked and that caused quite a bit of drama, but Adira can sense things. She says there's something different with you."

"Who's Adira?" I asked, not wanting to change the subject, but she'd lost me for a moment.

Cait lightly smacked her hand against the side of her head. "That's my wolf. I forget shifters don't normally have names for their wolf spirits. Given I was raised human, I couldn't not call her by something proper. It just felt wrong. She's lived a lot of lifetimes and has good intuition. We should try a few things with your magic when we have more time."

My heart ached and blossomed at the same time. I wanted to try these new things with Charlie. She would be so excited for this, but it was nice to have a new friend. Amersyn and Rachel had been nice yesterday, but they didn't understand me like Cait seemed to.

"Thanks. I'd love to do that," I said with a genuine smile on my face.

She nudged me with her shoulder. "We can wait for Charlie if you want as well. I have a best friend at home who's helping to watch the pack in our absence. I don't know what I'd do without her, so I don't take offense if you'd rather wait."

Seriously. How was she so damn nice and understanding?

I shook my head. "Charlie would kick my ass for wallowing." I laughed, then added, "Maybe we'll have some time once we're back from the council."

Cait shuddered. "I can't believe we're going back there, but I agree with Beatrix. Roman didn't think this was our fight, but I reminded him of all the people who stepped up for us. We owe this to Beatrix and the rest of the supernatural population."

Before I could reply to her and ask about what had happened to her, Roman and Foster appeared in our line of sight. Warmth traveled through the tether at my chest, urging me to run, not walk, toward Foster. I managed to keep my pace brisk before I threw my arms around his neck.

He kissed the top of my shoulder where he'd last left his mark on me. "I hope you don't mind that we left."

"No. It was good talking with Cait," I said earnestly.

Foster pulled back and pressed his forehead against mine, taking a deep inhale. "I'm glad. Beatrix is ready for us."

I glanced over at Roman and Cait. They were huddled close together like Foster and I were. Maybe it was a shifter thing or a mate thing, I didn't know, but seeing others I could finally relate to eased some of the stresses I'd been carrying.

Cait grinned up at Roman, and her cheeks reddened from whatever he'd whispered in her ear. I turned away so they could have their private moment and followed Foster to the meeting area we'd been in the day before.

We entered to find everyone else already there and all but one chair lined up in a half circle. Lucinda and Finn were standing at the center of the room with their backs to the others while they talked quietly amongst themselves. The four vampires were already seated on the right while the witches I hadn't met yet were as far from them as they could get on the other side of the room.

I shook my head and sighed as we continued forward.

"What's wrong?" Foster whispered.

My chin quickly pointed around the room. "Beatrix thinks we can end the council and create these communities, but I don't think it's going to be as easy as she hopes."

His eyes roamed the small space. "No, probably not, but we have to start somewhere."

His response surprised me. I didn't think he cared too much for this plan, but maybe that was a conversation we needed to have more in depth.

We took a seat in the middle of the half-circle. Roman and Cait joined us a few minutes later, and the room was awkwardly tense. In front of me, I eyed the two new witches Beatrix had invited whom I'd never seen before.

One was ridiculously tall. Maybe even more so than

Foster, but she was overly thin. I could see her shoulder bones poking through the thin cloak she wore. Her long, black hair fell to mid-back and her eyes were a murky, silver color that seemed to see nothing yet everything all at once.

The witch next to her watched each of us for a few seconds at a time, reading the room but giving no indication of what she thought. Her dark eyes and skin remained unchanging as she sat with her ankles crossed and hands folded in her lap.

Not even when Beatrix burst into the room from the back door did either of them flinch.

"Welcome, everyone," Beatrix said in an even tone. "I see nothing has changed yet. Don't worry. We'll work on that soon."

I assumed the crazy witch was talking about the segregation of the groups, as I'd already noted.

Evelyn and Ava walked in behind her, nodding at the witches, and then took a seat next to them while Lucinda and Finn sat on the opposite side of Foster.

Beatrix of course took center stage.

She toyed with the end of her long, silver braid before flinging it behind her. "Just to make sure we're all on the same page, let me recap why each of us is here in case anyone is having doubts." Her gaze moved to the new witches. "Mirra and Vi, the hunters have been circling your covens, and it doesn't matter how many you kill or cast away, more always show up where they don't belong, wanting something they have no right to."

Interesting, I thought as Beatrix quickly moved on in her introductions.

"Then we have Foster and Andie. While neither of them has become personally acquainted with the council yet, they haven't gone unnoticed by the nameless leaders. This witch and wolf are true mates, and if they're ever going to have a sense of security while living their lives freely, the council needs to be a thing of the past."

Then she glanced at Roman and Cait. "These two have already witnessed the mess that is the council. I'm sure they're only here because of Cait, but they both know what could happen if the council remains left unchecked."

Even the vampires nodded at Beatrix's words. I felt like there was a lot more history that I should have been aware of before working with these supernaturals.

"Lucinda and Finn. Some could say they have no reason to join us, other than Lucy here loves a good fight, but I say differently." Beatrix paused, challenging the fae, but she stayed quiet. "I say they have the most to gain here. They've lived separately for centuries. While they might feel safe in their bubble, that could change at any time, and I know they're smart enough to realize that."

Surprisingly, neither Lucinda nor Finn countered her statement.

Beatrix then pointed a crooked finger at Maciah. "And lastly, we have the vampires. Ones who don't kill for sport or food. They fight for human life on a near-nightly basis and despise dictators. They are the example all nests should follow, but we are far from that utopia unless we take actions to continue moving us forward."

She chuckled to herself, then straightened in her chair. "As you can see, we all have a reason to be here, but that's only the first step. The second is to understand that I don't mean to disband the council and leave our world without leadership. Everyone needs someone to look to for guidance and I'm not saying any or all of us will be those people should tomorrow go according to plan, but our leadership should be transparent. Supernaturals should know whose rules they're following and whose punishment is being issued. No more cloak and dagger. No more fear of the unknown. No more letting a group of faceless leaders do whatever they want because someone once thought it was a good idea."

My skin shivered as I listened to Beatrix speak more passionately than ever before. The depth of care she had on this subject was real and tangible to everyone in this room if the widening of their eyes was any indication.

Foster's chest rumbled next to me, but he was nodding his head in agreement when I glanced over at him. That was a positive change I hadn't expected to come so easily. I really wished we could do that mind-speak thing right then.

"So, how do you think we're going to do this?" Mirra, the taller witch, asked.

Beatrix grinned. "We're going to ask nicely."

Roman scoffed and chuckled at the same time. "And *when* that doesn't work?"

"*If,*" Beatrix corrected, "that doesn't work, then we will demand transparency and openness from them. *When* they don't comply with that, we will give the option to dissolve the council peacefully or by force. While there are only a few of us going tomorrow, we will have an army they can't beat standing behind us."

"How do you know they won't comply with transparency?" Amersyn asked.

Lucinda leaned forward and stared at Beatrix while grinning. "Because there is nothing more that people in power hate than giving up said power. They have very little outside of their anonymity. Beatrix saw through that the day they admitted to being compromised, didn't you, old friend?"

Beatrix nodded, fighting her own smile. "I did, and if they couldn't fight off an unstable witch, then there's no chance in hell they can fight us off. The council will surrender willingly, or they will die. Not all of them will see things that way, but I know enough will and they'll be smart enough to walk away with their identities hidden while they still can."

"Wouldn't we then need to worry about them coming

after us on their own?" I asked, because I didn't for one second believe the only power these people held was their anonymity. Something had gotten them to where they were, regardless of whether or not they were the *most* powerful.

"Maybe," Beatrix answered. "But that won't be a worry for some time, and when it is, we'll be ready for them."

Her confidence was contagious. I had to give the elder witch that. I believed her, and it seemed everyone else in the room did as well, considering there were no outward objections so far.

"Isn't the council hidden?" Foster asked.

Mirra spoke up again. "It is, and they've recently moved, but my coven has been keeping close tabs on them, considering the threats we've received. We know exactly where they are."

I was tempted to ask *how* she knew, but the haunted look of her murky eyes had me keeping my mouth shut.

"When do we leave, and how are we getting there?" Finn asked next.

Beatrix narrowed her eyes. "Are you trying to steal my show, Finnigan?"

He groaned and looked at Lucinda. "Please, stop calling me that in front of other people." Then, he addressed Beatrix. "Of course not."

She and the fae wore matching smirks as Beatrix spoke. "Of *course* not. We're leaving tomorrow around ten in the morning. We'll let the council at least have their breakfast before we ruin their day. Ava and Evelyn will open a secure portal to reduce the amount of notice anyone has of our arrival. I assume we'll be home before lunchtime."

Foster leaned closer to my ear. "We'll need to go to the pack and relay all of this to Holden."

I nodded as Beatrix continued.

"I recommend the rest of you spend this time getting to

know each other. Maybe set an example of how easy it is for us to all work together."

Zeke snorted, and a bolt of magic left Beatrix's finger before anyone could question what was happening.

"Have you learned nothing, vampire?" She *tsked*.

Rachel tended to the scorch mark on his arm while Zeke remained silent.

"Well, then. Everyone, have a good day and let me know if you need anything." Beatrix stood as if nothing had just happened. "I'll be around."

The last bit was said almost as a threat. Likely only for the vampire she seemed not to be terribly fond of.

Mirra and Vi disappeared as soon as Beatrix had left the room, but nobody else did. Surprising both Foster and me, Roman stood and shook hands with Lucinda and Finn. "How are things on the islands?"

"Better than they've been in decades. You should come visit again," Finn said with a laugh. "We promise not to intrude next time."

Roman glanced at Cait longingly. "It all worked out how it was meant to."

Lucinda gagged. "We see that."

"Sorry. She might have accepted a mate, but affection still isn't her thing," Finn said with love, but not at all jokingly.

"I told you before, you'll find me living in the depths of the ocean before I start accepting hugs," Lucinda replied with a shudder.

Finn merely shook his head, then addressed everyone still present in the room. "Well, we're going to our room, but we'll be back out later. Maybe we can all have dinner together."

I could sense the hesitation in Foster, but still, he nodded. "Sure. We'll find you when we're back from the pack."

Lucinda grabbed Finn's wrist and dragged him from the room. "There are too many mates in here. I can't breathe."

I chuckled at her parting words, then glanced at the

vampires and wolves. "Are any of you going to join us for dinner?" I asked since I hadn't heard or seen confirmations from any of them.

"As long as there are no surprise guests, then sure," Zeke grumbled, still holding his arm where Beatrix had zapped him.

"You'd think one day he'd learn to keep his mouth shut." Amersyn rolled her eyes. "Yes, we'll be around, and we'll bring our own food."

My stomach churned, but I hoped my face remained neutral. I hadn't thought about their *diet*. At least they didn't kill people to get their sustenance, according to Beatrix.

Roman and Cait hadn't replied yet. I turned to them, hoping they'd say *yes*. They were looking at each other, seeming to be having a private conversation before Roman finally sighed and turned to Foster. "Do you think Holden would mind if we went to the pack with you?"

I could hear the annoyance in his tone and clearly saw the grin on Cait's face, which made me do the same and answer before Foster could.

"He won't mind at all. Come on." I reached for Cait's arm, and she easily stepped forward, going with me out the door.

"They're going to hate us getting along," she tittered.

Maybe on the outside, but from what I'd seen, alphas were nothing more than big teddy bears when it came to their mates. They secretly loved that we'd both made a new friend. I had no doubts about that whatsoever.

14

FOSTER

Our mate is happy, my wolf said as Roman and I followed her and Cait to the edge of the coven.

She is, and we're going to do everything in our power to keep her that way, I replied. Finding Charlie and stopping Moira was the best way to do that for good, but the distraction Cait offered was welcome.

The alpha female respects our mate. That makes me curious, he added.

Curious? About what?

Things. He paused. *Very interesting things I wondered about before.*

My wolf was being purposely obtuse, but I wasn't in the mood to banter. His tendency to hide things from me wasn't new, and I knew he'd tell me more whenever he was ready. For now, I needed to make sure Holden knew I was on my way and arriving with guests.

Andie and I are headed to the pack with Roman and his alpha female Cait, I said to Holden through the pack connection.

Good. I was hoping to see Roman before tomorrow.

I grunted. *And you'll apologize to Andie as we previously talked about?*

I'm an alpha of my word, was his curt reply. If he'd been in front of me, I might have punched him.

If his apology wasn't the sincerest thing I'd ever heard, he was going to know how unhappy I was. I might have been in the mood to play nice with this council distraction, thanks to the Moon Goddess stating this was the right direction to go in, but that didn't mean I'd turned over a new leaf with all things.

Nobody disrespected my mate and walked away without injury.

Even my wolf couldn't disagree with me there.

"Holden is glad you and Cait are joining us," I said to Roman once I'd taken a calming breath.

Andie glanced back at me and gave me a onceover. I nodded in confirmation that I was still good.

"Great. I've only ever spoken to him by phone and email," Roman replied, then he quietly added, "I'm not a fan of the 'one community' ideal that Beatrix has, but I do see the benefits. She'll have to allow some leeway for those of us who have already created our own homes."

The coven barrier was just up ahead, and I waited until we'd passed through before responding. "I'm sure we're decades away from new communities forming, but I'm sure once they're ready, the wolves who would like to join them could live outside of the town. We're not meant for city living."

Roman looked up at the trees in front of us. "No, we're not, but *together yet separate* may be the way to compromise. Each state would have its own 'city' so to speak. One where there are still resources for all and are just large enough to not feel on top of each other while blending in with the humans as needed."

I was glad he immediately understood what I was saying. I'd slowly been trying to accept that Luna had advised correctly and following Beatrix on this insane mission was the right thing for our immediate needs.

While I still wasn't sure how all of this would work out, I *was* seeing that working together on this before facing off with Moira was a way to build trust between those who would continue standing by us in the coming weeks.

It wasn't until this morning that I'd allowed myself to picture the various futures ahead of us and not many of them were good if we didn't follow Beatrix's lead.

Having a mate who was a witch born from two powerful lines meant that there might always be threats to her if things didn't change.

If we lived somewhere where our protection had a much further reach... I couldn't deny the appeal there. Of course, my wolf and I wanted to keep Andie safe ourselves, but I wasn't foolish enough to believe that we could best every person who might want her power.

"Do you mind if we shift?" Cait asked Andie and I felt the decline in my mate's mood right in my chest.

My mate hated being different from me, but I hoped she knew how much I loved her, regardless.

Andie forced a smile to her face. "Not at all. We'll catch up."

Cait's eyes softened, and she grabbed Andie's elbow before reaching back for Roman. They locked hands briefly before stepping to the side.

I paused with Andie, and she watched with bated breath as their bodies shimmered before transforming and landing onto four legs.

Cait's wolf was undeniably unique. The first thing I noticed was how her dark coat pulsed with a soft, purple glow and how she was inches longer than any normal wolf.

She shook her fur out, and her tail sashayed back and forth while her wolf yipped. Roman's charcoal wolf sniffed at her, and I heard him rumble, but I couldn't tell whether that was out of concern over something we didn't understand or just excitement of being shifted together.

Andie grabbed my hand and glanced up at me. "I'm sorry I can't give you that."

Without asking for permission, I lifted her into my arms and squeezed tightly. "Why would I want that when holding you like this is so much better?"

She blushed and smacked my chest. "Lies, but I appreciate your words nonetheless."

I leaned forward and pressed my lips to hers, lingering for several moments until the shared heat between us got to a point that Roman and Cait probably wouldn't have appreciated.

"Never a lie," I said before running to catch up with the wolves.

Andie snuggled in as my speed increased. "Does your wolf have a name?"

Confusion struck me. "Um, no. Why?"

"Cait's does. Her name is Adira." Andie blushed. "I just thought maybe I could call your wolf something other than 'your wolf.'"

I waited for my wolf to respond since I knew he was listening.

Nobody has used my given name since my first shift, he said quietly.

Shit. I suddenly felt like an asshole for never asking him.

What can I call you? I asked.

Not you. Just Andie. He bristled. *She can call me 'Elias.'*

I relayed the message. "He said you can call him 'Elias' if you'd like."

Andie grinned widely. "I love that, and I will. Maybe I can see him again tonight."

After dinner, my wol—Elias demanded.

That was going to take some getting used to.

I said not you, he grumbled.

Or maybe not.

I glanced down at Andie. "We'll shift tonight after dinner."

She grinned widely in response and soon, we were at the pack. I slowed my steps, watching for the pack members I knew would have been out in the forest. A part of me hoped one of them said something rude just so I could set an example where it came to Andie, but so far, none of the wolves came closer as I set her down.

Cait and Roman were already back on two feet and beaming at each other.

"What's going on?" Andie asked.

The two of them shared a look, then Cait whispered, "We'll tell you later."

Huh. That was interesting.

Holden came out of the pack house before any other questions could be asked. His face remained passive as he strode toward us, hands in his pockets and only slight wrinkles around his eyes.

Roman stepped forward and shook his hand. "It's nice to officially meet you." Then Roman gestured to Cait. "This is my alpha female Cait."

Holden finally cracked a smile. "I'm glad you both could make it. Let's head inside."

My jaw ground together as he ignored Andie and me, leading Roman and Cait ahead.

Cait glanced back with a frown on her face, but Andie pulled me along before I could make a scene.

"It's fine," Andie whispered to me as I reluctantly followed her.

My arm wrapped protectively around her. "No, it's not, and he's going to know that as soon as we're in his office."

We went into the house and headed in just the direction I predicted. The others were just going through the office door when we caught sight of them, and Holden didn't bother waiting for us to enter before he took a seat.

"Hold—" I began to snarl, but Andie cut me off as we walked through the door.

"I'd like to apologize for the trouble I caused your pack, Holden," Andie said, moving a step in front of me. "I know if I hadn't been mated to Foster and he hadn't been part of your pack that Moira never would have come here. I also know that I wasn't in control of myself, and while neither Foster nor I agree with being kept apart, I do believe you made the best decision you could for the greater good."

She finished, and I was ready to rip Holden apart because Andie shouldn't have had to apologize, but Holden stood again and came around his desk.

He reached for Andie's elbow and I growled at him, but he paid me no attention. "Thank you, Andie. I'm sorry I didn't at least keep you updated about Foster. I was just worried that any news other than good news would make things worse for you. I couldn't risk another incident within the pack. Not with everything that had already happened."

Holden glanced at me and then back at Andie before continuing. "I'm also sorry for making you not feel welcome within the pack. I shouldn't have taken my anger out on you for my daughter being taken. You might have been the reason Moira came, but I know she's the person I was truly furious with. Never you."

My fury turned into a low simmer as he spoke. That was the apology I'd been wanting. That was the one Andie deserved because she wasn't the one who'd taken the witches and wolves. She hadn't sent witches here to kill us. My mate had only tried to make things better.

Andie smiled at the alpha and wiped at the tears on her cheek. "Thank you."

Holden nodded and released her arm before going back to

his desk. "So, tell me how things went with Beatrix and the others."

I quickly filled him in on Beatrix's "why" for wanting to disband the council, given it had been a bit more elaborate and eye-opening than it had been on previous occasions, along with the plans for tomorrow.

"Good. I assumed a lot of that, but it's nice to see Beatrix actually voicing her thoughts instead of thinking nobody else needs to know what's going through her head," Holden said. "I've spent the morning working with Mack and several others to choose who would go with me and who would stay behind to watch the pack not only here, but in town. We still haven't finished deciding, but I paused the meeting when I knew you were arriving."

"I don't know how you run such a large pack with only one alpha," Roman said with a grimace. "I thought mine was big, but what you have here is on a completely different level."

Holden shrugged. "Things work just fine most days. It's all we've known for years."

An awkward silence filled the room until Andie cleared her throat. "Do you mind if Cait and I go see Gemma?"

"Go on ahead," Holden answered. "I think I can keep these two busy for a while."

Andie smiled and stood. I followed her movements and went to the door with her. I kissed her softly. "You didn't have to apologize first."

She smiled. "Yes, I did, and if I weren't your mate, you would realize that's the truth. We'll be back soon."

I squeezed her hand. "Be careful."

Andie nodded at Cait. "We'll be fine."

With that, they exited the office. Before I got back to my seat, Holden's voice echoed in my mind, talking not only to me, but to every wolf connected to him.

I've given Andie permission to enter the pack again. If she has any issues with pack members when she comes to visit—at any time —punishment will be swift and severe.

He'd given the warning without telling them that she was already here. An interesting choice, but I appreciated the gesture regardless and trusted Andie would be safe with Cait.

"Thank you," I said to the alpha.

Holden nodded, then turned toward Roman. "So, tell me, how are things in Texas these days?"

Roman glanced between the two of us but answered the question anyway, going on about merging packs, betas, and a life that I hadn't known for so many years.

One that I hoped would be mine just as soon as we moved through these next obstacles.

Not only did I want that, but Andie deserved the kind of life that Roman described. Full of family, friends, and peace.

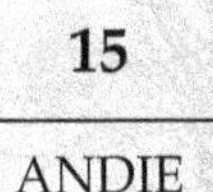

15

ANDIE

Cait and I had managed to make our way through the pack without incident. I'd invited her for several reasons, but I wouldn't deny one of them had been to make sure that if I ran into trouble, I'd have someone on my side and someone to contact Foster. She was just the person, thanks to her kindness and mind-speak with Roman.

Thankfully, there were no reasons to reach out to our mates and we spent an hour catching up with Gemma. Cait nearly cried when she held the baby and didn't relinquish him for the entirety of our visit, making me wonder if that was connected to the look she and Roman had shared earlier.

But when I finally got the chance to ask, her answer wasn't at all what I'd expected.

"We're definitely trying for a baby when my heat comes, but that's not what had us grinning earlier," Cait said, then she glanced around. "I'll have to tell you later, though."

Patience wasn't always my strong suit, and with her fidgeting hands, she seemed eager to talk.

I stopped us near a tree and created a small shield to keep anything we said private. "Better?"

Her eyes moved, taking in my magic as it settled and disappeared but remained just as effective. "Shifting is amazing, but tricks like that are something else altogether."

The awe in her voice only made me feel slightly better about not having a wolf.

Cait grabbed my hand and still kept her voice low. "So, my wolf hasn't glowed purple like that in some time. She told me that's the sign from the Moon Goddess that we're doing what we should be. Roman hadn't been completely on board with all this, but now, he sees I've been right this whole time."

I didn't know what her glow really had to do with our situation, but I returned her smile. "That's great."

"But that's not all." I didn't think it was possible for Cait's smile to widen, but it did. "With the Luna Marked energy, Adira says she thinks we can help you use your magic to shift. You wouldn't be a conventional wolf, but it could be interesting to see what happens."

I was trying to be grateful for their interest in me, but a part of me wasn't so sure. "Why would Adira think that?"

Cait lightly sighed. "She's a big fan of mates. Her respect of the bond is almost ridiculous. She's why I've been on board to help you guys. My stubbornness almost lost me Roman, but more than that, nobody should ever get in the way of a bond between mates."

I didn't want to get too excited. I didn't want to believe her wolf was right or could really give me the one thing I'd been dying to give Foster, but the more Cait spoke, the more hope rose within me.

Cait flinched then turned around. "Time's up. Our mates are panicking because they can't hear us. We'll talk more soon. I promise."

Sure enough, Foster and Roman popped into my line of sight just as I removed the privacy shield. Neither of them asked about why they couldn't hear us. Instead, they wrapped us in their arms and suggested we get back to the coven for dinner.

"How about instead of shifting or running, I get us there a little faster?" I suggested. Since the wolves had gotten time to show off their abilities, I figured it was my turn to do the same.

Nobody objected and I opened the portal to let out right in front of the meeting room, where I figured it would be easiest for everyone to gather, given our house wasn't big enough.

Foster walked through first with Cait behind him while she laughed at her mate. "Oh, come on, Roman. Nothing is going to bite you."

He grumbled but finally stepped through.

I chuckled as I closed the opening and we all got to work on setting up for dinner. We found all of the plates and silverware to set the table, checked in on the food that Ava, Evelyn, and some of the other witches were preparing and cooking, then brought out drinks.

Before we knew it, everything was ready and platters of food that smelled divine were being brought out for our guests.

Roman and Cait sat across from us at the end of the table while the fae sat in the middle and it wasn't long before the vampires showed up, spreading out along the table with their groups of two.

"How was everyone's day?" I asked to diminish the silence before things turned awkward.

Amersyn laughed. "It was uneventful. Something I'm not used to but am trying to enjoy."

Lucinda twirled a dagger with the point down on the table. "You should come to Fae Islands. I can't remember the last time we had a bloodsucker there."

"Maybe it's because you still call us 'bloodsuckers,'" Maciah deadpanned without looking at the snarky fae.

She smirked, tossed the blade in the air, and then tucked it into the holster at her hip. "Right."

"Serve up, everyone," I said loudly, but nobody made a move for the food.

Beatrix was out of her damn mind for thinking we could all live and work together.

Roman finally grabbed a steak from the tray in the middle, then a baked potato. "Who do we have to thank for all the food?"

"Beatrix picked the menu, but Ava and Evelyn would have worked with other witches to have the food made," I said, offering him a thankful smile.

Zeke gagged. "At least our food isn't magically processed."

Rachel cut a glare at him. "I'm sure she meant 'made' as in 'cooked.' Don't be rude just because you got in trouble with Beatrix again."

I grinned. "Thank you, Rachel."

Her smile was wide and lit up the room. "You're welcome."

Finally, those who were eating filled their plates. It wasn't long after that smaller conversations started up, and not just between those who lived together. It wasn't a grand party by any means, but it wasn't as uncomfortable as I'd foreseen it being in the beginning.

By the time we helped clean up, thanked the witches who'd cooked, and said our goodbyes for the evening, my head was beginning to ache. I wanted nothing more than to rest with my mate.

I teleported us back to our house because even walking a few blocks seemed like a feat too big to tackle after the busy day.

Foster wrapped his arms around me. "Why don't you go get ready for bed and I'll bring you something warm to drink?"

His eyes flashed brighter, reminding me of his wolf and the fact that we had a date tonight. "How about we go into the backyard and you shift? It's a nice evening for lying in the grass."

Any tiredness that I'd been feeling moments before was pushed down. After the talk I'd had with Cait earlier, my mind had begun to wander. There were definitely some things I was curious about, and it helped boost my energy to think about them again.

Plus, spending time with Foster's wolf—no, Elias—in any manner was the perfect ending to our day.

"Are you sure?" he asked. "My wolf doesn't mind waiting," he added, but I could hear the disappointment in his voice at the thought.

"Tell Elias his furry ass better be in that yard by the time I'm out of the bathroom or we're going to have words." I turned and walked down the hallway, grinning at the sound of Foster's deep chuckle echoing behind me.

Within a couple of minutes, I took care of business and went out the back door. I glanced left and right, but I couldn't see Elias.

I took a step farther into the yard. "Foster? Eli—"

Something large and imposing leapt in front of me, and I screamed much too loudly, considering all of the training I'd been doing.

Elias had jumped from the roof and was now sitting before me with his tail thumping.

I pointed and glared at him. "That was rude."

His head twisted back, glancing at his rear end.

"Ah, I take it you didn't like me calling your ass furry." I winked at Elias, but he glowered in return.

Kneeling in front of him, I pressed my head against his chest. "I promise it wasn't an insult. Your ass is perfect, just like the rest of you."

A rumbling vibrated beneath my temple, and I squeezed

him tighter before getting back up. "What do you want to do?"

I maybe should have asked Foster this before he'd shifted. At least he could have communicated for us, but there wasn't anything wrong with winging it, either.

Elias's already bright-blue eyes increased in luminosity, then he stared at my hands.

"Magic?" I asked, and his head moved up and down.

The wolf was more in tune with things than I had given him credit for.

"Okay, then."

The ball of power at my core lit up at my attention, and within the blink of an eye, a sphere of dark-blue magic hovered above my palm.

I tossed it up into the air, then caught it with the other hand. "Want me to throw it?"

Elias lay down and put a paw over his face.

I was absolutely kidding, but the insult was well worth seeing him pout as he was.

"I didn't get the chance to tell Foster, but Cait mentioned her wolf thinks I could shift in some way," I said, concentrating hard on my thoughts and the energy already swirling within my palm.

Elias stared up at me with an intensity I wasn't used to from him, but it encouraged me to continue exploring where my inner thoughts were leading me.

I extinguished the ball in my hands and kneeled to join him on the ground. My hands cupped his huge head, and, for a moment, I tried my hardest to read his mind, but still, there was no sound between us or the bond.

"I wish I could hear you," I said softly, resting my head against his.

The connection I did feel to Elias warmed inside my chest, and I smiled, knowing he was probably trying to say it was okay, but that didn't lessen my guilt that I wasn't the she-wolf he deserved.

As we stayed on the ground, connecting and soaking each other up, my thoughts focused on how it might be possible for me to transform into a wolf.

I was tempted to pop over to Cait and Roman's cabin to ask, but before I could do anything of the sort, something shifted in me. A new, elevated sense of awareness of Elias and our surroundings.

I stilled, listening for anything that didn't belong, but nothing was out of place...except for me.

My eyes closed and I breathed deeply.

What am I missing?

Energy pulsed along my skin, fighting to get out in a way I hadn't experienced before. The one thing I'd learned during the recent weeks was that I couldn't fight who I was. I had to embrace every part of myself, including the pieces I was afraid of, like the syphon energy. It wasn't until I'd done so that I'd felt like I had truly taken control of the power.

So, now, when I badly wanted to shove whatever magic was rising from deep within back where it'd come from, I didn't.

Instead, I reopened my eyes, stood up, and took a step back from Elias. He wouldn't get hurt because my energy decided to act out tonight or because I'd let my thoughts lead me down a path I probably shouldn't have stepped foot on without more guidance.

My eyes glanced over my arms. The same blue of magic— what I assumed was now my permanent energy color— glowed softly along my skin.

My focus remained only on the power that continued to grow and the more I concentrated, the tighter my chest became.

Elias stood on four legs and whimpered, but I held my

finger up. "Give me a minute before you let Foster shift back."

I didn't need my mate panicking and breaking my concentration. Whatever this was, I wouldn't sleep until I figured it out.

Another minute ticked by, and Elias's whimpers turned to growls. I knew that was Foster trying to break through, but I was so close to whatever this was.

The hue of light around me stretched and darkened with every beat of my heart. I was trying to examine it, but the harder I tried, the farther I felt the magic pull away from me.

Maybe I wasn't supposed to keep whatever this was. Maybe the magic Cait had mentioned wasn't inside of me.

"Back up a little more," I said, then added, "I promise if this doesn't work, I'm done."

The wolf nodded and walked backward, never taking his eyes off me.

Once I felt like we were a safe enough distance apart, I pushed the energy away from me. It expanded then quickly snapped back, burning my skin enough to make me wince.

That didn't deter me, though.

I tried again, pushing harder and focusing more.

Elias half-howled, half-barked at me, gaining my attention as I was midway through my second attempt.

He was sitting up and staring at the crescent moon in the sky, and I followed his sight.

Please let me be able to shift, I pleaded.

With those unspoken words, the magic pulsing around my skin stretched further and began to form into something in front of me, but the more power that left my body, the less I was able to focus.

My breathing was normal, and I felt physically fine, but my awareness was slipping and I didn't know how to stop it. That was when panic finally started to set in.

"Foster...help..." I whispered just as my body crumpled to the ground.

16

FOSTER

W atching Andie fall to the ground made my heart stop for the brief second that it took me to realize I needed to get my shit together and shift so that I could help. At least that was my plan until my wolf wouldn't let me. I was about to ground his ass for life before he spoke.

Look at her, he demanded.

My eyes refocused. At first, I only saw Andie's prone body, but then…there was something else.

Right next to her, magic swirled slowly, taking shape into something I couldn't believe.

She's shifting in her own way, my wolf whispered reverently.

I'd have never believed it if I hadn't seen the transformation with my own eyes, but sure enough, the energy that had left Andie's body was taking the form of a wolf. A petite, glowing blue wolf with silver eyes and a form that didn't appear solid moved fluidly and stepped toward us.

Andie? I asked, but there was no answer.

I told my wolf to give Andie's body more attention instead

of the magic outside of her. We listened to her heartbeat and focused on the rise and fall of her chest. Everything seemed as though she were sleeping and her face remained peaceful.

There was no way to know if she was aware of what was happening, but this wolf...spirit?...she'd created didn't seem to be concerned with anything as she pranced across the yard.

The she-wolf's form was a solid foot shorter than mine. When she bumped into my wolf, she only managed to nudge his front flank with her much-smaller head.

He growled quietly in reply, and then she leapt over the fence.

Shit, I thought.

I didn't want to leave Andie's body without knowing if that was her controlling the... Shit, I wasn't even sure what to call the thing. Except, there was no controlling my wolf now.

He chased after the spirit with pure joy coursing through his thoughts.

If Andie isn't okay when we get back, you're not getting out for a decade, I warned.

She's fine. I can still hear her resting from here.

He might have been able to while he was concentrating, but something told me the wolf wasn't going to be focused on our mate's body for long. At least, not the physical form.

This wolf spirit, however, pranced and turned in circles while we caught up to her. My own marveled at her movements and was practically foaming at the mouth to catch her.

Her silver eyes closed and opened slowly before she threw her head back and howled the most blissful sound I'd ever heard.

As much as I wanted to force both wolves back to the house, not even I could deny my wolf in having what happened next.

The two wolves chased each other through the trees and,

for such a small thing, Andie's outran mine tenfold. Not once did he catch her until the very end when she slowed down, a lopsided grin on her wolfish face.

He pounced playfully at her side, and I was surprised when his paws didn't go right through her form.

Even made from magic, the wolf was solid and tangible and smelled of roses and sage, just like her creator.

Can we go back now? I asked forcefully of my wolf.

He let out a happy sigh. *I think we can.*

The two wolves shared a look and then without another sound, Andie's ran in the direction of our house.

Can you talk to her? I asked him

No, but she seems to understand me. I don't know how and I don't care. This is the best day ever.

I wasn't sure about the "best day," but it was certainly a good surprise as long as Andie was still okay when we got back.

My wolf took chase once again, but when we came out of the trees, all we caught was a glimpse of a glowing tail jumping over the fence.

He raced forward, and when we were back in the yard, the glowing wolf was nowhere to be seen.

I pushed a shift forward and forced my wolf back into the recesses of my mind.

Within seconds, I was on two feet and running toward Andie.

She groaned when I reached for her. "What happened?"

"You don't remember anything?" That shocked the hell out of me.

She gently shook her head. "My magic was doing something weird, and then I lost consciousness. How long was I out?"

"About twenty minutes." I stroked her hair and helped her up. "You really don't remember *anything*?"

She frowned. "What happened? Did I hurt you? Is that why you were across the yard?"

"Not even close." I smiled. "You created a wolf."

Andie stumbled, but I kept her upright. "Holy shit. Cait was right?"

I nodded, trying not to be hurt that she'd failed to tell me about this conversation with Cait before. "Your energy turned into a wolf that looked more like a spirit, but it had a solid form. Elias couldn't hear her, but she seemed to understand him. They ran amidst the trees for nearly twenty minutes."

Her eyes bulged out, and her mouth popped open. "Seriously? How could I not remember that?"

"You were a little unconscious throughout the whole thing." I offered her a small smile and urged her to head back inside. "How do you feel now?"

She closed her eyes briefly once we were inside the door, then reopened them. "A little tired, but not abnormally so. I can't believe I did that."

I pressed my lips to the side of her head. "Neither can I, but what were you saying about Cait? What did she tell you?"

Andie's cheeks turned crimson. "With the dinner, I forgot to mention it. She said her wolf received some of her Luna Marked energy back. I'm not sure what that means, but because of that, she felt like she could help me shift. I didn't get the chance to ask what that meant, but apparently, I figured it out on my own."

If I didn't already know Roman and Cait were good wolves, I'd be more than suspicious. I tried to rein in any concerns I had over what had happened. While I knew her shifting should have been a good thing, it was different and something we didn't understand.

With everything else going on, I wasn't sure what to make of the whole thing.

"Let's try to figure this out later. Tomorrow is going to be a long day," I said softly, not wanting to hurt her feelings.

She made a humming sound and when we were almost to the bedroom, she brightened a little more. "What did Elias think?"

I didn't even need to wait for him to confirm his answer. "He thought it was the best day ever," I said with a smile only Andie ever saw from me.

That had her face lighting up with joy. "Good. That's what's most important." Then she frowned. "We probably shouldn't say anything to Beatrix until we're back from seeing the council. I don't want her to worry about anything else."

I had no issues with that, especially given all the extra guests we had around the coven.

After they all left would be soon enough to figure out what tonight had really meant.

THE FOLLOWING MORNING, WE HAD BREAKFAST, THEN MET WITH the others outside of the meeting hall. The group of people present was bigger than I thought we needed it to be, but this was Beatrix's show and I was just here to keep Andie safe.

Standing for the witches were Beatrix, Ava, the two visiting witches Mirra and Vi, and Andie. For the wolves, it was me, Holden, Roman, and Cait. Then Maciah, Amersyn, Rachel, and Zeke represented the vampires. I didn't see Lucinda and Finn around for the fae, but I was more than okay with their absence.

Andie and I joined Beatrix first. "How long until we leave?" I asked when she nodded in greeting at us.

She glanced at her wrist, where there was no watch. "About five minutes."

"Where are Lucinda and Finn?" Andie asked.

Beatrix glanced up into the sky. "They'll be here."

Mirra was staring hard at Andie, and I didn't like that, especially after what had happened last night. So I guided my mate toward Holden, Roman, and Cait.

As soon as Cait laid eyes on Andie, she gasped. "You did it, didn't you?"

Andie's worried gaze met mine, then Cait retracted. "Wait, no." Her nose wrinkled. "You just smell too much like your mate."

The tightness in my chest eased, but not by much.

Andie's nervous laughter rang out as others stared at our small group. "Yeah, it's been a good morning."

I knew it killed her to imply we'd been talking about having sex, but it was better fewer people knew what had really happened last night. Not until we understood whatever that experience had been.

Cait winked. "Nothing wrong with that. Do witches go through heat?" She fanned her face and whispered, "The best kind of torture."

Andie's eyes widened a bit, and she seemed speechless as she shrugged, glancing behind us.

Yeah, everyone was listening and staring.

Evelyn appeared, brushing back her hair and taking in everyone around us. "Are we ready to open the portal?"

Beatrix looked up again. "Yes."

Her answer surprised me, given I couldn't sense the fae anywhere near us, but the old witch must have known something we didn't. *That* wasn't a surprise.

Ava and Evelyn worked together on the portal with Beatrix right behind them. Andie observed their actions with rapt attention, and I watched her while keeping an eye on the others.

I didn't like the interest that was growing for my mate. Mirra, in particular, made me want to rip her throat out. I didn't know why, but I wasn't going to let my guard down.

I think the witch is just curious. Andie is unique in many ways, my wolf said.

I don't need your optimism right now.

He chuckled. *I thought you missed it?*

Fair point.

Within minutes, the portal opened and I grabbed Andie's hand. She smiled at me, understanding I needed her close, even if I knew she was powerful in her own right. My need was only a reflection of me and not her.

The groups went through one by one until only Beatrix was left on the other side. "Okay, Lucy. Enough is enough."

A clap that sounded like thunder echoed from above us.

"You're no fun," Lucinda said as she floated down the ground.

"And you're terrible at hiding."

Lucinda rolled her eyes. "You only knew we were there because it's your magic guarding the coven."

Beatrix's lip twitched, but she said nothing else to the fae. "Close the opening. I will call when we're done," she said to Ava.

The shimmering hole pulsed with energy, then began to shrink until it disappeared altogether.

Beatrix then turned to face the rest of us. "Thanks to Mirra's information, we know the new council location is just south of here."

"Where is 'here'?" Roman asked, glancing around just like I had been.

There were more mountains than there were trees, and it was as hot as Hades out here, even though it was still morning. At least, I thought it was...

"We're in eastern Montana," Beatrix answered. "Now, when we arrive, only I will do the talking unless you're specifically addressed by the council. We are going to do our best not to have a fight on our hands, but I have witches at the ready to open portals for others to come to our aid, should we need it."

Nobody objected. We already knew all of this.

Lucinda extended her wings, turning them into weapons within seconds. Beatrix glared at her. "No."

"No, what?" the fae asked. "You want us to look intimidating and worth listening to, right? I already swore to keep my mouth shut, which was hard enough. I won't play down my capabilities."

Unfortunately, she made a good point.

Beatrix must have thought that as well, because she said nothing more on the subject before turning and walking south.

Finn followed his mate, extending wings that were nothing like Lucinda's. They were smooth like leather, apart from the half dozen scars I could see on each one. The coloring was a green so dark, I first thought they were black wings until they glinted under the sunlight.

None of the others in our group did anything out of the ordinary, but only an idiot would miss the power within our group.

Beatrix's portal had put us only about a mile outside of the stronghold, and when we arrived, the only thing I could see was a stone wall, maybe twenty feet in height, that circled around the property with only one gate on this side.

On top of the wall were sentry points, barbed wire, and tall spikes. Each tower contained three or more supernaturals. It wasn't long before we heard commotion, confirming our arrival had been noticed.

Beatrix paused, halting the rest of us once we were about a hundred yards from the steel gate.

Three men shimmered into existence, and one stepped forward, wearing all-black clothing with a bright-green insignia on his puffed-out chest. His red eyes told us he was a vampire and not one like those who had joined us. This one, I would guess, freely dined on human blood.

"You don't have an invitation allowing you to be here," he said darkly.

Beatrix stepped closer and grinned. "No, but we do have a right to be here. We need a word with *our* council."

The vampire stiffened. "There's a process for that. You can't just show up."

"But we have." Mirra stepped forward. "And under Act Ten, Section Seven-Point-Four, we have every right to request to be seen. Unless the council has amended their bylaws and failed to notify their subsidiaries, then we *will* be meeting with them."

The vampire hissed before turning abruptly. "Notify Leader. I'll escort our guests through the gates."

Both of his cohorts nodded, then shimmered away as quickly as they'd arrived.

I was pretty sure one of them was a wolf shifter and the other a warlock, though I couldn't be certain. Either way, they hadn't been touching each other when they arrived or departed, and normal supernaturals didn't have the ability to teleport.

That was something we needed to be aware of.

My grip on Andie's hand tightened as we followed the vampire. I didn't like this. My eyes scanned the area constantly and I kept seeing more and more guards appear where they hadn't been before. We were being circled, and I wasn't sure how many of us were aware of that fact.

Do you see what I'm seeing? I asked Holden through our pack connection.

I do. Beatrix doesn't understand what she's getting us into. This is exactly why I didn't want to come here.

I could relate to his frustration, but I'd also understood Beatrix's reasonings. I guessed we'd know who was right soon enough. It was too late to back out now.

We should shift, my wolf suggested.

No, I need to be able to communicate with Andie for as long as possible.

I'm ready when you are.

Yeah, I knew he would be. My wolf might have been positive most days, but he fought with a ferocity very few shifters had within them.

Just as we got to the gate, the two guards who had accompanied the vampire returned. They wore matching smirks, and I leaned closer to Andie. "Be ready."

She stiffened at my softly spoken words and squeezed my hand in return.

This isn't good, Holden warned as he took a step back, likely to make room for a shift.

"Is there a problem?" Beatrix asked with a pointed brow.

The bald guy with dark eyes that I'd thought might have been a warlock answered. "No problem at all."

Vi, the witch with Mirra, hissed. "Lies."

Holden shifted at that moment, with Roman and Cait quickly following. Supernaturals of varying kinds jumped down from the tops of the stone wall and blocked us in.

"I'm going to shift, but I'm not leaving your side. Not this time," I said to Andie.

She nodded, hands already glowing a dark blue and eyes focused forward.

The vampires stood with their backs to each other and fangs extended. Finn looked ready to murder someone, and Lucinda wore her signature smirk.

The four witches remained together, standing in front of us as the first line of defense.

"You don't want to do this," Beatrix said. "All we want is to talk with the council."

The vampire who'd led us to the gate scoffed. "Right. And all I want is a salad for lunch when I'm done sucking the blood from your body."

Beatrix chuckled, and I shifted.

This wasn't fucking good.

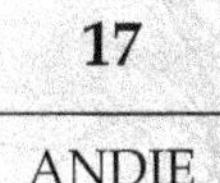

17

ANDIE

Foster's wolf stuck close to my side as a couple dozen guards closed in on us. My hands pulsed with energy, and the need to suck the life from these assholes grew exponentially by the second.

Beatrix cut a look my way and shook her head, as if she'd been able to read my thoughts.

I knew the less people who were aware of the full extent of my abilities, the better, but if my choices were between keeping my secret or saving anyone's life, my secret was about to become very public knowledge.

The lead vampire guard blurred into motion, and air whooshed at my back. I wasn't sure what from, but I didn't hesitate to act.

Energy pulsed off me, covering every inch of my body, and I charged forward with Foster at my side. A warlock sent a stream of power toward my chest, but I ducked and dodged before straightening back out and slamming my fist into his stomach.

He sucked in air and crashed into the metal gate behind him.

I pressed a hand over his forehead to knock him out with

my magic, but a growl distracted me. Several guards were headed toward us. Foster and I were the only ones blocked in by the gate. We had to move and quickly.

My eyes closed for a couple of brief seconds, then I thrusted my hands forward. Energy exploded from my palms and four of the six guards headed our way went to the ground.

Foster, or more accurately, Elias, leapt into the air, his teeth sinking into the neck of the incoming vampire who'd avoided my magic. The crunch and gushing sounds that followed made bile rise up my throat, but there was no time for queasiness.

More supernaturals began jumping down from the stone wall, and we were quickly outnumbered.

Beatrix had said she'd call for help if there was a fight, but I couldn't see any portals opening, so that left only one option.

With my back to the still-closed gate, I watched my friends fight for their lives, then closed my eyes again. I'd already spent time with each of them, focusing on their energy signatures so that I wouldn't put them in danger like I had before with the witches and wolves while fighting Moira.

Once I had a lock on the ones I wanted to keep safe, I channeled my syphon power, demanding it to take from anything other than fourteen bright lights I had my attention on.

A heaviness settled over me as I stretched the power and pushed it forward. Shouts rang out around me, but I didn't open my eyes. I wouldn't lose control. I wouldn't hurt another person I cared about.

A gust of wind tried to knock me over but was quickly blocked by something else. I trusted Foster to be watching over me and remained focused on the task I needed to finish now that I'd started.

"I knew there was something different about you." Lucinda's voice sounded close by.

Maybe she was the one who'd stepped in front of me.

My core strained from the added energy and magic I was taking in. The mix of supernaturals increased my already sensitive stomach until it was churning just as rapidly as the power gathering inside me.

Sweat broke out on my forehead, and my jaw clenched painfully tight.

There were so many fucking guards.

My only saving grace was I didn't have to take enough energy from each one to do major harm. Only enough to make them pass out long enough to stop the fighting.

Several minutes ticked by until the sounds of fighting ceased. I carefully pulled back my magic and reopened my eyes to find a snarling wolf beside Lucinda, who had her wings spread out and was standing like a blockade in front of me.

She slowly lowered them as I stepped forward.

"It worked." My awe was more because each of them was still alive and I hadn't just mass-murdered a bunch of supernaturals.

"Glad to know you had so much faith in yourself." The fae chuckled. "What do we do with these dipshits now?"

My gaze fell on Beatrix. She frowned at me. "You shouldn't have used your suppression power."

Suppression? All right. I was okay with that lie.

"I did what was necessary," I replied, wobbling a little from the overwhelming power inside me. "Where was the help we were supposed to have?"

"Unable to get through our safeguards," a voice boomed from above us.

I glanced up, and there was a cloaked figure floating toward the ground. Their covered arms lifted, and energy rippled from the form.

Groans from those still on the ground sounded.

"Go clean yourselves up and get back to your posts," the same voice demanded.

I couldn't tell if they were a man or a woman, but I could feel their power. Though, it didn't scare me. While strong, I didn't get the feeling that they could do much on their own.

The navy-blue robe billowed around them, and the cloaked figure turned back toward where I was standing with Beatrix, Lucinda, and Foster's wolf. I tried to see through the shadows within the hood, but there was nothing other than darkness.

"Why are you here?" the voice demanded.

Beatrix stepped forward. "We want to meet with the whole council, as is our right."

A strange noise came from the figure. "Why?"

"Because we have things to discuss," she retorted, then added, "Privately."

Sensing movement above us, I flicked my eyes toward the sky and saw two more cloaked figures hovering where the first had just come from. They looked forward, as if the scene beneath them were nothing of importance.

"We are busy. You'll need to come back when you're able to set an appointment," the voice said with agitation rising in their even tone.

Cait and Roman moved closer, and she tilted her chin up. "What about that 'great service' we did for you last year? After we saved your asses, you can't even spare a bit of your day to hear us out?"

Roman grimaced next to her, and I didn't blame him. A full-on war would start if they hurt Cait. I knew that without a doubt in my heart.

"We already issued our *thank you* for your role in that event," the voice deadpanned.

Roman's chest rumbled. "Sending a healing stone and a letter to us months later I'm sure took a lot of effort."

The council member turned toward Roman. "It was your mate who'd said a thanks wasn't necessary. We could have ignored you completely after helping with your fallen fighters."

Shit. This wasn't going well at all. If they refused us, I wasn't sure what Beatrix planned to do. If the others couldn't get a portal open to join us, the likelihood of us making it out of here together and alive seemed slim.

The steel gate behind me groaned as it began moving forward. We stepped out of the way, moving closer to Roman and Cait just as another cloaked figure appeared.

Shit. How many of these assholes were there?

"Let them in and quit wasting time," the voice bellowed, surprising more than just me.

"If we—" the one who had been addressing us before tried speaking but was promptly cut off.

The newest arrival floated higher into the sky. "Do as I said. Now." Then, they disappeared into thin air.

Maybe they weren't all assholes. I guessed we'd be finding out soon.

The first one rushed past us. "Follow me."

Foster shifted back to two feet and wrapped an arm around me, but I brushed him off and kneeled to the ground like I needed to retie my boots. Except I was expelling the additional power inside my body.

My fingers dug into the gravel ground, and I shivered as the foreign energy moved through me once again. Foster stood over me and helped me up as soon as I was done, but we didn't have time to catch up. The others were almost out of sight, causing us to jog ahead and rejoin our group.

Behind the rock walls were more stone buildings like ones I'd only ever seen in historical movies. Castle-like structures had been erected everywhere around us, higher than the barriers, but we somehow hadn't seen them when we'd arrived.

Magic shields seemed to be everywhere around here.

It was daylight, but I didn't miss the old lantern-style lights that flickered above as we walked the cobblestone pathways toward the biggest building of them all.

Energy pulsed around us from every direction, and my skin crawled, ready to soak up more than what I'd already had if needed again.

Two more cloaked figures flanked the one currently guiding us up a long set of wide concrete steps. Neither said anything as they floated next to the first.

"How are they floating?" I whispered to Foster.

"They must have a powerful sorcerer among them, which isn't surprising," he answered, holding on to me tighter.

Sorcerer. I'd yet to hear anyone use that term to describe a witch or warlock. Beatrix was rather powerful. Did that make her a sorceress? Given her cockiness, I'd assume if she were one, she'd have made a point to make sure people knew that, but maybe not.

We entered through massive, detailed carved wooden doors. They opened without anyone touching them and closed just the same. The entry was open with four sets of stairs leading toward different levels of the building. The floors were black marble with grey swirling inside them, and the walls were a cream color adorned with old oil paintings framed in gold trim.

The three council members led us up the third set of stairs, and we all followed wordlessly. Being able to mind-speak would have been super fucking helpful, but instead, I continued to try to focus on my surroundings instead of what was coming.

The steps beneath my feet had been made from some sort of marble, and the railings were silver metal with flourishes between the bars that were cool to the touch.

A shiver ran through me as we got to the top landing.

Something about this didn't feel right, but I was trying to remain positive. Only, the silence wasn't helping.

Foster pressed his lips to my temple as we turned left down a hallway. I sighed in relief from the contact and remembered the most important thing: I still had him by my side.

I reached for the tether that bound us and closed my eyes, letting Foster be my eyes while I got my shit together.

With calming breaths, I focused on his heartbeat, on the steady stride with which he walked, and the confidence he exuded. There wasn't an ounce of fear in him. Only a worry that I assumed was from what I'd done.

His love seeped through our bond and warmed my insides until I felt my chest loosen. With one last steadying breath, I reopened my eyes and found him looking down at me.

"Better?" he asked.

I nodded. "Thank you."

We entered a room to find eight throne-like chairs sitting on top of a dais at the back of the room. There was also a long, stone table in the middle that was surrounded by more lackluster wooden chairs.

Five of the grander seats were already filled with more cloaked figures, and the three who had led us here took the remaining spots.

The leader who had stopped the fighting sat in the middle with their chair pushed a little more forward than the others. "Have a seat and tell us why you're here." The monotone voice echoed through the room.

Apparently, they weren't going to reveal any part of themselves.

We each found our seats, and surprisingly—or maybe not so much—there were just enough places for each of us.

I held Foster's hand under the table as I waited to hear what Beatrix would say on our behalf.

Seconds ticked by with no noise in the room. I wasn't sure if that was a tactic on Beatrix's part or just her nerves making themselves known, but either way, I didn't like it.

Whatever combined energy these eight beings shared wasn't something I wanted to be around for long. Beatrix had had me thinking these beings were nothing in comparison to our combined power, but that didn't seem to be the case to me. Not after everything we'd seen so far.

Finally, Beatrix placed her folded hands on the tabletop and grinned. "We're here, representing the different races, to ask that the council cease to exist."

Okay, so she was just going right in. No foreplay with small talk.

None of the eight opposing figures flinched at her words. "Why would we do that?"

I'd heard the same voice, but this time, I couldn't tell who was speaking.

"Because you no longer put the needs of the races above your own," Beatrix answered with confidence. "Your hunters are out of control. When there are real issues that we need help with, you fail to answer the call. Most importantly, the fact that none of you will reveal yourselves is very telling."

We were met with silence for several tense minutes, but the more Beatrix spoke, the less I let my nerves bother me. She was right, and I blamed the initial, not-so-warm welcoming, for my lack of faith.

"We see," said the same voice. "Are you here to de-throne us yourself?"

I didn't miss the amusement in their tone.

Beatrix grinned. "No, we're here to ask nicely, but we aren't afraid to act however necessary to make sure that the supernaturals as a whole are taken care of."

None of the cloaked figures moved. They remained hidden within their shadowed hoods and frozen in their chairs, but I sensed a change in their energy. A miniscule change, but a change nonetheless.

They didn't like Beatrix's implied threat.

"And what will you do for authority? Do you just expect all supernaturals to live in peace without anyone to put them in their place?" one of them asked.

This time, it was Finn who answered the council, even though Beatrix had told us not to speak. "The fae have lived decades without any assistance from your council or hunters. We have a community of people who abide by laws and the proper people in place to enforce said laws. The same can be done here. There can be communities with whoever wants to live within them and the protections they offer."

"Protections or restrictions?" they challenged.

Finn stood his ground proudly. "If someone thinks of laws as restrictions, then that's another problem to be handled separately."

"And if none of the other races want to join these 'communities,' what then? You'll have forced us to disband, and the world will be left without structure."

It was getting really annoying not knowing which one of them was speaking to us.

"That's a risk worth taking," Cait said this time. "We're not saying that everyone has to uproot their lives and move to a community in order to be part of one. There wouldn't just be one central location; there would be many of them all over the states. A pack could be several hours from a mixed-race community and still be part of them if they chose."

Roman nodded, adding to Cait's well-given thoughts. "And those who wish to keep their lives as they are now are welcome to do so, but those communities would have their own enforcers. Should someone go on a rampage or risk our secrets being exposed to the humans, then they'd be dealt with swiftly and efficiently."

Silence once again descended on the room as we waited

for another question to be asked that wouldn't actually make a difference. We all knew it didn't matter what we said. The council was going to do whatever they wanted. They were either going to take us as a threat or they weren't.

Beatrix stood before speaking again. "We have the approval of our ancestors and makers to do this. You might think you're gods up here on your thrones and with your hidden identities, but gods you are not. I won't stand down from this. You have reigned over supernaturals for too long and without accountability. We shouldn't have to live in fear just because of who we were born to be or who we are mated to. You have no right to step in or toss threats around just because something doesn't fit into one of your little boxes. You either agree to disband the council or you prepare for a fight. Either way, your time as our supposed leaders is up."

Her hands gestured to our group. "And if you think these are the only people who support our idea of communities and having more control over our lives, then you're sorely mistaken. We have covens, packs, and nests at the ready to fight for a better life, much like the fae have already done. So the choice is yours: Walk away peacefully or risk your lives when we force you out. We are no longer afraid of the consequences."

Well, shit. Even I was ready to bow down to Beatrix. Her words were spoken with such surety and power that my skin was covered in goosebumps.

"Are you going to allow us to consider our options?" they asked.

Beatrix was still standing and smirked. "You don't need time. You already know what you're going to do. So let's not waste anyone's time. What is the choice your council is going to make today?"

Some days I loved her so much more than others.

The council members finally broke from their frozen

states, and several of them turned to glance at the one in the center, who stood, matching Beatrix's stance.

"You know very little of what we do, witch. You don't have the numbers to dethrone us," they said.

Without needing to be able to communicate, we all stood as a united front, and Beatrix grinned. "As I said before, what you see here isn't all that we have. You have the resources to know that my words are the truth. You no longer intimidate us. The fact that you remain faceless tells us all we need to know. It is you who are afraid of us. As our covens, packs, and nests grow stronger, you stay here behind your guarded walls, afraid of what's to come. When your precious council was overtaken by a mere witch on her own, that was enough to show us the truth you can no longer hide from."

A member on the end raised their hand, but I wasn't going to stand by and let one of them hurt Beatrix while she was having a stare-off with their leader.

I lifted my palm and directed energy toward Beatrix just as a black orb of magic flew across the room. When the power impacted with the shield I'd barely erected in time, I had to grab on to Foster and take from his energy to keep myself upright.

Whatever I had prevented from hitting Beatrix felt as if it had traveled through my magic and attacked me at my core.

My knees buckled, but my hold on Foster kept me from falling down. Once the pinpricks had stopped attacking my center, I released Foster and squeezed his hand in thanks. I turned toward the cowardly council member.

"You are not the threat here," I forcefully reminded them.

I took a steadying breath, waiting for the next attack, but none came. Instead, the leader in the middle stepped forward. "We will announce the withdrawal of our leadership under one condition." A shimmer rippled around them before they continued speaking. "*When* your plan fails, you will all be bound to us. Each of you standing here will be forced to live within our strongholds and your bonds to each other will be broken and replaced by fealty to us. That is the only way you walk out of here without a fight."

Fuck. All the mother fucks.

I shared a glance with Foster. The fire in his eyes and the wrath bouncing between our bond was strong. Neither of us liked this scenario.

The thought of our bond ever being forcefully severed wasn't something I was okay with. I knew Beatrix believed in her plan, but this was a risk I wasn't sure I could take.

Maciah was the first to respond this time. "We can only speak for ourselves, but the vampires agree to your condition."

Lucinda was next. "As do the fae."

How the hell were they agreeing so easily? Did they not have the same bond Foster and I shared? I didn't know and I wasn't sure I could make this decision as swiftly as them.

"The witches agree as well," Mirra said next. Though, I wasn't sure if she was speaking for her and Vi, or if Beatrix and I were supposed to be included in that as well.

It was down to me and Foster plus Roman and Cait.

Foster's hand gripped my cheek, and his gaze held mine captive. "The Moon Goddess didn't lead us down this path just for us to be torn apart. I can't believe that."

His words were quiet, but sure and strong with the kind of strength I wished I'd had in that moment. I wanted to have such beliefs, but I didn't know this goddess. I wasn't a shifter. Hell, some days, I wasn't even sure *what* I was.

But Foster wasn't just my mate. He was the light that kept guiding me forward. The anchor that grounded me. The other half of my soul.

If he believed this risk was worth taking, then I wouldn't doubt him. Not now and not ever.

I turned toward the council with piercing eyes that fell on

each one of them before I spoke. "We, too, agree to your condition."

Roman was next. "The wolves from East Texas agree as well."

It wasn't until Holden cleared his throat at the end of the table that I remembered the alpha had come with us. He'd been so quiet during the conversation.

"I have been alive for many decades. I have seen the rise and fall of many. The ultimatum you are issuing here is a disgrace to what the council once stood for. So much so, I'm tempted to disagree with the others." Holden paused, and the tension rose within the room to an all-time high.

Until he continued. "That would be my decision if I suspected you'd fight us fairly. Though, I don't presume you expected a unanimous agreement between the fifteen of us. You have given us a way to leave here with our lives intact, and that is the condition I'm agreeing to."

Shit. Holden was furious. Though, I couldn't tell if his anger was with the council, Beatrix, or just the situation as a whole.

The council moved back to their chairs, each of them mirroring each other's movements. "Condition granted. We will make an announcement that the council will cease to exist."

Lucinda waggled a finger. "I don't think so. You don't get to trip us up with words, or a lack thereof. You'll also call all of your dogs back in, and you'll wipe their memories just like you used to do for anyone who came to work for you. More importantly, Finn and I are going to be here to make sure everything is handled accordingly or our agreement to your conditions will be null and void."

A wave of energy blasted forward from the council. "How dare you—" one of them said before the leader lifted their robe-covered hand, silencing them.

"We accept," they said calmly. "You are welcome to stay

for as long as you feel necessary to make sure we've done as agreed upon."

"And we'll be back with many more if Lucinda and Finn are not released within an appropriate timeframe," Holden added.

His threat to the council shocked me, given his earlier comment and previous silence.

"Noted," the council leader, or at least I assumed, said. "You're dismissed."

Beatrix chuckled but stayed silent as we began to file out of the room. When I got to the door, I turned back and found the old witch giving Lucinda something. I couldn't tell what it was or hear what they were saying, but I hoped whatever it was would aid in making sure the fae both got back to where they belonged.

18

FOSTER

When we got back to the coven, my intent was to take Andie home, let her rest and strengthen our bond, but as soon as we stepped through the portal, the energy in the air was frantic. Ava was pacing, and Evelyn was constantly biting her check to the point I assumed she was swallowing down her own blood.

"What's wrong?" I asked, but I was ignored as Beatrix came through behind us.

She met their worried glances. "Where?"

"Where what?" Andie asked before they could answer.

Evelyn stepped forward. "South of Denver. In a gully between mountain ranges."

"How long ago?" Beatrix asked next.

"Only ten minutes ago."

Andie grabbed Beatrix's shoulder and spun her around. "What the hell are the two of you talking about?"

Holden stood next to me, equally as eager to hear the answer to that question.

"They found the location of the missing witches and wolves," Beatrix replied calmly.

Andie's nails dug into my flesh. "Charlie."

"What mountain ranges?" Holden demanded, his alpha power pressing down on each of us.

Beatrix *tsked*. "Not so fast, wolf. We don't know what kind of traps may be set up there. We need to send a smaller group in to check things out."

Holden snarled, elongated teeth peeking out from his gums. "My daughter is with that group, Beatrix. I will not wait for anyone." He stepped forward. "Now, what fucking mountain ranges?"

I'd never heard the alpha swear before. I'd never seen him truly lose control. Beatrix needed to choose her next words very carefully.

"I'm not trying to keep you from your daughter," Beatrix said. "I'm trying to make sure you stay alive long enough to see her again. If you can give me—"

He roared. "I've given you more than six weeks. If you know where my daughter is, you're going to tell me right now."

His pain carried through the air and punched me right in the chest. The agony he felt from missing Piper made it hard for me to breathe.

Beatrix pinched the bridge of her nose before nodding at Evelyn. "Tell him."

"Between the San Luis Peak and Mineral Mountain," Evelyn said. "We can be there within the hour, but Beatrix is right. A smaller team should be sent ahead to warn us how many others we'll be facing and what kind of magical traps we could be walking into."

The veins in Holden's neck and the ones on his forehead pulsed. "There won't be enough of them to keep me from my daughter."

He spun around and faced me. "Are you coming with me?"

I hesitated, and he snarled, turning away and shifting before racing out of the coven.

Fuck.

"Get a team out there now," Beatrix demanded of Evelyn. "Hell, I'll go myself. We can't let that alpha ruin our chances of getting everyone back alive."

Andie frowned. "But he can't beat us there without our help."

The old witch sighed. "He can if he has another witch helping him, and I fully believe he does."

She wasn't wrong about that. Holden had spent decades cultivating relationships with many of the supernaturals around LA. I wouldn't put it past him to call in favors if needed and do whatever it took to get to his daughter quicker.

Beatrix, Ava, and Evelyn rushed off toward the houses, and I turned to Andie. "What do you want to do?"

"I want to be there for Charlie. I want to be the one who brings her home," she said confidently.

Damn it. I'd known she was going to say that.

I didn't blame her. Charlie was family, but at least she wasn't asking me to rush in like Holden wanted.

Roman clasped my shoulder. "What can we do?"

"Agreed," Maciah added. "We're here to help. Not just with the council, but whatever you need."

I thought about our interactions with Moira in the past. She was known for playing games and testing what we were capable of. We couldn't let this be another bloodbath like the attack on the pack.

"Maciah, can you four stay here at the coven and make sure that nothing goes wrong while we're gone?" I asked. The vampire nodded, and I turned to Roman and Cait. "Go to Holden. Maybe he'll listen to another strong alpha. Ask him to wait. Beatrix will do everything she can to get our people back."

Even I could hardly believe the words coming out of my

mouth. I'd once despised the old witch, but she'd come a long way in the last couple of months. I couldn't deny that.

Roman and Cait both nodded, but it was the latter who replied, "We'll do whatever we can to keep him rational."

Zeke and Rachel stepped to the side. "We'll go do a run around the perimeter of the coven to check on things."

"And we'll go find something to check on while the two of you chat," Amersyn said, tugging on Maciah's hand.

Once it was just Andie and me, I wrapped my arms around her and held her tightly. "I don't like your life being in danger twice in one day."

"I feel the same way about yours, but we can't let them do this on their own," she said. Then, she quietly added, "Not when I can help."

I fucking hated the syphon power of hers sometimes, regardless of the fact that it had saved our asses earlier.

Before my rage could spike too high, I focused on the steady beat of her heart. "Okay. Then we go, but we stick together. Just like earlier."

Her body weighed heavily against me. "When will the fighting end?"

"Maybe never," I answered honestly. "But I'll fight until my dying breath to keep you safe."

"That's what scares me most," she replied, then she pulled back enough to push up on her toes and press her lips to mine.

My hand tangled with her light-pink strands, squeezing the nape of her neck. "I love you so fucking much."

"I love you equally. Now, let's go so we can get home sooner."

Gods, I hoped she was right.

NEARLY TWO HOURS LATER, A GROUP OF TWENTY WITCHES AND twice as many wolves moved through the trees at the base of the Colorado mountains. The scout team had already been through and said they could sense bodies, but no magic.

That didn't make me feel better about proceeding, but also didn't stop us.

We had to save the others if it was at all possible. They'd been gone for too long and had likely been tortured for days on end.

I wasn't sure my mate had considered that. Even if we brought Charlie back tonight, I wasn't sure if Andie was going to *really* be getting her friend back yet.

"Just over this hill," Peter said. He'd been with the group that had arrived before us and was now leading us on the same path they'd previously taken.

Beatrix paused and pointed at Andie. "Help me look for traps."

Andie didn't hesitate to step forward. They locked forearms and when I moved to step closer, their combined energy shoved me back.

My mate shot me an apologetic look.

This was a new trick she'd yet to tell me about, and I wasn't sure it was one I liked.

Silver and blue waves pulsed off of them, becoming transparent after a couple of feet, but I could feel their potency and wondered if whoever was waiting for us at the bottom of the hill would as well.

It didn't make sense to me that Moira wouldn't have her best guards on this group.

Another minute later, Andie and Beatrix pulled apart and their energy slowly disappeared from around them.

Beatrix nodded at her. "Your control is almost impeccable."

"Thanks." Andie smiled as she walked back to me, and I was near certain I knew what she was thinking. "Almost" *meant* perfect. Beatrix just didn't want to admit Andie had come so far and mostly on her own thanks to the time we'd been separated.

The old witch tossed her silver braid behind her shoulder. "There is very little magic present."

"Then we're walking into a trap," Mirra said, mirroring my previous thoughts.

Holden growled, stepping forward. "I don't care. Our pack is going in there with or without the rest of you."

Beatrix stupidly placed a hand over his chest. "Wait a minute."

His eyes turned nearly black, and his nose was touching her as he snarled in reply. "If you want to keep that hand attached to your wrist, I'd suggest removing it very quickly."

She sighed and rolled her eyes, not helping the situation. "All of you alphas are the same." Beatrix removed her hand and pointed to four other witches. "Teleport around the area. Look for anything we've missed. The rest of us will go in on foot from here."

Holden stepped back, but his shoulders didn't relax as he commanded a few of our pack members. "Do the same and report any details, no matter how small, as you go."

Three shifters nodded before backing away and transforming to their wolf forms. Two silver wolves with varying markings and a tan one darted into the trees, moving silently away from us.

Holden turned on his heel and stomped toward where we sensed the others. Neither of us could communicate with any of the pack members who had been taken, even though we were now so close to them. I worried about what that meant and what we'd soon find, but I wasn't going to leave Holden to do this himself.

I grabbed Andie's hand. "Please stay with me. Whatever this is, it isn't good."

"I agree." Her teeth scraped over her lower lip. "But we can't leave when we're so close."

I already knew that. I just hoped I didn't soon regret that decision.

The rest of our large group traveled up the hill and around the corner of a mountain. The trail leading forward was littered with large rocks and brush that went to my knees, but none of it was enough to deter us.

Holden was out in front, storming his way through everything and not trying to be quiet while Beatrix kept pace just behind him, hands out and ready to act at a moment's notice.

Andie was the same. Her shoulders were tense, and her eyes never stayed in one place long.

Their nerves aren't going to help anything, my wolf said.

I know that. Why do you think I'm not letting myself lose control?

He paused. *Even if she'll hate us, we'll need to take Andie and run if this is worse than we think.*

I already knew that, which was why I was attempting to keep my emotions in check. I needed every wit about me. There were a couple of scenarios I saw playing out and neither were good.

The first being a mass slaughter as soon as we were close to the structure holding the others. The second being that there really was no one waiting to attack us down there and one or more of those taken had been turned into trojan horses. That we'd get them back to the coven and pack, only to have them turn on us when we least expected it.

Both weren't ideal situations, but there was no convincing anyone else here that we couldn't bring these supernaturals back home.

We were finally headed downhill again and had a clear view of the old barn building where we could sense the missing coven and pack members. There were no others around that I or my wolf could sense, and Beatrix assured us that there was no one else waiting in the wings.

Option two is looking rather likely, my wolf said, and I agreed with him.

I glanced at Holden's rigid back as his speed increased. I needed to warn him of my thoughts, but waiting until he had eyes on Piper was a better idea. I doubted he'd listen to me if I said anything just yet.

A few witches and shifters spread out and circled around the barn, inspecting its aged, grey wood and peeking in the dusty windows while the rest of us went around to the front, where there were huge double doors nearly falling off their hinges.

Holden jerked one of them hard enough that it nearly took out the five shifters spread out around him when the door fell to the ground.

He didn't wait for the thudding echo before stepping inside the dark space.

Andie made a ball of light magic in her palm and then tossed it up to the high ceiling. The energy grew brighter as soon as it found purchase on a rafter and shone down on the group huddled in the middle.

Nearly two dozen witches and wolves were clinging to each other, covered in dirt, sitting on straw that was covered in what I assumed to be patches of black mold.

My eyes searched the area, but there truly was nobody else here.

Holden gently moved through the unresponsive supernaturals until Piper's auburn hair came into view. He picked her up and held her like a child draped over his arms, tears streaming down his cheeks as every part of him trembled.

I moved forward to help him, but he shook his head. "I have to do this." The emotion in his voice nearly broke me.

The pang in my chest increased tenfold as I watched him

whisper softly into her ear and carry her from the barn. My attention moved back to Andie, who was helping others stand if they were able and laying those who couldn't down for Ava and Camille to inspect.

Finally, Charlie's blonde hair came into view, and Andie gasped. The once-vibrant witch had hollowed cheeks and dark circles under her eyes, and her hair was in a tangled mess up to her shoulders. Her eyes stared blankly ahead, offering no acknowledgment that she'd been rescued.

Fuck. This was almost worse than the other two scenarios I'd thought up.

"We need to get out of here," Ava said, a shudder in her shoulders as she leaned over a witch I recognized as Sheila.

Beatrix nodded, then turned to me. "Gather the wolves. We're opening a portal and it closes within five minutes."

We're leaving within five minutes, I mentally said to Holden. *Are you still close?*

I'm just beyond the trees. His voice was gruff as he responded. *What this witch did is unforgivable.*

Shit, that must have meant that Piper was unconscious like Charlie.

We're going to find her, I promised him before bending down to help Andie with Charlie.

"Let me carry her," I said quietly.

Andie nodded stiffly, swiping tears from her cheeks. "If I hadn't lost control… If I hadn't tried to take Moira on by myself just so I could get my magic… This is all my fault."

I already had Charlie in my arms and badly wanted to hug my mate, but since I couldn't, I reached out to touch her in even the smallest of ways.

My hold on Charlie adjusted to one arm and I grabbed Andie's wrist. "This is not your fault. You did exactly what you were supposed to do. Moira will pay for this. Not you." My voice deepened. "Never you."

She nodded but dropped her glossy eyes, a move that told

me she didn't believe my words. I was going to have to keep an eye on her. Guilt could drive even the sanest person to do things they shouldn't.

Quickly, witches and wolves were helped through the portal that had been opened, and we arrived in front of the infirmary. Dozens of coven members were standing around, watching, whispering, and pointing as more dazed supernaturals were carried through.

I headed into the infirmary with Charlie still draped over my chest and Andie at my side. We took the bed at the farthest end and Andie stepped up, roaming her hands over Charlie's prone body.

"I'm going to fix her," Andie said. Her voice was forced and tense.

"Maybe we should wait for Camille or Ava," I suggested softly, placing my hand at the base of her spine.

Her eyes flashed with fury as her head twisted slowly toward me. "I'm going to fix her," she repeated, but this time, her tone was frantic.

I grabbed my mate by the shoulders and forced her to face me again. "Listen to me, Andie. Charlie doesn't and won't blame you for this. Your emotions are all over the place. You need to let someone else help her."

A sob tore from her throat. "But I…"

My arms pulled Andie in tight against me. "You did everything you could to make this right. Now, let someone else do their part."

She wept against my chest, the sound shattering pieces of my heart because I wasn't going to be the person to make this better. Hell, at this point, I wasn't sure there was a way to heal what had happened.

Even killing Moira wouldn't fix this mess.

Camille nudged past us, and I moved with Andie still in my arms another step out of the way. Camille's hands moved over Charlie, much like Andie's had been, but there was a steady thrum of yellow energy that pulsed from her fingertips.

"Each of them seems to be heavily sedated in some way," Ava said when she joined Camille's side. "None of them have any response to what's happening around them. Even more curious, there are no injuries to be seen. Their bodies aren't even malnourished, and there's no dark magic. Nothing other than their consciousness having been tampered with."

"Can you pull them out of it?" Andie asked, her voice broken.

Ava moved on to the next bed, but Camille nodded. "Slowly. We can't jolt their minds since we don't know how they came to be in this state, but I'll be taking this side of the room while Ava is working the other. It might take several tries, but we'll find a way to get them back."

I noticed how she hadn't said "back to normal" and I wondered if that had been intentional or if I was reading too much into it.

I turned my head and searched for the wolves, but I couldn't see them. "What about the pack members?"

"Holden took them back already." Camille grimaced. "Beatrix sent him with two other healers, though. Hopefully, they'll be able to manage there without additional assistance if anything else comes up."

Yeah, like one of them waking and losing their damned mind before trying to kill people.

Holden wasn't in the right state of mind to be making decisions.

How are things looking over there? I asked Mack through a private pack link.

His response was immediate. *Not good, but we're handling it.*

What does that mean?

That Holden isn't cooperating with the witches, but I've almost got him calm.

I'd help if I could, but I can't leave Andie.

There was silence for a few beats. *How is Charlie?*

My eyes cast over the witch in question. *Camille says she's going to find a way to snap her out of whatever this is, and there are no physical injuries or dark magic.*

The mental damage that they could have done to them doesn't require dark magic, Mack said flatly, a fact I had already thought of.

I'll keep you updated.

Same, he said sharply.

Fuck. I wasn't okay with any of this.

Camille finished the first round of healing on Charlie and moved on to the bed next to us. I tilted Andie's chin up. She still had fresh tears falling from her sad eyes, and I hated that there was literally nothing I could do to make her hurt go away.

Well, nothing other than stand by her side and hope enough for the both of us that everything would be okay once people came out of their catatonic states.

19

ANDIE

The agony over seeing Charlie had nearly destroyed me. I'd had flashbacks of watching my mom slowly slip away, of processing that Aunt Junie was gone without being able to say a proper goodbye to her. So many people had been taken from me, and I couldn't possibly lose another. Not yet.

Then, when her parents had shown up… I'd been tempted to run away like a coward, given how long I'd avoided them, but Marlene had wrapped me in her arms, holding me like I was her own child and thanking me for bringing her daughter home.

A war of emotions erupted inside me. Pain burned through my muscles, and tears leaked freely down my cheeks as I held the woman I'd considered a second mother as a child.

"I'm so sorry," I muttered over and over, but she and William insisted they understood and hadn't once blamed me.

Foster stood by, holding me when I needed the extra strength and just being present when I needed to stand on my own.

As the hours ticked by, Beatrix called William and Marlene away to discuss the council, but I promised to update them as soon as anything changed.

Camille and Ava continued to move about the room, tending to witches non-stop. None of those brought back had woken yet, and I finally forced myself to leave Charlie's side and check on the others.

Chase, Sheila, and Merrit were the only ones I'd talked to in depth before, but that didn't mean my heart didn't further shatter as I passed by all eleven of them. Family and friends all huddled next to the beds with their heads bent and hands folded in front of them.

We might have had magic on our side, but there was nothing wrong with asking the higher powers for a little assist.

When I noticed Ava at Charlie's bed again, I hurried to make my way back, surprised it wasn't Camille.

"What's wrong?" I asked, not understanding why they'd switched places.

Ava offered me a small smile, and the dark circles forming under her eyes from the overuse of magic nearly matched that of Charlie's hollow face.

"Nothing is wrong," she answered defensively. "We're doing our job the best we can."

I reached a hand to her elbow. "I know. I'm sorry. Can I help?"

Foster got up from the chair he'd been resting in, a grimace on his face, but his concern wasn't necessary. I was in a better place than I'd been when we'd returned. There was no reason for me to just stand here any longer.

Ava nodded. "Share some of that power you've got stored away with me." Her tone was tired but joking. Though, maybe she was onto something.

"Where's Beatrix?" I asked since I hadn't spoken with her since we'd returned to the coven.

"She's either still in the meeting about the council or she's back at the pack," Ava answered. "She keeps going back to make sure the wolves have all the help they might need."

I glanced at Foster, needing his input since Beatrix wasn't here to ask. "What if instead of trying to pull dark magic out of people like I've done before, I push my original power into them?"

His brow creased. "I don't like that."

"Neither do I," Ava said. "I was only kidding before."

I glanced between the two of them. "What is the point of being who I am if I can't help people? There is nothing to syphon, but maybe what everyone needs is a boost of magic. And not just healing energy, but true, unfiltered power."

Ava held her finger up. "Don't do a damn thing until I come back." Then she hurried toward Camille at the other end of the room.

Foster gripped my hand. "I know you want to help because you feel responsible, but how do you think Charlie would feel if she woke up and you weren't okay because you helped her?"

"I've learned a lot about myself over the weeks," I said defensively. "I'm not a child who can't control her magic."

He took a step back, as if I'd slapped him. Sure, my tone had been sharp, but I'd listened to him before. I'd taken a step back, realizing that I wasn't going to do any good while I'd been crying my eyes out.

That wasn't the case any longer. My thoughts were on the right track, and my emotions were under control. I knew that without a doubt in my soul, and I needed him to know as well.

Foster reached for me, but I stood my ground. I loved him and I knew he loved me, but he had to trust me like I did him.

When I didn't budge, he moved closer again, resting his forehead against mine. "I'm sorry. You should do whatever you feel is right. Your instincts haven't been wrong so far, and there's no reason to believe they'd be now."

There was the mate I needed.

"Thank you." I peeked over to where Camille and Ava seemed to be arguing, then at Charlie before glancing up at Foster. "I'm not waiting for them."

He kissed my temple. "Just be careful. That's all I ask."

"I promise." I stepped away from him and grabbed Charlie's hand. "I'm going to fix this. Just like I said before."

Oh, how I wished she could have responded, but that wouldn't be possible until I did what needed to be done.

I closed my eyes and placed both palms over her chest. I could do this. I just had to focus. I was from two original witch lines. The Abbotts and the Bishops. We were strong and capable. Most importantly, I knew I had my family standing behind me.

A presence that was different from my mother and aunt pressed in around me, wrapping around my body like a familiar blanket.

Dad.

It wasn't often I felt him without Mom, which meant that I needed to focus on the power I got from him and not Mom's syphon energy, something I'd already assumed, but it was good to have confirmation.

Okay, Charlie. You better be ready to wake up now, I thought as I dug deep inside myself. I couldn't use the magic from Junie or from Mom. I had to pull from the original well of energy. The power that had always been inside me, just silenced.

A pulsing orb of light glowed within my mind, dark blue in color just like my magic these days, but I pushed past that, finding the purple I'd associated with Aunt Junie. That was thicker and not as easy to wade through, but I wasn't giving up.

Not even as my chest tightened and breathing became

harder. Instead of dwelling on those reactions, I concentrated on the strength from my father and knowing that if I could do this, Charlie would be okay.

She had to be.

There were no other options I'd accept.

Foster pressed his hand over my spine. "I'm right here."

I must have been looking as bad as I felt, but the fact that he offered his support instead of demanding I stop meant more to me than I could say with words.

With the added strength seeping into me, I squeezed my eyes tighter and pushed through the final layer of Aunt Junie's energy. My breath *whooshed* out of me as I did. Then, I felt like I was covered by ice, and a pink glow blinded me.

The hair on my arms and neck stood tall as I focused on the pure energy. I'd thought exploding into the ether had been powerful, but this was something else entirely.

Not stronger, but more...pure. I wasn't sure how to describe it.

The magic wasn't anyone else's. I knew that.

This power was mine and mine alone to do with as I needed.

This was likely what Moira was looking for, and she'd have never found it in my necklace because *this* had never left me. It had just been buried deep with my lack of knowledge and a spell.

I took a small piece of the glowing pink orb and pulled it along the tether I'd created as I'd pushed through the other layers of my core.

Protecting the energy as best I could, I tugged and tugged until its warmth moved to the palm that was right over Charlie's heart. Instead of letting the power fly forward, I stopped its momentum and moved my hands to her sternum.

She didn't need help getting her heart to beat. She needed a jolt to her core.

"Don't let go of me," I whispered to Foster as I kept my

eyes closed tight and prepared my body for whatever was coming next.

His hands squeezed around my waist. "Never."

With that reassurance, I pushed the tiniest piece of my origin magic forward and through to Charlie. As soon as the power passed through her skin, I lost control of it and was blasted backward.

Well, not just me.

A ball of energy had exploded around Charlie, sending Foster and me crashing to the ground, along with the blanket that had been covering her lower body. Hell, even her bedside table was now knocked over on its side.

"What the hell was that?" Ava shouted, but I ignored her rage as I scrambled to get to my feet.

I needed to see Charlie's face, to hear her heartbeat and be sure that I hadn't killed my best friend.

Foster lifted me up when I couldn't get my feet beneath me. "Let me help you now."

There was no denying him. Whatever I'd done had knocked every bit of strength from my body, and I wasn't even sure if I could do it again without causing serious damage to myself.

As my mate carried me back toward the bed, my eyes searched Charlie's person. Her chest was still rising and falling, and nothing else seemed changed.

"It didn't work." The devastation in my voice tore through me, and the tears I'd cried earlier threatened to come back with a vengeance as my throat burned with defeat.

Foster lifted my chin with one finger. "Look closer at her face."

I blinked back the glossiness in my eyes and did as he suggested. I couldn't see anything different, but I kept my gaze focused on Charlie anyway.

Another minute ticked by painfully slowly, and I finally saw what his enhanced eyes had already seen.

Her cheeks were regaining color and expanding. The dark circles under her long lashes were fading, and her cracked lips were healing to a soft pink.

"Charlie?" I whispered, leaning closer over the bed as Foster held on to my waist, still keeping my body upright with his assistance.

She didn't reply, but everything about her body was improving when before, no matter how many times Ava and Camille had come by, there had been no changes.

I grabbed her hand. "I'm right here. You're going to be okay. Nobody is ever going to take you from us again."

There was a twitch in her eyelid, but no other movement.

Evelyn stopped at the foot of the bed with Ava and Camille flanking her. The senior witch had awe in her eyes, but a tightness in her tone. "What did you do?"

"I gave her a piece of my origin magic," I said without an ounce of regret, even though I had no idea what the consequences to my actions might be.

Evelyn shook her head, but instead of reprimanding me, her lips rose ever-so-slightly. "Beatrix isn't going to be happy with you."

"I don't care. I'd have traded my life for Charlie's if that was what it would have taken."

As soon as the words had left my mouth, Foster growled in my ear. "Over my dead body."

Yeah, I probably wouldn't have gotten away with sacrificing myself, but I'd have tried anyway.

I frowned. "I can try to help the others, but I need time to recover."

Evelyn waved a hand flippantly. "That's not a problem. They're all resting peacefully. We have the answer we didn't see before. We'll get them awake one by one. Beatrix might have other solutions as well when she's back."

My head swiveled to Foster. "The wolves. They don't have magic like us. What if this won't work on them?"

He brushed a loose strand of my hair back. "I already reached out to Mack. Holden and Beatrix are taking care of them. Piper is already awake. Apparently, the alpha command when combined with some of Beatrix's magic was powerful enough to help."

A relief like I'd never known pressed over me like a warm blanket, and I collapsed into his arms. Between the morning with the council, and then the afternoon and evening dealing with this, I had nothing else left in me to give.

Thankfully, I had a mate who gladly picked up my slack and lifted me into his arms.

"We'll stay here until she's awake, and then I'm taking you home," he said softly into my ear.

That, I couldn't and wouldn't argue with.

20

FOSTER

The last forty-eight hours had been equal parts torture and joy. Charlie had woken up for about an hour. Long enough to eat something, be overly confused, then fall right back to sleep. According to her parents, she'd only been awake for a few minutes at a time since then, but she seemed to be getting more coherent each time. Though, Andie and I hadn't seen her since the first waking.

Andie had been using her ability to help others to keep her distracted while also tiring herself out to the point I wasn't sure she was going to be able to fully recover. I'd about had enough with her pushing herself and everyone else letting her.

I'd thought Beatrix would be in my corner on this, but the old witch didn't seem to mind Andie doing the heavy lifting while she interviewed each person who had been taken. Sure, Ava and Evelyn were helping, but their powers weren't as strong as Andie's, and there were more repercussions for them.

All of them had the same story. In fact, their descriptions of what had happened were eerily similar, as if the words weren't their own.

They'd been taken in the fog by the witches and brought to a warehouse, where they'd been questioned peacefully. Then, their magic had been tested and they'd been fed and clothed and provided with books and television to keep them distracted.

The group had all slept in the same room with mattresses on the floor and had had use of a proper bathroom and shower. Hell, it almost sounded as if they'd been on vacation instead of being tortured like we'd all thought.

But what had been even stranger was that none of them remembered anything beyond the first week. Which made me think that they'd been in those catatonic states for over five weeks. Not asleep, but not awake, either. It was no wonder that Charlie, and I assumed the many others, were sleeping like the dead.

When I woke up this morning, Andie was gone and I knew where I'd find her. She'd be in the infirmary already, tending to those she hadn't helped yet. While I admired her drive to fix this mess, she wasn't the only witch here who could. She was just the one who seemed to be able to help the quickest.

I showered in record time and dressed for the day, donning jeans and a plain, black T-shirt before heading to Andie.

When I arrived, she was standing over one of the witches, but not for long. As soon as the door closed behind me, her knees began to buckle, and she fell to the ground in a heap.

I raced forward to catch her but only managed to save her head from thumping against the tile. Fury immediately rose within me, and I picked her up, walking swiftly toward the door and without her permission.

Andie groaned against my chest, barely able to keep her eyes open. "I need to finish."

I stayed silent, afraid that if I said something to her too

soon, she'd be the victim of my wrath, which I knew she didn't deserve.

Her hand pressed over my chest after we'd already made it outside. "Foster. You need to take me back."

Still, I kept my words to myself.

She wiggled against me—only slightly stronger than she'd been a minute ago—but my hold around her back and legs increased in pressure, locking her in.

"Seriously, Foster. Let me down. I'm fine now."

My head reared back, and my chest rumbled. "*Fine?* Have you looked in the mirror today, Andie?"

She winced at my sharply spoken words. "No."

I stopped my forward momentum. We were halfway between the infirmary and the main area of the cottages. I took a moment to focus on the grass beneath my boots and the wind that blew over us. I didn't want to be angry *with* Andie. I just couldn't let her continue to sacrifice her own wellbeing.

Finally, I moved my gaze until I saw her staring up at me with wide eyes. "I'm sorry, Andie. I can't let you heal the last few witches. You need to let Ava and Camille finish with them. They know what needs to be done now."

"But—" she started, though I didn't let her finish.

My gaze darkened. "No, Andie. I won't stand here any longer and let you hurt yourself. I'd rather them die than continue watching you suffer."

She gasped. "You don't mean that. You agreed with Beatrix's plan. You've been so understanding."

"And now, I've reached my limit." I growled. "I love you, and I know you might hate me for this, but I'm taking you back to the house, where you're going to eat a proper breakfast. After that, I'm taking you back to bed. The place you're going to stay all day."

A sliver of guilt ate at me, given I'd never spoken to her so harshly, but she was *my* mate. It was my responsibility to keep her safe. Even if that was from herself.

Without waiting for a reply from her slack mouth, I continued toward the house. It wasn't until we hit the cobblestone road that she began hitting my chest. "Put me down right now, Foster Kline."

"No."

She huffed. "Don't make me hurt you."

My lips twitched at that. "Go ahead. Use your magic on me. You're dead on your feet right now. Your well is empty. Do your *current* best."

She turned her head away from me and crossed her arms, a deep scowl forming between her brows.

I ignored the way hurting her made my chest ache and continued toward our house. When we arrived and I reached for the door, she surprised me by jumping out of my arms, but she was still too weak.

Her attempt at running was more like a quick walk, which I caught up to with three strides. My arms wrapped around her waist, and I threw her over my shoulder, clamping my forearm around her thighs.

"Let go of me!" she screamed.

I ignored her and opened the door. Just as I kicked it closed, a hand smacked on the door frame.

"What's going on here?" Beatrix asked with a quirked brow when I turned around.

"He's holding me hostage," Andie complained from behind me.

I rolled my eyes at her choice of words. "I'm saving her from herself. She collapsed in the infirmary trying to heal another witch. She's done. The rest of you can handle the few who still aren't awake."

Beatrix stepped forward and poked a finger into Andie's jean-clad thigh. "I told you to stay away today." Then she looked up at me. "I'll put a spell around the house that will last until sunrise tomorrow. She won't be able to get out."

Andie's fist beat at my back as her legs tried their best to kick through my hold. "You can't keep me locked up like some prisoner."

Beatrix grinned. "Have fun with that." She shut the door.

I felt energy press down around us and waited an extra few seconds before letting Andie down finally.

She bolted for the door. I watched, ready to run if Beatrix's spell didn't work how she intended, but instead, I ended up thrusting my arms out and catching Andie as she was blasted backward.

"Son of a bitch, that hurt." She groaned, rubbing a hand over her face.

Beatrix's head peeked in the door, a shit-eating grin on her face. "Oh, that was so much better than I thought it was going to be."

"You're a terrible person," Andie grumbled.

I merely waved at Beatrix and thanked her for the assist before closing the door again.

"Now, how about some breakfast?" I asked as I released Andie and walked toward the kitchen.

Her loud stomping followed me, and then a pillow hit the back of my head. "This isn't fair."

"French toast or cereal or eggs? Maybe all three?" I asked, though I was more thinking out loud. I had little faith that she'd answer me.

"You have to let me go," she whined. "What if Charlie wakes up? I want to be able to see her. You can't keep me from her after all the time I spent wondering if she was dead."

This time, pain leached into my heart from our bond. That, she was serious about.

"If Charlie wakes up tonight and wants to visit, I have a feeling anyone who wants to come inside the house is more than welcome to," I replied, knowing I could call Beatrix if that situation came up.

A bottle of water came flying at my head, but I snatched the plastic from the air. "I didn't realize you were so violent."

"And I didn't realize you were a psycho." A heavy breath of air puffed out from between her lips as she sat down. Then her gaze flicked up to me briefly. "French toast."

I turned so she wouldn't see my smile, then got to cooking.

The only sound that filled the room was that of my cooking and when I turned back to check on Andie for the third time, she was leaning her head against the counter and fast asleep.

With a shake of my head, I moved the sizzling pan from the hot burner and turned everything off. Once I was sure everything was as cleaned up as it needed to be for the moment, I picked up Andie's limp form and cradled her against my chest.

"I have you, love," I whispered against her forehead while I carried her to the bedroom.

Putting her on the bed, I wanted to make sure she was comfortable, so I removed her shoes and jeans before tucking the comforter around her.

The fact that she hadn't woken during all of that proved how exhausted my mate was. I'd done the right thing, even if she was pissed with me. I had a feeling after some solid sleep, she wouldn't be so upset.

I undressed myself and got into bed with her, bringing my phone and a book from her dresser. There was no way I'd be able to sleep. At least I could be entertained for the day and make sure we didn't miss any updates.

21

ANDIE

When I finally woke up, the sky was dark and all the lights in the house were off. I couldn't see a damn thing, but I knew Foster was still next to me. I wanted to still be furious with him for locking me up, but after some sleep, I realized he'd been right. I was being stubborn—and possibly a little stupid—by continuing to chip away at my core energy.

Beatrix had confirmed it would regenerate, but it wasn't something that happened as quickly as it did with the magic we normally accessed. After a day's rest, I couldn't deny I was feeling more like my old self.

"Am I safe to touch you again?" Foster asked quietly with a bit of a chuckle in his voice.

I rolled over and wrapped an arm and a leg around him. "Of course you are." I pressed my lips over his chest. "Thank you for what you did."

He pulled me up until I was laying across him. "I told you. It's my job to protect you. Your own actions aren't excluded from that. Not that I would stop you from doing what you wanted with just about anything, but you went too far this time."

I rested on my forearms over his chest, letting my hair create a curtain around our faces. "I really don't want to agree with that, but your logic unfortunately makes sense. Just so you know, you might be bigger than me, but at full strength, I could stop you from doing something you shouldn't."

His laughter vibrated through me. "Noted." Then his hands moved down my back, stopping just over my ass. "Now that you're rested…"

I leaned forward and pressed my lips to his. "Would you like something?"

His eyes narrowed, and before I knew it, I was on my back, staring up into his perfect blue eyes. "You. Always you."

With one quick tug, he ripped my underwear and pulled the material out from under me. Heat slammed into my core, and the energy I'd been lacking these last few days lit up like fireworks inside me.

How had I not realized that it was Foster I'd needed? That it was this connection that only he could provide me?

He slowly aligned himself with my wet pussy and rubbed the head of his girth over my clit. My back involuntarily arched, and a moan escaped from me. "Don't be slow. Not today," I begged.

Foster's answering smirk was everything.

He slammed inside me, and every muscle in my body clenched painfully yet blissfully until I adjusted to his hard cock.

"Nothing feels better than being inside you," he whispered against my ear, then he pulled nearly all the way out before thrusting forward. Hard.

My nails dug into his sides as I held on for the ride. My legs wrapped around his ass, and one of my hands moved up to tangle with his long hair.

I moved my hips, needing him impossibly deep. The feeling that there would never be enough closeness between us overwhelmed me to the point where I grabbed his chin, needing his lips on me to calm my raging nerves.

His tongue twisted with mine, and we rocked together, rough and passionately.

"You're okay, Andie," Foster murmured against my lips. "I have you. Just let go of everything else."

Let go. How was I supposed to do that?

How was I supposed to let go of every fear and stress currently storming through me? No matter how much I loved Foster and needed his touch like I needed my next breath, I didn't know how to let go of everything else when I felt so fucking responsible.

His mouth covered mine again, distracting the worst of my thoughts just as I needed him to, and love bloomed through our bond. Not only that, but there was admiration and respect and faith there as well.

All emotions I didn't feel like I deserved.

A tear trickled from the corner of each eye as I held him tighter, not wanting to break down while we were having sex.

Foster paused his momentum and lifted up until he could lock gazes with me. "Let me heal you, Andie."

His words hit my chest with the force of a tornado.

He wasn't just giving me sex or a distraction. He was trying to take it all away, and he didn't care that I was ready to fall apart. He was there to pick up my shattered pieces and put me back together.

Finally, I let the floodgates open.

I gave myself permission to cry.

To mourn and process the weeks that I'd been without Foster.

To accept the blame I'd earned over the missing witches and wolves—Charlie especially—and forgive myself, too.

To let myself go.

Even if it was just for this moment, I was okay with that, because I trusted Foster so completely. I knew that he held no judgment toward me for my previous decisions, and he didn't expect the same penance from me that I expected of myself.

He only cared about me being happy and alive.

He was who I could trust to help guide my decisions moving forward.

Foster.

My mate.

My everything.

Understanding that, remembering what having a bond with Foster meant, allowed me to do as he'd first asked. It allowed me to let go.

My heart opened, and the tears continued to trail down my face as Foster transitioned from sex to lovemaking.

His movements were no longer the rough distraction I'd begged him for. They were slow and purposeful.

Every stroke reminded me how much he loved me. Every longing gaze reminded me that I was perfect as I was—flaws and all. Every light kiss he placed on my heated skin reminded me that, no matter what came next, we'd always find a way through.

Finally, the tears stopped, and the depressing emotions were quickly replaced with need. Need for Foster and need for a release I was long overdue for.

My hips moved and circled underneath him. "Love you so much."

"Love you so fucking much," he said roughly over my lips.

Our eyes stayed locked as our passion for each other took over and we were both ready for the orgasms we desperately needed.

I felt him tense above me, and his speed increased once again.

A tingling built at my core and spread through the rest of my body until Foster reached between us, rubbing a thumb over my clit.

Like a bomb, I ignited around him and called his name out with a cry.

He shuddered above me, and by the time tremors had stopped racing through my body, I felt the comforting weight of him pressing down on me.

His head was resting on the pillow I was using, and he smiled softly. "How do you feel now?"

"Better than I thought I deserved," I said honestly.

"Do you finally realize that none of this is truly your fault and you can move forward without guilt holding you back?

I nodded and traced a finger over the stubble on his cheek. "Thank you for reminding me of all the things I've been forgetting."

He leaned forward and pressed his lips to mine. "Always. Even when you don't want me to."

I didn't miss the smirk that flittered over his face.

"If you ever hold me hostage again, we're going to have a few big words." I poked a finger at his shoulder several times as I spoke.

"Big words." He feigned a shudder. "Sounds scary."

"I can be very scary, thank you very much." I tried to shove him off me, but without using magic, I was no match for his dead weight.

He raised a brow. "Going somewhere?"

"I'd like to take a shower and then make sure Charlie hasn't called."

Foster reached across the bed and grabbed my phone that I hadn't realized was there. "I've had it with me. I wouldn't have kept you from her."

When he shook the phone, the screen turned on and showed that it was after four in the morning. I considered trying to go back to sleep, but my mind was already moving.

"Has Beatrix's spell lifted yet?" I asked as I finally wiggled out from underneath his heavy form.

"I texted her last night and she said at sunrise, it would be over," he answered.

I let out a huff. "I want to say I can't believe she sided with you, but really, I can. I knew she secretly liked you since that moment we were in the attic looking for information on my syphon powers. That old witch can't deny it any longer."

He sat up in bed, watching my every movement as I grabbed clothes from the dresser. "Eh. Let her have her hatred. It's mildly entertaining now that I don't want to rip her head off every five minutes."

God, I didn't miss those early days.

Well, maybe I sort of did.

I glanced at the window and prayed the time would go by quickly. As much as I'd needed the rest and time with Foster, I missed Charlie. The brief moment I'd been able to see her over the last couple of days hadn't been enough.

Though, as I walked to the bathroom to shower, I realized the heaviness I'd been carrying around was gone, even without needing to be—literally—connected to Foster.

That brought a bit of a smile to my face.

I still wanted to help however I could, because Moira wasn't going anywhere until she got her soulmate back. If he died… Well, I didn't want to picture what might happen then.

As I was rubbing shampoo in my hair, Foster stepped into the shower. His wide body took up space quickly. His hands raised, moving mine out of the way, and began massaging the soap into my long strands while I faced him.

With nothing to do with my hands, I trailed my fingers over his abdomen, circling the individual muscles there, and smiled each time they twitched under my scrutiny.

"Andie," Foster warned while he was rinsing my hair and my hands crept lower.

"Yes?" My eyes flashed up to his, and I batted my lashes at him.

He grunted and reached for the conditioner, but while he

was distracted, I dropped to my knees and had the head of his already half-hard cock in my mouth.

A breath hissed from between his lips, and he grabbed my head. "Fuck, that feels good."

His length hardened under my hold, and I took him as deep as I could go while I let my fingers fondle his balls, enjoying the way he flinched above me.

Once he was fully hard, I swirled my tongue around the thick, veiny shaft, bobbing my head as I moved forward and backward.

Foster's hold tightened on my hair, and his hips began to thrust in time with my head, fucking my mouth while I sucked him off.

My grip tightened at the base of his dick and my other hand squeezed tighter on his balls, doubling my efforts in hopes that my mate would have the explosive release he deserved.

"Shit, Andie." He groaned. "I'm going to come already."

He tried to pull me up, but I switched a hand to his thigh, holding on and staying right where I wanted to be.

I heard a thud, assuming one of his hands slammed against the shower wall when I lowered my tongue and sucked hard, drawing his cock to the back of my throat.

His body shuddered underneath my touch, and cum shot into my mouth. The salty taste covered the inside of my cheeks, and I swallowed as quickly as I could with his dick still in my mouth.

Foster finally pulled out of me and lifted me up, fighting a smile. "I didn't join you for that."

I returned his grin. "I know, but I wanted to thank you again for saving me from myself."

His lips pressed to my forehead. "I'm glad you don't still hate me for that."

"I could never hate you for anything," I replied as he reached for the conditioner.

I grabbed a loofa and body wash, taking care of him as he took care of me.

In that moment, nothing had ever felt more right.

No matter what shit happened, this was all I needed to feel centered again. I hoped I wouldn't forget that ever again.

As soon as we were done, Foster walked his naked ass out of the bathroom and tossed on a pair of shorts. "I'll make breakfast while you take your time getting ready. Any requests?"

I tapped my chin and hummed. "That French toast you were cooking yesterday smelled pretty good before I fell asleep. Oh, and maybe some bacon?"

He winked and nodded. "As you wish."

Once he was gone from sight, I rubbed the towel over my face and wondered how in the world I'd gotten so fucking lucky.

22

ANDIE

The sun came up while we were eating breakfast, but instead of running out the front door, I suggested we finish eating on the back porch to fully appreciate the new day.

"I've missed this version of you," Foster said as I sat across from him, grinning at the golden colors rushing along the horizon.

I glanced at him and frowned. "I'm sorry I wasn't myself when you came back."

"That's nothing you should ever apologize for, Andie," he said forcefully. "You were exactly who you needed to be to survive all the shit that had been happening around you. There is nothing wrong with that, as long as you're taking care of yourself while you do what you need to."

The sureness of his words sent a shiver down my spine. Damn, I really did love this man.

I took one last bite of bacon and groaned. "Food is good."

"You haven't been eating enough of it lately."

I ignored the dig, because I knew he meant well and took his "job" of taking care of me seriously.

My phone started vibrating on the table between us. Charlie's name was on the screen.

"Charlie?" I asked, trying not to get too excited.

"Oh, good. You're up. Can I come over?" she asked with a yawn.

My head was shaking as a few tears trailed my face. "Absolutely not. I'm coming to you, assuming you're home?"

She made a grumbling "uh-huh" sound, then added, "Feel free to bring Foster, too. I haven't pissed him off in much too long."

My cheeks hurt from grinning so widely. "You got it."

She hung up, and Foster was already standing from his chair and grabbing our plates. "Go get some shoes on and I'll make Charlie a plate. Maybe then she won't try to 'piss me off.'"

He said the words with a layer of seriousness, but he couldn't hide the spark in his eyes.

"Thank you," I said quickly before placing a chaste kiss on his cheek and rushing past him to our bedroom.

I was going to hug my best friend again.

After the night I'd had…or was it morning? Either way, I didn't think my heart could handle any more goodness, but I was going to soak it up for as long as it lasted.

If there was anything these last couple of months had taught me, it was that everything you cherished most could be taken away at any time.

Life had to be lived for the moment and not for what could be.

Within a minute, I was waiting near the couch, ready to go, and Foster came out of the kitchen with food for Charlie.

I bounced on the balls of my feet, then grabbed Foster's hand without telling him what I was doing. In the next second, we were standing in front of Charlie's house, and Foster nearly dropped the glass plate of food.

"Shit, Andie." He groaned. Oops. Now that I'd thought

about it, I was pretty sure I hadn't teleported with him since he'd been back.

I took the breakfast from him and rubbed a hand over his back. "Sorry. I got excited."

He offered me a half-smile and straightened. "It's all right. Just need to get used to that again."

Elias probably did, too, I thought.

When I stepped up to the door, it was already cracked open, so I walked right in with Foster behind me. The lights were off, so I ventured through the small, two-bedroom cottage and finally saw a lamp shining from Charlie's bedroom.

She was struggling to sit up in bed, so I raced over, set the food down, and helped her with the pillows behind her back.

The color was back in her face, and her hair shone with the golden color I was used to seeing on her. My throat burned as we reached for each other.

Of course, I'd seen her when she'd woken up before, but she hadn't been fully aware then. This was different. This was finally having my best friend back.

Her grip was loose around my shoulder, and she shook against me. I'd yet to see Charlie cry since returning to this world. Knowing how badly she'd been affected by the past few weeks broke me apart.

I squeezed my eyes shut and held her close. "I'm so sorry, Charlie."

She shushed me. "This wasn't your fault." She paused. "I'm just glad I'm back with no permanent damage that I can tell."

I pulled back, checking her over a little closer for my own peace of mind. "Are you sure? None of the others said they'd been hurt or tortured, but I'd thought…" I had to stop before I completely lost it.

"Whatever you'd thought was wrong," she said softly.

"Unless our memories were wiped, nothing happened to us besides a little malnourishment."

I took a shuddering breath. "I really hope so."

We still didn't know for sure that there wasn't a trojan horse within the witches or wolves. It was a theory that Foster had presented to both Beatrix and Holden. They took his concern seriously, but all of the tests to check for dark magic came back negative, which meant none of them were being— at least within the coven—watched.

Still, I wasn't trusting Moira that much. She'd taken them all for a purpose. We needed to know what that purpose had been before we could rest easy.

Charlie nodded toward the plate I'd set at the end of the bed. "Is that for me?"

"Of course." I grabbed it and took the foil off, glad Foster had even thought to put a fork on the plate before we left.

Once Charlie had a good hold on the food, I turned toward her bedroom door, but I didn't see Foster lingering. I closed my eyes briefly and searched for his proximity through our bond. He must have waited in the living room.

My attention went back to Charlie, who was moaning over her French toast. "I don't know what I did to deserve such deliciousness, but thank you."

I chuckled. "You can thank Foster when he's done giving us some privacy."

She peeked around me. "He doesn't have to hide away."

"He knows that." Or at least I assumed so from the contentment I could sense from him through our connection.

I squeezed her thigh while she shoveled the remnants of food into her mouth. "So, they really didn't torture you for information or ask questions about our coven?"

I hated to bring this up now, but it was better to do so without preamble, considering time wasn't on our side.

She finished chewing as she shook her head. "Seriously. It was really weird. As soon as we came out of the mist they'd taken us in, we were locked in a room, squeezed together like sardines. The wolves panicked first because they couldn't hear their other halves, and when the witches couldn't muster even the smallest amount of magic, I knew we had to be in some sort of containment pod."

My brow creased. "Those exist?"

"Unfortunately, more than you'd think," she answered. "Beatrix has one here."

I sucked in a breath. "Seriously? Where?"

Charlie shrugged as she took her last bite. "No clue, but I know it exists. I've heard her mention it before, and I don't take her for the kind of person who bluffs, you know?"

No, neither did I.

I shook off the eeriness I felt at knowing that and waited for Charlie to continue. "After we left the pod, we went somewhere with more space and beds for us to sleep on. I don't remember how many days passed before that happened, though. Then it wasn't too long after that everything just goes black in my memory."

Again, it was the same story everyone else had already told.

I tried to relate to Moira. To think of what I would do if I were her and had leverage against the coven who had something I wanted.

Giving my hostages any sort of comfort and letting them go mere weeks later without ever using them as bait wasn't at the top of my list.

Something must have happened. Something that I badly wish we knew about.

"Enough about me." Charlie poked at my knee. "What about you? You're different than before. What happened?"

I let out a heavy breath. I wasn't even sure where to start. The last couple of months felt like they had gone by torturously slow, yet at the same time, everything seemed like a blur.

"Well, let's see. When you were taken, Foster went into some sort of magical coma and he didn't wake up until last week," I said first.

Charlie's jaw dropped. "Noooo."

"Yeah. And during all that, Holden wouldn't let me see him."

"But you fixed everyone else. *Is he an idiot?*" she practically yelled.

I just lifted my shoulders. "I spent my weeks searching for you and the others, while also trying to find a way inside the pack that wouldn't require me to fight a wolf. When I wasn't doing any of that, I was practicing with my magic." I grimaced. "Well, more like trying to control it."

"What do you mean?" she asked with utter interest.

"I syphoned most of my magic from the necklace while I was fighting with Moira that day," I answered. "She didn't know I could do that. Hell, she might not realize what I've done, even now. The energy made me erratic. I had to be by myself most every day so that I didn't hurt anyone else."

A lone tear streaked down her cheek. "I'm so sorry, Andie. I wish I'd been here."

"Me, too, but not so that you could have helped. Just so that you hadn't been where you were."

"That, too." She laughed and the sound warmed my chest. She leaned toward the edge of the bed. "Yo, wolf boy. You going to come say *hi* or did you not miss me?"

Charlie winked at me when she'd finished yelling across the house. I could sense Foster's amusement as he got closer.

When he entered the bedroom, there was a scowl on his face. "You know I'd never miss you. It was more like a vacation."

She scoffed. "Says the shifter who just woke up from a coma."

Foster stood behind me and squeezed my shoulders.

"Seems like we both had a hellish time. I'm glad you're back, though. You know, for Andie's sake."

"Of course," Charlie said seriously.

Then Foster shocked the hell out of me by adding, "Mack was pretty torn up about you being taken. He's texted multiple times asking how you're doing since we brought everyone back."

"Oh." Charlie's cheeks reddened, and I didn't think I'd ever seen her blush before. "Well, you're welcome to pass along my phone number to him so he can find out that answer for himself."

I grinned. There was my sassy Charlie. Maybe she was going to be okay after all and my worrying had been for nothing. Of course, her being deprived of her senses and magic for weeks on end wasn't nothing, but at least she hadn't been tortured—that we knew of.

If they had been while they'd been in that weird zone-out, I was okay with accepting that none of them would have anything to tell us that could be helpful in locating Moira or figuring out her plans.

"You'll get to see him tomorrow if you're feeling up for going to the meeting Beatrix is hosting here," Foster said to Charlie.

I glanced up at him. "What meeting?"

"Holden told me he'd be at the coven tomorrow and was bringing Mack with him to meet with Beatrix and the rest of us. I'm assuming we didn't find out yet because of your timeout." Foster shot me a pointed look.

"What timeout?" Charlie asked quickly.

I waved a hand. "It was nothing."

Foster then raised a brow. "Nothing? You collapsing from using too much of your core energy isn't nothing, Andie. It was dangerous, and a 'timeout' was necessary to keep you alive."

He was being a bit dramatic, but he also wasn't wrong, unfortunately.

Charlie punched me in the thigh. Hard. "Were you trying to make up for something that wasn't even your fault?"

I shook my head "no" as Foster said, "Yes."

She rolled her eyes. "I should have known you'd have a guilt complex. Seriously, you need to let that shit go. Not a single person who was taken blamed you while we were locked up and conscious."

"Yeah. Well, that wasn't the case here," I muttered. "At least not with the wolves."

Foster growled from next to me. "They were wrong, and we both know that had nothing to do with you and everything to do with Holden not knowing how to process his daughter being among those taken."

My mate might have been right, and I understood that a little better now, but still. I didn't think the guilt would ever truly go away until the threat of Moira was dealt with.

It was something I hoped happened rather soon, because continuing as we had been, not knowing what to expect next, wasn't going to work forever.

At least not for me.

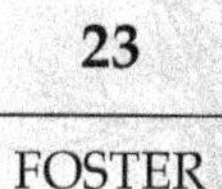

23

FOSTER

Even though Charlie had invited me over, I left her and Andie alone while I went to the pack. It had been much too long since I'd gone of my own accord and without being furious with everyone for having kept Andie away.

Given I hadn't asked Holden to remove me from the pack, I figured it would be good for me to go back to checking in regularly with him and Mack.

I didn't have a specific job within the pack yet, but I figured once things settled, I'd have more responsibilities, which would mean less time with Andie. I tried to tell myself I was okay with that, but it was harder than I thought it would be.

Once I was within the boundary lines of the pack, I reached out to Holden and he invited me to join him and Mack in the alpha office.

I headed straight there, only nodding at others as I passed by them on my way.

My knuckles knocked on the wooden door, and Mack was right there to let me in. "Welcome back, Foster."

The grin on his face wasn't something I'd expected. Not

that Mack wasn't normally jovial, but this was different. His smile as I took a seat put me on edge.

"What's going on?" I asked, glancing between him and Holden, who was sitting behind his desk with his arms resting behind his head.

He gave Mack a narrowed glance. "Tone it down, Beta."

Mack nodded at me, dropping the shit-eating grin. "How's Charlie?"

"She's good. Finally not falling right back to sleep," I answered.

My eyes fell back on Holden, waiting for him to say whatever they were keeping from me.

And here I'd thought I was finally going to have a normal visit at the pack.

"Damn it, Mack. You couldn't keep your emotions in check for five minutes?" Holden groaned, then leaned forward, sorting through some papers on his desk. He handed me two sheets. "Foster, I'd like you to look this proposal over and tell me what you think."

I accepted the documents and glanced over the first paragraph. "You're leaving the pack?"

He shook his head. "No, keep reading."

Doing as he said, I nodded in agreement to many of these things. "Splitting the pack is a good idea. Having things divided between the city and woods isn't feasible for the long term as the pack continues to grow."

He smirked. "I'm glad you agree. I'm going to be presenting this idea to the others who assist with running the pack. Keep reading."

I flipped to the second page, and the words began depicting how the separation would take place and the duties would be assigned if it all went accordingly.

At the very end, there was a suggested hierarchy order for each of the packs. My head shook, and I tossed the papers on the desk. "No fucking way, Holden."

My mood immediately plummeted. I couldn't believe he'd assume something so huge.

Holden sighed. "Just keep those papers and give it some thought. You wouldn't be on your own out here. I'd leave Mack as the beta with you. Plus, the pack already respects your authority."

Yet most of them probably didn't know that I'd failed to protect the wolves I'd once been honored to care for. My blood family. My pack family. All of them gone in one night because I'd made the mistake of trusting two evil beings.

Mack grasped my shoulder. "Come on, man. Just think about it. Talk to Andie. See what she says. You were born to be an alpha. You won't survive merely belonging in a pack."

"Sure, I will," I grumbled. "I've been fine the last decade that way."

Holden *tsked*. "There's a difference between *surviving* and *thriving*. Do you want to be the mate for Andie who merely survives? Or do you want to be the one who overcomes his fears and doesn't let the past decide his future?"

That was a low blow and one I hadn't been prepared for.

My eyes cast down, and I stared at my fists. *What do you think?* I asked my wolf.

His reply was slow to come, which I appreciated. *I think that what happened before was completely out of your control and that you're not to blame for someone else's evil. Just like Andie isn't responsible for Moira's actions. That being said, if you truly don't want to lead a pack, then don't. It's a disservice to the wolves here if you take a job that you don't really want.*

Fuck. He wasn't wrong. About any of it.

I wouldn't have been able to admit that before, but seeing what Andie had been going through and trying to convince her otherwise, I couldn't be a hypocrite and still hold myself accountable for something I'd had no control over.

Sure, I'd invited those shifters into our pack, but they were the ones who'd chosen to deceive me and kill everyone else. And for no damn reason, either.

I glanced up at Holden. "Can I think about this?"

"I'd be disappointed with any other answer." He smiled and pushed the papers I'd thrown down back toward me.

This time, I folded them carefully and sat up to tuck them into my back pocket. This wasn't only a decision I needed to think about, but one Andie needed to be okay with as well. It would mean leaving the coven and living with the pack full-time.

"So, I didn't see your name on that list of new assignment proposals," I said, wanting to move the conversation off me.

"No. Losing Piper, even temporarily, reminded me too much of when I lost my mate," he replied solemnly. "I decided that, when she's mentally ready, it's Piper's turn to take over. She's practically been running the city anyway, and we're overdue on officially splitting the pack. We'll just need to find her a good beta since Mack would stay with you. Nothing will really have to change besides the amount of time I get to go fishing."

I chuckled softly. "That sounds like a boring retirement plan."

"After the last few months, boring is just what I need."

Shit, that was the truth.

Mack nudged me. "Are you really going to think about the alpha role, or are you just placating us?"

I glanced over at him to find a hopeful expression on his rugged face. "I'm going to think about it, but I don't know how long I'll need. It's not an easy decision. Not only because of my past, but I have to consider Andie as well. She's not an alpha female."

But isn't she? my wolf said. *She might not have shifted in the conventional sense, but she produced a wolf.*

Holden cocked his head. "What's that look for?"

I hadn't told anyone else about Andie's wolf spirit because

of several reasons, one of them being we hadn't really had time to sit and consider what it meant that she'd passed out during the whole thing and couldn't remember what had happened.

As Holden and Mack both waited patiently for me to reveal what had shifted my mood, I knew I could trust them.

"Andie might have a wolf, but it's not like ours." Then I added, "Hell, I don't even know if it's an actual part of her, given how the wolf appeared."

Holden moved forward in his chair, leaning over his desk further. "What do you mean? What happened and when?"

I explained the whole evening to them in vivid detail, hoping that even the smallest thing might explain what it all meant, but not even talking about the spirit wolf helped make sense of the event.

Mack let out a low whistle and ran a hand over his buzzed hair. "Man, you've certainly got one hell of a mate. I've never even heard rumors of such a thing."

"Yeah, neither have I," Holden added. Though where Mack was intrigued, the alpha was just as concerned as I'd been since it had happened.

"But this is a problem for later," I said. "My mate is fine, and we have enough to deal with right now, still searching for Moira. Unless a wolf starts leaping from Andie's chest randomly, let's keep this between us."

Holden steepled his fingers. "Does Beatrix know?"

"Not that I'm aware of, and let's keep it that way. She doesn't need to add this to the list of things to stress over right now."

He chuckled. "Has the old witch finally grown on you?"

I shrugged. "We have come to an unspoken understanding that I'm okay with."

"And this is why you'd make the best alpha for this pack," Mack said sincerely. "Anyone who can come to *any* understanding with that witch has talents most don't possess."

He wasn't wrong about that. Not by a long shot.

"What about the shifters who returned?" I asked, purposely diverting the conversation. "Are they all awake and back to normal with their wolves?"

I'd known Beatrix had been here helping, but since I'd been busy keeping an eye on Andie, I never had gotten any details on how things had gone with the returning pack members.

Holden nodded at Mack, who answered me. "All nine are awake. There are still a few too weak to shift, but they're younger pack members and we're not worried at this point. None of them have been acting out of character, either. We have them all staying with a friend or family member who also happens to be a guard or once was. So, if anything happens, we'll know about it quickly and someone will be there to minimize damage."

Unsurprising that they'd taken extra precautions after James's mind had been taken over before and he'd nearly killed Andie. What did surprise me was that Beatrix hadn't done the same for the witches.

"How long do you plan to have someone keeping watch over those taken?" I asked.

Holden *hmmed*. "Depends on a few things. I'm hoping tomorrow's meeting will be insightful as to what Beatrix plans to do next. Once word gets out about the council, things could get out of hand quickly. She might have been better off waiting for that bomb until we all had less to deal with."

"You know, if the Moon Goddess herself hadn't told me to trust the old witch's judgment, I'd agree with you." I laughed darkly. "Maybe that's why I've been less annoyed with her lately. Either way, it seemed to be a *now or never* thing. The hunters were harassing innocent people, and the council was interested in my bond with Andie to the point that our old wolf council advised against our mating. That's something I'm happy to not have looming over my head."

Mack nodded in agreement. "Plus, it's not like the council or hunters ever did much to help us as of late. We could send messages to the rest of the packs letting them know the announcement is coming so they can prepare like our shifters in town have."

That made me think about the vampires staying in the coven. "Maciah and his crew have already been trying to clean up the murdering bloodsuckers. I'm sure they've already alerted the nests they've aligned with. We'll be prepared for the fallout."

"We don't really have a choice now," Holden muttered as he sorted through more papers scattered about his desk, then began going on about the amended training schedule with Mack.

I only half-listened as I thought about everything we'd already talked about.

I'd come to the pack in hopes of just a casual visit, and now I was leaving with a weight on my shoulders that I wasn't sure I wanted.

What I needed was to talk with someone who wanted what was best for me and not themselves or the pack.

What I needed was Andie.

24

ANDIE

Foster's emotions were all over the place, so when he texted that he was on his way back after I'd made lunch for Charlie, I parted ways with her and met Foster at the barrier entrance I expected him to come through.

I wasn't sure I could handle another problem, but I stuffed down my own worries and focused on Foster's pinched expression when he walked through the opaque wall.

His arms wrapped around me and he squeezed hard. "Missed you." His voice was rough and fear that something terrible had happened rushed through me.

"What's going on with the pack?" I asked gently.

He sighed and pulled back, running a hand over his shoulder-length hair. "Too much. Let's go back to the house."

"Quickly or leisurely?" I asked with a raised brow.

He frowned. "Quickly."

I grabbed his hand and teleported us without waiting for him to change his mind. He wobbled a bit, but not as much as last time, then picked me up and carried me inside the house.

We ended up on the couch with me in his lap and his head resting against mine.

"Foster, you're starting to scare me a bit," I said. "What happened?"

One of his hands reached into his back pocket and pulled out folded papers. I took them from him and started to scan the contents. I didn't see anything alarming there. Some changes within the pack that were probably long overdue, given how spread out they all seemed to be.

Then I flipped to the second page, and I immediately knew what had my mate on edge.

"Hey, just because he wrote it down doesn't mean you have to accept," I said earnestly.

He nodded and looked straight ahead, avoiding my gaze.

I forced his chin toward me. "Talk to me."

"I don't want to be an alpha again," he said immediately.

"Then don't be."

Then his frown deepened. "But my only reason is because of what happened before and my wolf kindly pointed out that by using the past as an excuse not to move forward, I'm doing exactly what I told you not to do. I'm taking the blame and punishing myself for something I didn't have complete control over."

A knife felt like it was burrowing in my chest. Everything inside me hurt for Foster. I knew exactly how he was feeling, and I hated that he still carried the past with him so heavily.

My hands stroked his shoulder and arm and then grabbed hold of his hands. "There is nothing I can say to make this better. I know that, because while you helped me to see the bigger picture, it was still on me to accept what happened and move forward. You don't have to forget your old pack, but you are allowed to keep living the life you were meant to have. And you were meant to lead."

He seemed to already know that, and I was pretty sure he already knew what he was going to do. It was just overcoming the "what if" scenarios probably running through his head and moving past his guilt.

Foster's eyes blinked slowly. "It's not just me who has to make the decision, you know?"

I tilted my head. "Uh, no. This has nothing to do with me."

His lips finally twitched upward. "Actually, it very much does. You're my mate, Andie. If I chose to be alpha, then that would make you alpha female of the pack. There would be no splitting our time between the coven and there. The pack would be our home, and the wolves would be our people."

Well, shit on a stick.

I hadn't thought of that, and I wasn't sure if I was qualified for such a role, but if this was what Foster wanted— and I was pretty confident it was, deep down—then I'd figure out a way to handle whatever being alpha female meant.

Ignoring my own nerves, I smiled and said, "I have no objections to living with the pack full-time as long as I'm still allowed to practice my magic, have Charlie over, and work with Beatrix on occasion."

"Of course," he said. "Nothing in that regard would have to change, but you would be busier, helping the wolves with issues and other things around the pack."

I started to picture that life and what it would be like to have a true purpose. Before finding Foster, I'd felt lost for so many years. I hadn't known where I belonged, but picturing us in the pack house, the thought of helping others in the capacity he was describing…

Well, it made my chest light and fluttery.

"I'm all in if you are," I said with assurance.

His stare bored into mine. "You're positive?"

"You'd be able to sense if I were hesitant, so you already know the answer to that question," I pointed out.

He dropped his head back onto the couch and groaned. I poked at his stomach and laughed. "You're going to be pack alpha."

"Keep that from even Charlie until this mess with Moira is

done," he said. "Holden isn't making changes anytime soon. So I'd rather focus on one thing if we can."

That, I could agree with.

Hopefully, tomorrow's meeting would include news that brought us one step closer to being done with all this nonsense.

THE MEETING WAS CHAOTIC. I DIDN'T KNOW HOW ELSE TO describe the scene before me. There were dozens of people present. Most of whom I didn't know, but apparently, they were here to help. Though, I had a feeling that Beatrix's throwdown with the council had more to do with their presence than our need in figuring out where Moira was hiding.

"Silence!" Beatrix finally shouted, and the room quickly quieted. "Thank you. Now, if you'd all take a seat or stand in the back, I'd like to get started."

I was already sitting in the second row with Charlie and Foster. I'd told Charlie to stay home, given she still wobbled quite a bit when she walked, but she'd insisted on being present.

While she didn't remember any torture, I suspected as more of her awareness returned, vengeance was rising higher on her priority list.

"All right, so I'm going to make this intro quick," Beatrix started. "We have Maciah's nest representatives on the left. These are vampires who deserve our respect, and if they're not treated as such, then you will be seeing me soon after. Then, we have Mirra and Vi with a few more of their coven members from back east."

She pointed toward the middle where most of the wolf shifters had congregated. "First is the East Texas Pack along with the South Carolina pack alpha and alpha female. Behind them, joining us late"—Beatrix glowered—"are Holden and Mack from next door. Lastly, we have some of my coven members, whom you can meet later."

Heads swiveled around, getting a better look around the room.

"Now that you know who is present, I should also mention that we are working with the fae as well. Lucinda and Finn, whom I'm sure most of you have heard of, are working to make sure the council doesn't do anything we didn't agree on. They should be back within a day or two, and they'll be bringing more of their people with them."

A few murmurs sounded throughout the room, but nobody seemed overly surprised by that announcement.

"Now, as you can see, we have plenty of help, but we still have no idea where Moira is," Beatrix said with disdain. "The witches have been working around the clock to track her, but even the little blips we'd been getting before have ceased. Has anyone else heard or seen anything that might give us a clue as to where this…witch is hiding?"

I glanced around, hoping someone would say something, but the room stayed relatively silent.

"Okay. Well, we're going to need more eyes and ears out there," Beatrix said. "She is *somewhere*, and we need everyone looking for her. There's no telling if she's going to give up on Andie and start looking elsewhere for a solution to her problem."

Oh, Beatrix. She was the queen at making people side with her crazy.

Fear was a powerful thing.

"If she comes for us, we'll be ready," an older alpha with salt-and-pepper hair and who was missing one of his legs said with eagerness in his light-brown eyes.

I wasn't sure I believed him, but he had enough confidence in his voice that nobody else questioned him.

Well, except for Beatrix.

"Ready for what?" she counted. "To die? Have you ever fought dark magic, Perry? Oh, wait. Yes, you have, and we all know what happened when you did. I'm not saying you're not capable, but we shouldn't be ready for defensive moves here. Just waiting for Moira to show isn't going to keep people safe. We need to be actively tracking her with every available resource. This might seem like a 'Beatrix and Holden problem,' but if Moira isn't stopped, I assure you, she will become a 'supernatural problem.'"

Her words were spoken with such conviction, I found myself nodding my head as she spoke, hoping that everyone else in the room believed that, after all Moira had done, the chances of her slipping off into the sunset once she got her soulmate back were slim-to-none.

"We will send more wolves out to search the Midwest," Roman said proudly.

Maciah nodded next. "We have nests of vampires who can scour the north and parts of the east as well, plus what we've already been doing here."

Perry shared a glance with his mate, who nodded, then stood. "We will do more as well. We'll fill in at the territories not covered."

Well, at least now we had a plan. Sort of. More like a continuation of what we'd already been doing.

"And the witches will continue searching for dark energy signatures," Beatrix added. "We'll be following up on each one and keeping track of what we find. All notes will be emailed to each of you at the end of every day. Hopefully, between all of us, we will find enough information to figure this out."

Gods, I hoped so.

Foster gave my hand a squeeze as Beatrix ended the meeting. We finally stood, and the room was immediately loud as people moved back into their circles, catching up with old friends.

Mack came right over to us. His eyes were focused only on Charlie, and there was a longing in them I'd yet to see, but the slight line between his eyes made me wonder if he was also confused or conflicted.

Charlie stumbled next to me again and I grabbed on to her, but Mack took her from me.

"Would you like help getting back home?" he asked. "Seems like you should be in bed a while longer."

Charlie's cheeks reddened, and I stepped back, sharing an interested glance with Foster.

"That would be lovely," Charlie cooed.

Lovely? Who was this woman and where was my snarky best friend?

They pushed through the crowd, completely ignoring the looks they were getting from others in the room.

We weren't the only ones confused by what the hell had just happened.

"Do you think…" I trailed off, not knowing if I should ask the question out loud.

Foster shrugged. "Crazier things have happened."

If Charlie and Mack were indeed mates, I was pretty sure my heart might explode. I didn't know why they wouldn't have felt anything before, but maybe we'd find out soon enough.

Foster took my hand in his and guided us forward. "We should visit with the other alphas."

Given our conversation yesterday, I agreed with him. I needed to be an alpha female, and making friends with the others here probably wasn't the worst idea.

Plus, Cait was with the shifter group alongside Roman, so at least I knew one of them.

Foster shook hands with Holden, Roman, then Perry, and greeted Perry's mate last. "Silvie, this is my mate Andie."

I stepped forward to shake her hand, but she pushed her

way through the crowd. "I don't do handshakes. I prefer hugs."

I laughed against her tight hold. "Well, okay, then. I'll remember that."

She nodded against my shoulder, then pulled back. "Good, because I was just telling Holden here that it's time the alphas met more often. It shouldn't take shit like this to get us all together. I assume you and Foster will be joining us for such future gatherings?"

I shared a look with my mate. He kept a straight face and smiled. "If you'll allow just anyone to join you, then sure, we'll be there."

Silvie narrowed piercing eyes on Foster. "Uh-huh."

Well, she might not have known of Holden's plans to make Foster an alpha, but she sure suspected something.

Perry adjusted the hold on his cane and nudged Silvie. "Leave the man alone. We'll have your gathering, and whoever comes, comes."

She poked at his thigh. "Do you want me to cut your other leg off, too?"

My eyes widened and my jaw dropped, but before they could catch my surprise at her statement, Cait leaned in and whispered, "Long story. She only did it to save his life. Don't worry. They love each other."

Well, that was a bit of relief.

"Silvie is right, though," Roman said once the bickering had stopped. "I vote for quarterly meetings. A half day for business and the rest for fun." Then he nodded at me. "Andie here can help shuttle us around, too."

Cait backhanded him in the gut and air rushed from between his lips. "Don't assume that because she's a witch, we suddenly have access to portals whenever we want. That's rude."

I considered telling her it was okay, that I'd be happy to

help, but something told me Cait was enjoying this moment a little too much for me to ruin it.

Foster, however, didn't catch on to that. Or didn't care. He wrapped an arm around my shoulder. "I'm sure we can figure something out."

Cait winked at me, and I grinned in return. Oh, how I couldn't wait to spend time with her under better circumstances.

After chatting a while longer, the portals were opened by the coven witches to get everyone home for the time being, and we said our goodbyes. Silvie hugged me again, then smirked over her shoulder as she left. I didn't know what she thought she knew, but her coyness made me like her more.

I leaned my head against Foster's arm. "Shall we head home as well?"

"Yeah, but let's walk," he said. "I need to stretch my legs."

Then another thought occurred to me. "You also need to shift. It's been a few too many days since you've run with your wolf."

He frowned and nodded. "I will tonight. Maybe we can start in the backyard again."

I liked that idea. I still hadn't mentioned anything to Beatrix. I wasn't sure if pushing a spirit wolf out of my chest was safe or not, but it sure made Elias, Foster's wolf, happy and that was important to me.

When we were halfway home, I saw Benjamin and Reah walking toward us. Guilt immediately consumed all of my feelings. I'd told them I'd come by for lunch sometime and I never had. Considering how thrilled I'd been to know I had family still, I was sure doing a shitty job of conveying that I cared about them.

I waved awkwardly. "Hey, guys."

Benjamin's bright eyes lit up. "Hi, Andie. We just stopped by your house."

I glanced at Reah. There was a tightness around her eyes. I

knew she didn't like leaving the house much and felt bad she'd had to come to me.

"Oh, yeah?" I said. "We're just heading back if you want to walk with us."

Benjamin glanced at his mom. "I think we'd better get home, but we were just checking in to see how you were doing. Seems like you're better?"

I smiled in return. "Definitely better. I'm sorry I haven't been by. Things haven't been the calmest over the last couple of weeks."

"We understand," Reah finally said. "I didn't want to bother you, but Benjamin insisted you wouldn't mind."

"And he was right. You're welcome anytime. Hopefully, things settle down soon and I'll have more time for visits."

Her cheeks lifted and she nodded. "That would be nice. I found some more pictures of me and your mom when we were children. I kept them out to show you."

The hopefulness in her voice made my throat and eyes burn. She was just as thankful to have more family again as I was.

"I promise. I will be there." I glanced at Benjamin. "Text me reminders until I do."

He chuckled. "You got it, Cuz."

Reah shook her head and tugged on his arm. "Come on. Let's let them get back to what they were doing."

"It was good to see the both of you," Foster said as they continued by.

I looked up at him as we kept walking. "I can't believe I forgot to go over there."

"Reah was right. It's not like you've been ignoring them for recreational activities."

While true, that didn't make me feel less shitty about the situation.

I'd make a better effort, even if we didn't find Moira soon.

25

FOSTER

The next day, Charlie was back to her normal self. She was laughing and playing and poking fun at everyone, including me. I tried not to be annoyed with her, given she'd practically died and Andie seemed so damn happy to have her friend back.

The two of them spent most of the morning practicing with their magic so Charlie could see everything Andie had learned. They both ended up teaching each other a few things, and then Holden reached out to me just after lunchtime.

Are you busy? he asked.

Just finished eating. What's going on?

I know you haven't given me your answer yet, but I was hoping you and Andie could come over for a bit.

I glanced at her and Charlie laying in the grass together. *As long as Charlie can join us, I don't think that will be a problem.*

Has Charlie said anything about Mack in front of you? he asked hesitantly.

No, but I did notice the way they looked at each other after the meeting. Do you think there's something there?

Mack does. Bring her, and make sure Andie knows to tell me if

Charlie isn't feeling anything in return, he said. *I'll handle Mack myself if he's crossing a line he shouldn't be.*

I didn't think we were going to have that problem, but I'd pass along the information anyway.

Absolutely. We'll see you soon.

I got up and walked to stand over Andie. "Do either of you want to go to the pack with me? Holden asked us to visit."

Charlie was up before Andie. "I'm in."

My knees bent, and I helped Andie to her feet. She smiled and nodded. "Sure. Are we leaving now?"

"I figured we would unless you had anything else going on."

Holden hadn't said what he needed, but I also wanted to talk to him more about Andie's spirit wolf. She couldn't generate it again last night when I'd shifted, which had frustrated her to no end and was likely what led to her practicing with Charlie this morning.

She wanted it too badly, like I said before, my wolf chimed in to my thoughts. *She put too much pressure on herself. We need to get her to relax more.*

Easier said than done.

It was something I could tell Andie really wanted, which meant she wasn't going to stop trying until she mastered it, just like she'd been doing with the magic she'd acquired.

"Portal?" Andie suggested once she and Charlie had finished brushing the grass off themselves.

I nodded, given that was another thing she enjoyed practicing.

Charlie watched with rapt attention as Andie pressed her palms together, called her energy forward with precise control, and then thrusted her hands out in front of her.

The opening immediately became visible, but Andie wasn't done yet. She still had to concentrate, and that seemed to be the hardest part for her. The rift in the air was only the size of a baseball and she had to use her magic to make it big enough for us to walk through.

Slowly and carefully, she did just that while moving her hands around one another. Tethers of her energy shot forward, circling around the opening until it was oval-shaped and tall enough for them to walk through standing, but required me to bend forward a little.

We stepped onto the gravel driveway in front of the pack house, and Andie quickly turned to pull the energy back to herself. Once she was done, she dusted her hands off. "I feel like that should be easier than it has been lately."

Charlie nudged her arm. "Most witches can't create a portal for several years after they've begun practicing. You should be proud of how far you've come over these last few months."

I took Andie's hand in mine. "For once, I agree with the blonde."

Charlie sneered at me. "My hair color has nothing to do with who I am."

Oh, I knew that, but I'd missed pissing her off just a little.

"Uh-huh," I replied.

She opened her mouth to no doubt berate me, but something over my shoulder caught her attention.

No, not something. *Someone.*

She pushed past Andie and me without a care and hugged Mack. His face buried into her shoulder, disappearing into her long, golden locks.

They just stood like that, even when Holden came out to greet us. He eyed the two but only shook his head before nodding for us to follow him.

When we were inside, Holden turned to Andie. "I was thinking you might like to go into the kitchen and help Patty instead of being bored by pack talk. She's preparing meals for the monthly meetings hosted around the pack."

Andie smiled. "Sure. If you see Charlie before I do, just let her know where I am."

Andie's going to be in the kitchen. Make sure Charlie knows, I said to Mack privately.

"Already done." I pulled her in for a hug and a quick kiss.

She sighed. "I am seriously jealous of your pack communication."

I wished I could give her that gift, but maybe in time, she'd have it. Who knew what would happen when she became alpha female? Shifter magic worked in weird ways, and I had a feeling that was all thanks to Luna, the Moon Goddess.

She had a plan for things that very few of us were privy to.

Holden gestured for me to continue following him and we ended up in his office. He had old textbooks piled all over his desk, and he rubbed his eyes as he sat down.

"Have you slept since I last saw you?" I asked with concern.

He shrugged. "Some, but I found something you need to see."

He picked up one of the leatherbound books that was still open and handed it to me. "What's this?" I asked, barely able to read the faded text.

His arm reached across the desk, and he pointed to an image in the lower left corner. "That seems to meet the description of the wolf Andie created that you told me about."

My eyes focused on the area. Shit, it did. "What does the rest of this say?" I didn't see the point in struggling to read something he had probably already memorized.

"That when the spirit wolf arrives, so will change," he said ominously.

I froze in place. "What kind of change?"

"That's what I called you here for," he said before taking a seat.

I set the book back down and situated myself in the chair behind me. "So, you think Andie could be this spirit wolf?"

His hand rubbed over his jaw. "My wolf thinks she's the host for the spirit wolf. That they're not actually the same being like we are with our wolves."

That would make sense, given what I'd seen. Andie hadn't shifted when the wolf had appeared—she'd passed out.

"I'm going to keep reading, but I wanted you to see this for yourself so that you can keep an eye out for anything unusual," Holden added. "I don't know that it's something we have to worry about at all, but if you're going to accept the alpha role—which I still think you should—then figuring this out could be key to your leadership."

I heard what he wasn't saying. A powerful alpha was needed to rule a pack as desired as ours. Otherwise, we would constantly be challenged, or worse, Andie could be challenged for her alpha female position. It was rare but had happened recently, in fact. If she were the host to an ancient spirit wolf, that would give her added protection that I couldn't.

"Thank you for researching this," I said. "When I told you about it, I didn't expect you to do this much."

He waved off my sincerity. "I can't leave the pack to help search for that witch, so it was good to have the distraction."

I raised a brow. "Why did you need one to begin with?"

He grimaced. "Piper. She wants to take control now, but she's acting out of vengeance. Now is not the time for her to lead when she's furious over what happened to her." He sighed. "It's not that I fault her emotions—you saw me before we found her—but just like I want you to be as prepared as you can be for taking over, I need the same for my daughter when we split the pack."

I understood what he was saying, but I could also see how tired he'd grown over the last few months that I'd known him. He needed to put some things into motion sooner rather than later or it was he who would need to be worried about a challenge.

"What if you made her co-alpha?" I asked. "It's been done before. You can let the public see it's Piper running the city side of things and you holding them down here, but inside the pack, you can join Piper in the city while I help Mack more here."

He leaned forward, pressing his palms to the desk. "Are you saying you accept my proposal?"

I fought a smile, because I'd known this would make him happy, but I didn't want him getting too excited. "I'm saying that I *will*. One day, but not yet. I'm not ready yet, because Andie isn't ready yet. When she is, I will be too. As long as you're okay with not knowing when exactly that will be, then yes, I accept."

He let out a heavy sigh. "This will be perfect. I promise you, Foster. You were meant for this. I've known that since the moment you showed up in my territory as a rogue wolf."

For the first time in much too long, I felt the same way.

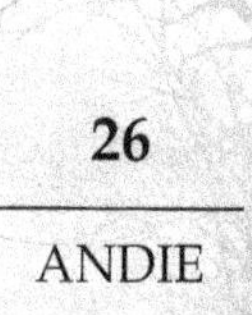

26

ANDIE

Going into the kitchen to help wasn't exactly how I'd seen my time at the pack going today, but once I was there, I realized Holden knew better than I did.

Patty was incredible. She was friendly yet firm and knew exactly how she wanted her kitchen run. I was immediately bossed around once I'd washed my hands, but as soon as I got into my groove with packaging already-made sandwiches, her tone lightened.

"We're glad to see you around the pack again," she said, blowing strands of ash-colored bangs out of her hazel eyes.

The rest of her hair was French braided just past her shoulders, and she wore a simple blue denim dress under her green apron. Slight wrinkles formed around her face as she concentrated on the food in front of her.

"Thanks," I said, a little uncomfortable. "Hopefully, the rest of the pack feels that way after what happened."

Her pale lips pressed together in a thin line. "Don't you worry about what everyone else thinks. Holden made a choice to welcome Foster into our pack, and we accepted that choice. You are Foster's mate, which makes you one of us, regardless of the juju magic flowing through you."

Comfort filled me, and I had to blink back some of my heavier emotions. "I appreciate that."

"Good. Now, stop what you're doing and grab the box of mason jars from the top shelf." She arched her back. "I'm too damn old to be climbing that stepladder."

I did as she asked while continuing to talk. "Does anyone else help you in here?"

"Yeah, but they're setting up the tables and decorations. They'll be back soon to start carrying all of the food out there for the women."

I set the heavy glass jars on the counter. "Women? Like only women are allowed to attend the meeting?"

She nodded. "We love our mates, but sometimes we just need a bitch fest, you know?"

I laughed, not having expected her to say those exact words. I also didn't really understand. At least, not yet. Foster and I had barely had the chance to spend long periods of time alone. I still cherished every moment I got with him, and even his "overbearing" qualities were endearing to me.

At least, for now.

She growled at me, actually bared teeth and everything. "Ah, the honeymoon phase. It will be a distant memory one day."

Her mate must have been a real peach. I couldn't wait to meet him. Not.

Foster entered the kitchen, and I tried not to brighten at his appearance, given Patty's previous comment.

"Do you ladies need help?" he asked, looking around and seeing the boxes of sandwiches I'd wrapped up and the mason jars Patty was now filling with lemonade.

"Nope. I have this," she grumbled. "Just like always. You two run along now."

"Are you sure?" I asked. "I don't mind helping finish up."

She nodded toward the back window. "Betsy and Chloe are on their way back. Thanks for your help, and don't be a stranger around here. You're welcome to join our next meeting if you have any reason to." Her eyes cast over Foster. "Though, I can see why you might not."

I choked on a laugh and pulled Foster from the kitchen before she said anything else.

Once we were halfway out the front door, he asked, "Do I want to know what she was talking about?"

"Nope. Not even a little bit."

"Okay, then." He went silent, then added, "Charlie is going to stay here with Mack. He'll bring her home later."

As happy as I was for her, I really hoped that whatever was building between them was a true bond and not something that might later break her heart.

Foster wrapped an arm around my shoulders. "She'll be safe with Mack."

"Can't say the same for him," I joked.

He grinned. "No, but she'll be good for his ego, as long as she stops using words like 'lovely' with him."

I shuddered, remembering how doe-eyed she'd gotten before. "Yeah, I doubt that will last forever."

We teleported back to the coven, and I went to the center of town instead of back to our house. Beatrix was just coming out of the meeting hall with Ava and Evelyn right behind her.

"Hey," I said, directing the greeting to all three of them.

"You smell like dog," Beatrix deadpanned, then she looked behind us. "I thought Charlie was with you."

"She's still at the pack," I replied, trying my best to ignore the *dog* comment, given Foster had stayed silent at the insult. "Do we need to get her back here?"

The old witch shook her head. "Lucinda and Finn should be returning shortly, but as far as I know, there are no updates. A fact that really makes me want to poison someone."

The worst part of that statement was I believed she'd do it. Not a deadly poison, but something just torturous enough to bring her joy.

"Well, we'll be around whenever they get here," I said, guiding Foster away from Beatrix before she could take her wrath out on him.

Ava and Evelyn waved a brief goodbye as they stoically followed behind Beatrix, who was stomping her way around the meeting house.

"What do you—" Before Foster could finish asking the question, a shimmer rippled in the sky and then Lucinda and Finn appeared with a tall, brooding, and bald older man behind them.

"Who the hell did that?" Beatrix's voice screeched, and she came rushing back around the building.

The man Lucinda and Finn had brought with them turned around, narrowing his midnight-colored eyes, standing on the cobblestone path in sandals and socks... Interesting fashion choice for a grown man.

Beatrix's steps faltered. "You've got to be fucking kidding me."

"You? No. No way." The man, whose accent sounded almost Russian, snarled.

The two of them were glaring at each other like long-lost enemies.

"Uh, what's going on?" I asked.

Finn watched the two of them carefully. "I thought you two hadn't met before."

Beatrix sneered. "We hadn't, but that doesn't mean I don't know of the idiot sorcerer who wears socks with sandals who Lucinda told me all about and who has interfered with my spells in the past, putting his fingers where they don't belong."

"Ha," he barked out. "You are blaming *me* for Panama? That was your fuck up."

She pointed a finger at him, and I swore she was going to zap his ass, but then she threw her arms in the air. "I can't deal with this right now."

Then the witch disappeared from sight.

"What the hell just happened?" Foster demanded.

The maybe Russian, whose name I still didn't know, turned back toward us. "The fates are cruel beings." Then he snarled at Lucinda. "I blame you for this. I went centuries without this…whatever this is. And now you have ruined everything. How could this have happened?"

His pacing was getting closer to Lucinda, but Finn stepped between them. "You knew we were coming to Beatrix's coven. What are you freaking out for?"

His unibrow scrunched. "That…that thing… She's my mate."

Holy shit. I wanted to be happy for Beatrix at hearing that, but given the way she'd stormed off, I wasn't sure how to feel. Though, eager to know how this was going to work out was something to start with.

Lucinda rolled her eyes, stepping to Finn's side. "Oh, for fuck's sake, Yury. Go hide in a tree and calm down. You'll survive this. If the two of you hate each other that much, I'm sure you can figure out how to reject the bond."

He grumbled something under his breath and then disappeared just like Beatrix had.

Soulmates. Holy hell. I couldn't believe it.

Lucinda finally grinned wickedly. "This is the universe finally thanking me for all the hell we've been through."

Finn shook his head. "And here I thought you loved me."

"Oh, you know what I mean," she said. "The two of them deserve each other. I hope they torture one another for the rest of their miserable lives."

Her words were harsh, but her tone was soft, as if the fae actually thought Beatrix and Yury could somehow find happiness.

Though, maybe she wasn't wrong. I'd just been thinking about how Beatrix would find joy in poisoning someone.

Maybe Yury needed to be warned…

"Well, that was interesting," Ava said, joining us with Evelyn at her side.

Evelyn nodded at the fae. "Did everything go as expected with the council?"

Finn answered first. "Yes. They were difficult and tried to trick us more than once, which wasn't a surprise, but we used the blocking potion Yury gave us. By the time we left, all of the hunters were accounted for and their memories stripped. The groups they've been harassing shouldn't have to worry about them any longer."

Relief at knowing that lifted a chunk of the weight that had been pressing down on me lately.

"We'll let Mirra know first, and she'll send word to the others," Evelyn responded.

"Anything on Moira?" Ava asked.

Finn grimaced. "Unfortunately not. That's why we brought Yury with us. He has powers unlike anything we've ever seen. He should be able to locate the witch if Beatrix will work with him."

Yeah, I wasn't sure that was going to happen anytime soon unless we forced her hand, which I wasn't opposed to doing. I knew Foster wouldn't be, either.

"Why didn't he help before?" Evelyn asked. "We've been searching for weeks on end." The judgement was clear in her tone as well as from the scowl on her face.

"Did you not hear him before?" Lucinda asked with a huff. "Getting that bastard to leave the island took bribes I doubt I can follow through on."

"Oh," Evelyn replied softer. "Well, we appreciate your efforts. We'll also talk to Beatrix."

I wished them all the luck, then added, "Let us know if we need to step in."

Ava frowned. "I hope it won't come to that."

Then the two of them shimmered out of sight.

"I'm fucking exhausted," Lucinda said. "We're going to have sexy time and then take a nap. Don't need us anytime soon."

Finn blanched next to her, but before he could say anything, Lucinda teleported them away and it was back to just Foster and me.

"Today hasn't gone at all like I expected," I said, unsure how I felt in the moment.

He pulled me into his arms. "Let's just hope Yury will help things and not cause Beatrix to lose her shit more than she normally does."

For many reasons, I couldn't picture that happening, but I tried to hope right alongside my mate.

I tried really hard.

27

———

FOSTER

Two full days. That was how long it took for Beatrix to leave her cottage. She'd fortified herself inside, locking everyone else out with a spell neither Andie nor the others were able to break.

We couldn't even hear what had been going on inside. Hell, about an hour before she'd finally stepped out the door, I'd begun to think she was dead.

When she'd finally graced us with her presence, I'd done a double-take. Her skin was brighter than usual. The normal scowl she displayed when things weren't going her way was replaced with a soft smirk, and her long, silver hair was braided then wrapped into a perfect bun at the base of her neck.

For all intents and purposes, she looked younger and more refreshed than I'd ever seen her.

"Holy shit," Andie muttered next to me.

"Nothing like a woman scorned," Ava tittered.

Well, it wasn't like Yury had done anything to the old witch other than arrive in her coven, but I guessed he could have been the motivation for this new version of Beatrix.

She strode toward us with her head held high and went

straight to Andie. "Good afternoon. I need you to gather this list of items." She handed my mate a small sheet of paper. "You'll be able to find everything you need at Spell House. Bring them straight to me."

Beatrix pointed at Ava and Evelyn. "You two bring the tracking maps to my cottage. We're going to try things a little differently today."

Nobody moved. We all just stared in shock from her calm tone and soothing voice.

Beatrix raised a brow. "Do I have something on my face? In my teeth? Is there toilet paper stuck to my foot? I'm not sure what you're all still doing here, but I'd rather you be gone already. We have things to do."

Some of her snark was back, but not all of it. Either way, it worked, and the rest of us went in different directions.

Andie glanced up at me. "I think she's broken."

"No, I think she's motivated," I said. "If Yury finds Moira first, then it will make her look bad."

My mate's mouth turned down. "You'd think being soulmates would make things easier."

"You didn't get the displeasure of meeting Yury more formally yesterday like I did." I honestly hadn't thought there was a being on this Earth who was worse than Beatrix, but I was wrong.

The giant of a sorcerer had been poking around the coven when I'd gone home to get us lunch and left Andie keeping watch at Beatrix's cottage. He'd seen me and stomped my way, then scowled, demanding I tell him where Beatrix kept the power source.

I'd had no idea what he was talking about and when he'd pointed a finger at me, flashbacks of my early days with Beatrix had returned. I'd partially shifted and moved until our noses had been nearly touching, warning him of what could happen if he so much as "poked" me.

He'd gone on a tirade then, but I'd ignored most of his

bitching and continued to the house. He'd been petulant and pulsed with power he hadn't bothered to keep contained like most magic users did.

I hadn't liked it.

At least Beatrix knew her worth and didn't feel the need to overpower others unless it was necessary. Well, she wasn't always right about *when* it was necessary, but still.

Shit. Was I really sticking up for that old witch?

Beatrix really *had* grown on me.

Like fungus on a tree.

Andie teleported us to Spell House, and we went straight upstairs to the cabinets. I read off the ingredients like frog's feet, wolf's blood, and names of other things I probably wasn't pronouncing right, but I didn't really care.

"Got them," Andie said, then she took a bag from the hook on the wall. "We'll just put everything in here and get back."

She seemed nervous and her emotions were being held back through the bond. "What's going on inside that head of yours?" I asked, taking the bag from her until she answered.

Andie shrugged and avoided eye contact. "What if this doesn't work?"

I grabbed her hand and rubbed a thumb over her palm. "What do you mean?"

"What if we don't find her? What if Moira stays hidden forever? Do we just move on with our lives as if none of this ever happened and hope it doesn't come back to bite us in the ass? If so, how the hell are we supposed to do that?" Her voice rose with every question, and her chest heaved as she seemed to be getting less and less air to her lungs.

I moved around the counter and pulled her into my arms. "You haven't rested enough. I didn't think anything of it because you weren't doing anything other than watching Beatrix's house, but you need to sleep."

She shook her head against my chest. "No, we need to

know our contingency plans, because too much time has passed. Moira has had too long to do whatever she wanted and it's not as if anything she's done has made sense. How do we prepare for something we don't understand?"

Maybe her panic wasn't completely unwarranted.

"Let's give Beatrix one last chance and then see what Yury has to offer," I suggested. "He could have run, but he didn't. Let's see what that means."

Her shuddering breath warmed my skin, and she looked up at me with hopeful eyes. "Do you really think this will work?"

Damn it. I didn't want to lie to her, and I wasn't the kind of person to "hope" for the best, but it wasn't just my life I had to worry about now. I had to consider Andie's happiness above all else. Hope was all we had right now.

"We'll find out soon," I said, tossing the bag on the counter. "Let's get this stuff back to Beatrix."

Andie chuckled. "Maybe if we take a while, she'll yell at us for wasting her time and things can feel more normal."

She had a point, but at the same time, I just wanted to know what the crazy witch had planned and why she hadn't thought of it sooner.

Once everything was together, we teleported back to the coven and arrived at Beatrix's house. Andie went up to the door first and opened it, then dropped the bag of vials. I reached out and caught it before it could hit the floor, then finally looked over her shoulder.

Beatrix and Yury were inside the cottage, standing a good ten feet apart, but both of their chests were heaving, and Beatrix's perfectly braided bun was now in disarray.

"I take it you saw something you weren't expecting when you opened that door," I whispered to Andie.

She shook her head. "Yep."

Yury scowled at us. "Out."

Beatrix flicked a bit of magic at him. "Don't talk to them like that."

There was a smirk creeping up on her face, and her words weren't as harsh as I'd expected.

Something had happened, and I was positive I didn't want to know what.

Beatrix strode forward, smoothing the wrinkles from her loose, cotton shirt as she crossed the room. "Thank you for the bag." She glanced between the two of us. "Next time, knock."

"Yeah, that won't be a problem," Andie said with a shiver.

We backed out of the doorway and away from the cottage.

"I swore he was eating her face off until they panicked and separated," Andie said with a bit of horror in her voice. Then she began to laugh hysterically. "Oh my God. Beatrix was just making out with Yury."

"What?" Ava gaped with Evelyn behind us.

Fucking hell. This was too much drama for me.

Andie joined the other two witches and began recounting everything that had happened in more detail than I cared to hear, so I stepped away.

At least her earlier panic had subsided.

Lucinda and Finn flew over the house and landed next to me. Great. I wasn't in the mood for the snarky fae, either.

Thankfully, she brushed past me and joined the other ladies. Finn, however, stayed behind.

"What's going on with them?" he asked with a nod of his head.

I shuddered as I tried to pick up on their conversation with my wolf hearing. "They're discussing Beatrix making out with Yury."

Finn recoiled. "I understand why you're standing over here then. Mind if I stay, too?"

"Not at all," I said. "How were things at Fae Islands?"

They'd gone back home yesterday at the request of their

new king. Lucinda had invited the rest of us to join them, but Andie had refused to leave until Beatrix came out. Honestly, I was kind of glad. I'd only ever heard stories about the fae, and going into their world when we had so much other shit going on didn't sound the least bit appealing.

"Oh, everything is fine," Finn answered. "He just wanted to confirm the list of those joining us when we find Moira and to make sure Yury was behaving."

I cocked my head. "Could the king do anything about it if Yury *weren't* behaving?"

Finn laughed. "Not likely, but he'd like to think he could."

"How the hell did you stumble upon the sorcerer anyway?" I asked. "I don't imagine he was living on the islands this whole time."

"No, he wasn't," Finn replied. "Lucinda had a friend who was living with her here in L.A. before I found her. Neva is a brownie elf, and she's rather convincing when she wants to be. She somehow persuaded that big ogre to help us and then he just never went away, much to our shock. Though, he did get his own private island as payment for his services."

Shit. That was one hell of a payment. I was suddenly curious what had happened over there, but there was no more time to ask questions.

Beatrix threw open her front door, and Yury was standing beside her. She was grinning and he was...maybe smiling? I wasn't sure, but his lips were raised with lots of teeth showing under his beard.

"I found her," Beatrix declared.

Yury grunted and poked her side, and Beatrix amended her statement. "*We* found her."

I shared a confused glance with Andie. Holy hell. Whatever bond was between Beatrix and Yury was already changing the normally obstinate witch.

"Where is she?" Lucinda asked first.

Beatrix glowered. "New Orleans."

"I thought groups looked there several times already," I said.

She glared at me. "Thanks, Captain Annoying. Yes, they did, but clearly, they missed something."

Apparently, she hadn't changed *that* much already.

"Then why are we waiting?" Andie asked, stepping forward. "Let's go."

I went to my mate's side, holding her hand in case she got any bright ideas about taking off on her own.

Beatrix huffed. "I literally just found her. We need a plan, and we need to gather everyone who has committed to the fight. We won't be unprepared like before."

Andie stiffened next to me. I knew she just wanted this over with, but Beatrix was right. We couldn't go rushing in or we'd be risking death.

"I'll get on the phone now," Evelyn said just before teleporting away.

Yury pointed at Lucinda. "Call that fae you consider king. Tell him we're ready."

She chuckled. "Right, big guy. You get to call the orders now, and we're all just here to follow along."

Yury sneered at her. "Yes." His accent grew heavier with his irritation.

"We'll go to the pack and contact the other wolves," Andie said, then she looked up at me.

I nodded in confirmation. "Holden already has a line to each of the alphas ready to go."

"Good, then why are you all still here?" Beatrix deadpanned.

Without warning, Andie teleported us to the pack.

I sucked in a breath, but other than that, I had no side effects.

She took a step forward, but I jerked her back and spun her around until she was staring at my eyes. We held gazes for a few moments until she finally nodded. "I'm okay."

"I know you are," I said. "I just wanted you to know that as well."

She took a heavy breath and brushed her hair from her shoulders. "This is it. We're going to finish this."

I nodded. "We are. Moira won't be able to hurt anyone else again."

Andie smiled widely, then grabbed my hand. "Come on, then."

28

ANDIE

Less than eighteen hours later, our plan was finalized. That evening, we would storm into New Orleans, and we would end Moira's reign of terror, causing the dark witches to fall.

The packs, covens, nests, and even the fae were all coming together to make sure that was the case. Many of them were interested in the community idea that Beatrix had also been telling them about.

All in all, this seemed like a win-win. We were all working together to remove a dark spot within our world, but still, as I tried to remain positive, each time someone talked about killing every dark witch we crossed paths with, my heart hurt a little more.

I kept picturing my mom's cousin being so young and naïve and joining Moira at one point. She'd gotten lucky in having a soulmate who'd gotten her out, but not everyone had that. There were a lot of innocent people who would die tonight, and the thought made me physically sick.

So much so that I was now standing in front of Beatrix's house by myself and wondering how she was going to take my request.

Before I could knock, she opened the door with a hand on her hip. "How long do you intend to stand there?"

I shrugged both shoulders. "It's a nice morning. Could be here awhile."

"Bullshit." She sighed. "Get in here and tell me what has you annoying me this early in the day."

Gladly, I thought as I stepped forward.

When I got inside the door, I peeked around for Yury, but I didn't see him. "Where's your…not-nemesis?"

She rolled her eyes and sat on the couch. "Not here."

I joined her and swiveled to face her. Beatrix was probably the most complicated person I'd ever known, but she was still part of my chosen family. While I'd never point this out verbally, seeing the glow around her—now that she was over hiding from Yury—made my heart happy.

She'd been alone a long time, and she'd lost more than any one person should have to lose in their lifetime. I might not have always agreed with her methods, but I could understand them in a way. They were her defense mechanisms. Ways to protect her heart from further hurt.

The crass witch would never admit it, but she cared about all of us more than anyone else ever could.

And that was a big reason I'd snuck out of the house before dawn to come see her.

"Don't look at me like that," she complained. "It's too early for feelings."

Ignoring her drivel, I leaned forward and wrapped my arms around her. "I love you, Beatrix."

She stiffened briefly, then softened and hugged me tightly in return. When I'd have expected her to let go, her grip only increased in strength.

We sat there together, without speaking, for what felt like an hour. Words weren't necessary. Not when I understood that Beatrix was the kind of person to show her feelings with actions.

When we finally pulled apart, she swatted at her cheeks and sneered. "I'm allergic to whatever disgusting perfume you're wearing."

I patted her leg. "It's called love, and I think you'll eventually get used to it."

Her lips pursed. "What brings you here when you're supposed to be sleeping after our night of planning?"

"I couldn't sleep," I said, fidgeting with my fingers. "I wanted to know if you intend to kill all of the beings we face tonight."

All emotion dropped from her face. "Why?"

"You know Reah. You know her story," I said. "What if there are more like her inside Moira's compound? What if not all of them deserve to die?" I was looking more at the hole in my jeans than at Beatrix.

She stayed quiet for several beats before speaking. "If someone is trying to kill me, then I won't hesitate to take their life. I won't make you any promises, but if there are witches present who wish to surrender, they won't be slaughtered."

I glanced up. "Maybe we could make sure everyone else knows that."

"I know you haven't been back in this world long, Andie, but everyone whom I have aligned us with already thinks the same way," Beatrix said with a softness I hadn't expected. "None of us are murderers, and we don't ever want to be. Otherwise, I'm sure this concern would have been brought up already."

"Oh," I said, feeling a little stupid for thinking the worst of everyone.

Beatrix groaned. "Don't get all mopey on me now. You didn't ask a stupid question. Is there anything else bothering you? I don't need your head clouded when we leave tonight."

I thought about that for a moment, but there really wasn't. Sure, preparing for a battle was mentally harder than just being thrown into one like before, but I'd known this couldn't be avoided. We had to fight our way to Moira. That was the only way to stop her.

"I'm okay. As long as I'm not expected to murder people" —I grimaced—"then there's nothing to worry about with me."

She patted my leg awkwardly. "Just use your syphon power when you need to, and everything will be fine. You've worked hard to command that energy and it will serve you well."

I hoped she was right. I'd found the control I needed for the syphon magic. It no longer overwhelmed me or took charge. I was the wielder, not the wielded.

She stood and shoved at my shoulder. "If there's nothing else, you need to go rest and leave me alone."

I got up and hugged her again, mostly because I knew she would pretend to hate the action.

Her arms remained at her sides. "You're going to annoy me," she grumbled.

"Yet you love me anyway, even if you don't say it," I countered, pulling back and grinning at her.

She sighed heavily. "Yeah, yeah. Now get out of here."

I chuckled as I walked out the door and then teleported to my house. Foster was waiting for me in the living room, sitting in the chair. His eyes lifted and darkened.

My steps faltered, and heat consumed my inner being as I stopped behind the couch.

His one look reminded me of every moment, every emotion, every ounce of love shared between us until I was frozen in place, torn between jumping him and crying from the sheer joy of being so lucky to call this man mine.

He used his hands to slowly push up from the cushion. His steps were slow and calculated, and his eyes never strayed from mine as he inched closer.

My chest heaved as I tried to remember to breathe, and I reached for him as soon as he was close enough.

I grabbed onto his shirt and jerked him closer. His heart thundered under my touch, and the world, along with all of our problems, disappeared.

His bearded cheek scraped over mine. "Did you get to talk to Beatrix?" he asked, and I nodded. "And you're all better?"

I moved my head again, feeling incapable of anything else. My skin warmed, and my legs tightened together. The bond pulled us together in a way like never before.

My body was mesmerized by him. My eyes could only see my mate. My heart only beat for him.

Everything else I'd recently been worrying about was a foreign thought as Foster raised his hand and gently traced his fingertips over my suddenly overheated skin.

By the time he made his way to my hand, I was putty. He pulled me forward, and I stumbled after him until he turned and picked me up.

No other words were shared between us. I didn't see the need to speak when I could feel so thoroughly.

My hands roamed over his arms and chest as he walked us toward the bedroom. He gently laid me onto the comforter and bent down on one knee.

Our eyes locked again, and I swore I was going to melt in a puddle or combust right there on the spot with the intensity of his gaze.

His fingers tugged at my shoes, pulling my socks away at the same time, then grabbed the ends of my leggings as he stood back up. He yanked those from my legs with ease, then leaned over me, his breath heavy over my shoulder where he kissed my sensitive skin.

When he pulled back, my shirt came away with him. I moved to stand and help him do the same, but he put a hand up to stop me. I rested back on my elbows in nothing more than my underwear and bra while he removed his jeans and T-shirt.

Foster stepped between my legs, spreading them apart

before grabbing my thighs and urging me to lock my ankles behind his back.

This whole *no speaking* thing was turning me on more than usual. I used our bond to track his emotions and offer him mine in return while his eyes and kisses did most of the speaking for him.

His lips explored my neck while his fingers reached around to remove my bra. Once that was out of the way, his arm wrapped around my waist, and he moved us further onto the bed.

His body lay over mine, burning my skin until I wiggled beneath him, needing more.

Without making me beg or wait, Foster ripped another pair of my underwear and kicked off his boxers. Something told me he got a thrill out of the former and I couldn't deny that I did as well.

Foster's forehead pressed against mine, and I breathed him in, closing my eyes and just soaking up this moment. This togetherness and the feeling of so much love that I didn't know what to do.

He tipped my chin up with his finger, and I reopened my eyes to find him still staring at me. A small smile played at his lips, and he slowly slid his cock between my legs.

I opened wider for him and gasped when he thrusted forward, stealing all of my breath. His movements were slow and gentle after that first move. We got lost not only in each other's eyes, but in our bond and all the emotions that went along with being fated together.

Foster was the other half of me. He'd shown me that I wasn't alone in this world anymore. What had happened in the past no longer mattered, but what was right here, right now, was all that I needed to concern myself with.

As the tether between us grew stronger, a raw urge grew within me—almost animalistic. I needed Foster, and while I had his body and heart, there was a part I suddenly knew was missing.

I needed his mind.

Without that, I didn't have all of my mate, and I wasn't okay with that.

My grip on his back tightened, and I pulled him closer, but instead of pressing my lips to his, my instincts had me moving toward his shoulder.

I breathed him in, just like he so often did to me. The earthy tones of his scent deepened, adding in layers of mint and a stronger wood tone like pine that I'd never noticed before.

My teeth nipped at his corded muscles that rippled beneath my touch.

Foster groaned above, still making love to me, but also inhaling me just as I was him.

The need to bite him overwhelmed me.

I had no idea what I was doing, but I couldn't stop my actions. I had to taste him in every way possible. There were no other options as I opened my mouth further, ignoring the ache in my gums, and sank my teeth into his skin.

Blood trickled into my mouth, coating my tongue with its coppery taste, but that wasn't what held my attention. It was the blasting light of emotion that slammed into me and tripled when Foster bit me in return.

The moment lasted only seconds, but it branded my soul for life.

We drank from each other, tightening a bond between us that was already unbreakable into something else entirely.

I didn't know what, but I knew, whatever we were, we were stronger together.

When I pulled back from his shoulder, my eyes watched his skin heal, and when my mind was no longer overwhelmed with new emotions, an orgasm unlike I'd ever known ripped through me.

Foster roared above me, increasing his speed and succumbing to his own release while he wrapped his arms tighter around me.

My right hand gripped his hair while the left pushed hard against his lower back, keeping him pressed against me while we both twitched with aftershocks.

I didn't know how long we lay there, but my mind felt numb.

Fuck, that was…indescribable. Foster groaned.

"It was otherworldly," I replied breathily.

His head jerked back. "Did you hear me?"

"Of course I did." My brows pinched together. He'd better not be losing his mind.

Andie.

Holy shit.

He'd said my name, but I was staring right at him and his lips had never moved.

Foster?

The grin that grew on his face had me falling in love with him all over again.

"You bit me and now we can mind-speak," he said excitedly. "I don't know why I didn't think of that before." Then he frowned. "How *did* you bite me?"

I wasn't sure. It wasn't like I'd savagely torn into his skin. I could see the two small holes I'd made, yet we were both aware my very human-looking teeth couldn't have done that.

My tongue smoothed over my incisors, and I winced before remembering my gums had ached.

"I think my teeth…shifted," I said hesitantly. "I'm not sure that's the right word for it, but my gums briefly hurt before I bit you."

He kissed me hard and quick. "I don't care how it happened." Then he added, *I just love you so fucking much, it shouldn't be possible,* through our new connection.

This was what I'd been jealous of before. Even if Foster didn't have a romantic connection to his pack, they'd had something with him that I'd thought I could never have.

Now that I did…I knew one thing for sure.

We were going to be unstoppable.

29

FOSTER

We were all supposed to have spent the day resting before we left for New Orleans. Except when I'd seen Andie walk through the door after visiting Beatrix, something had come over me. I'd needed to touch her, to love her thoroughly before any sleep could be had.

When she'd bitten me, I hadn't thought anything of it. Hell, thanks to the frenzy of our bond, I hadn't even realized she'd broken skin and imbibed my blood until she'd heard my thoughts.

This new connection between us... I hadn't thought we could get any closer, but I'd been wrong. We'd stayed in bed all day, and every time we'd made love, my strength had grown.

Not just in the physical sense, either.

I had more energy, and I felt like I could bulldoze a building with my bare hands, but my other senses, like smell and hearing, had also improved.

It seemed to be the same for Andie, which told me, while we were seriously lacking sleep, it wasn't going to affect our fighting tonight.

Not after everything that had happened throughout the day.

As we stood together under the waning moon with Beatrix and the other witches, I knew there was never a time when we could be more ready for this battle.

"We have placed some of our strongest witches at the packs, nests, and with the fae in a remote location," Beatrix announced with Yury by her side. "In less than five minutes, we will time our portals and descend into the outskirts of New Orleans. Moira doesn't seem to have left there yet, but her signature is harder to identify, which means the dark energy around her has increased."

She glanced up at Yury, and he nodded before she continued. "Yury will spell as many of us as he can with something that will assist in keeping their dark magic from affecting us, but still, use extreme caution once we break through the compound Moira's staying in on the outside of town."

"And what if we arrive and are outnumbered, regardless of all the help you've recruited?" Peter asked.

Beatrix looked down her nose. "Then you're welcome to flee. Nobody here is being forced to fight. You are still welcome in this coven if you don't join us, but I won't be leaving New Orleans until Moira is no longer breathing."

Silence was the only response to her statement.

"Make your choice now," Beatrix added ominously. "You might not get the chance to later."

At least she wasn't luring them to battle with a false sense of confidence.

Murmurs began to rise, and Beatrix stepped back.

I glanced down at Andie beside me. "Are you ready for this?"

"I am," she answered without hesitation.

And I knew she was.

As much as I didn't enjoy the thought of walking her right

into a fight, I knew there was no holding her back. My mate was strong and capable and smart.

She's more than anyone knows, my wolf added.

He'd been on an extra high since earlier as well. Though his thoughts weren't wrong.

Yes, but nobody else needs *to know*, I countered.

That we agreed on, which I was grateful for.

Beatrix and Yury began working on the portal, and I heard Andie's name being called. We both turned around to find Reah there without Benjamin.

Her eyes darted every which way, but she kept moving forward and Andie met her in the middle. "Is everything okay? Where's Benjamin?" Andie asked.

No matter how many times he'd asked, Beatrix hadn't let the kid join the fight. I was glad to back the witch up on that. He might have been an excellent tracker, but he was too young for war. His innocent mind deserved happier years for as long as he could have them.

Reah nodded. "Nothing is wrong. I left Benjamin at home, but I fell asleep on the couch after dinner and when I woke up, I knew I had to see you before you left."

Andie grabbed Reah's shaking hands. "Do you know why that is?"

"Death is inevitable, but it is not always the answer," Reah said cryptically.

Andie tilted her head. "Why would you say that?"

Reah glanced around again, then lightly shrugged. "I don't know, but you needed to know that. I must have dreamt something, and I had to come tell you."

"Okay." Andie looked over Reah's head at me, but I had no idea what the witch was talking about. "Thank you, Reah."

She bit her cheek and nodded. "Yeah. No problem. Be safe over there."

Then, just as quickly as she'd arrived, Reah disappeared into thin air.

Andie stared at the empty space where her cousin had just stood. "That was weird, right?"

"More than usual, yes." The portal was now open behind us, but I wasn't in a hurry if Andie needed a minute. "Are you okay?"

She took a deep breath, closing her eyes briefly. *I am.*

I loved hearing her voice in my head nearly as much as I loved her.

Let's go then.

Her fingers intertwined with mine, and we got into the line of witches and warlocks waiting to move through the portal. Once we got to the front, Beatrix stopped us.

"Wait for Yury," she said.

Andie stepped aside without question, and I stayed with her.

When everyone else was through, Yury stepped back onto the coven side of the shimmering rift and, without asking for permission, pressed his palm over Andie's chest.

She yelped, and I growled, immediately shoving him back. "Don't fucking touch her again."

Yury shook his head. "Calm down. I didn't hurt her. I only scared her."

"He's right," Andie agreed. "I shouldn't have yelped. What was that?"

"Power booster." Then his eyes narrowed. "Though I'm not sure you needed it. She's stronger than you told me."

Beatrix poked at Andie. "What did you do? Never mind. It's too late now. We have to go."

We stepped through, and Andie sucked in a breath at the scene before us.

Hundreds of supernaturals were gathered in a field. Vampires, shifters, witches, warlocks, and fae. All of them present and co-mingling together for one purpose: to strip the world of unnecessary darkness.

"Do you see Cait?" Andie asked. "What about Amersyn and Rachel?"

A dose of anxiety bled through our bond from her, and I gave my mate a tight hug. "I'm sure they're here, and I'm even more sure they're going to be fine. They have Roman, Maciah, and Zeke watching their backs, just like you have me."

She stared up at me and nodded. "You're right. There's no extra reason to worry."

Her words sounded surer than she felt through our connection, but that was understandable. Adrenaline would kick in soon enough and override most of her fears.

We were in some sort of clearing surrounded by large trees. The sky above us was dark, not because there were no stars or moon to be seen, but because of the black energy seeping from Moira's compound.

I couldn't see the physical structure, but only a fool wouldn't have been able to sense its nearness.

There's no way someone missed this before, I told Andie.

They were either working against us or this is a trap, she said. *Either way, we're here and we're not leaving anytime soon.*

Charlie joined us with Mack at her side. While they caught up, I reached out to Holden.

How's the pack?

Ready and eager for the fight, he answered. *The coven?*

Mostly the same, I said, then added, *Be safe out there.*

Always.

Mack nodded at me when I looked over at him. "You good?"

"Yeah, just checking in with Holden." I grabbed Andie's hand and noticed Mack had his arm wrapped around Charlie.

Clearly, they were moving forward with a relationship. Good for them.

The heaviness beating in around us from the dark magic increased once all of the portals were closed.

Beatrix levitated herself into the air and increased the volume of her voice with magic. "Yury and I are going to break the shield around this compound. We have no idea what's going to happen once that's done, but before we do, you will all feel a trickle of magic settle over you. This will help combat the effects of the darker energy. After that, it's up to your mind to keep the worst of the effects at bay. If anyone is having second thoughts, now is the time to turn around."

Nobody in my line of sight moved, and then it was Yury's turn to rise up into the air. He thrusted his hands out. Silver mixed with blue sparks shot from his palms, arching over the crowd before coming back down like soft rain.

The beads of magic embedded into my skin, and while my wolf bristled from the foreign power, I could immediately feel the difference of pressure around us.

Then Yury and Beatrix moved north and stopped. One of their palms connected with the other and a white glow emitted from them, almost bright enough that I had to turn away.

The light spread above them, forming a fifty-foot-wide circle, then it began to crack with black lines. Beatrix's and Yury's bodies shook, their backs still to us but visible.

The crowd beneath them was silent, and we all watched in awe as those burgeoning crevices splintered and shattered the shield around Moira's compound.

Andie hugged Charlie. "Don't do anything stupid."

Mack stole Charlie back with a tight grimace on his face. "I won't let her."

"You can't stop me from doing anything I want to," she countered. Though her words were sharply spoken, the longing look in her eyes told a different story.

Andie stepped back to my side and took my hand again. I

looked down at her, not needing words to share how much I loved her and believed that, no matter what we faced next, I would fight by her side with everything I had. Nothing could keep me from her. Not ever again.

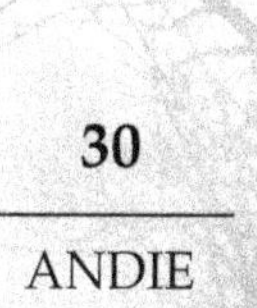

30

ANDIE

There was no time to think once Yury broke through the opening. Chaos descended and, even with the magical buffers we'd been given, breathing was difficult at best with all the darkness pressing in on us.

My eyes scanned the area, searching for Moira, while Foster shifted and Elias watched my back.

There was a mansion-sized brick house ahead of us with dead shrubbery surrounding it. There were no leaves or grass to be seen. Just dirt and dried-out branches.

None of the windows in the house displayed lights, but I didn't take that to mean nobody was inside. There could have been more than one shield around this place, and I wouldn't be assuming anything.

I jerked forward and caught myself by grabbing on to Elias's fur. There was a burning in my shoulder, and I turned around just in time to dodge another attempted hit.

A black orb flew over my head, and I threw up a shield to prevent the next one from hitting me. Foster's wolf moved to fight other witches at my back while he checked in with me.

You're hurting already, Foster said.

I'm fine.

I didn't need him getting distracted within the initial few minutes of the battle.

My instinct was to use my syphon ability and put the warlock attacking me on his ass, but instead, I leapt forward and kept my shield close in front of me.

I landed right in front of the dark-eyed magic user, then thrusted my palm forward while he was still gathering energy to hit me with.

Electricity raced through me and shocked him so severely that a hole burned through his black shirt and I began to smell burnt skin.

Though it wasn't until he shuddered and fell to the ground in a heap that I stopped forcing the heated power into him.

I gave the fucker a solid kick and heard a faint heartbeat. I tried not to be disappointed by that. Considering my earlier opinions, I reminded myself that I wasn't into being a murderer like the ones attacking us.

Elias whimpered ahead of me, and I quickly laid eyes on him. *Shit*. We'd barely even made it twenty feet into the compound.

I raised my hand, intent on sucking the energy right out of the bitch who had hit my mate, but Mack's wolf was quicker than me.

The tan beast leapt into the air and took the head right off the witch who had hit Elias's front flank.

While racing forward, I healed my shoulder with the light touch of my hand and some magic, then reached toward the wolf and did the same for him.

Elias says thanks. Foster grunted through my mind.

Based on his tone and Elias's snapping jaws, I'd say they were both rather pissed.

Mack ran off and rejoined Charlie, who had a minor cut on her cheek but was whipping tendrils of magic around like a seasoned pro.

Elias and I pushed on, and I still searched for Moira. When I once again couldn't get eyes on her, I had a feeling I wasn't going to find her out here.

We need to get into the house, I said to Foster.

His wolf nodded, but there was no verbal reply as they soared through the air and raked claws down the back of a warlock who was choking one of the vampires on our side.

Supernaturals were dropping left and right. Thankfully, not all of them were from our side, but still. There were cloaked figures popping up everywhere I looked, and I began to put the pieces together as to why we kept sensing Moira in different parts of the world.

She'd been biding her time, recruiting her own army.

A bright light from up ahead had me blinking several times until I made out Yury's and Beatrix's forms. They were sticking together and blasting through several shrouded beings at a time, breaking whatever connections the dark witches had to each other as they did.

Shouts rose into the air, and some of Moira's army started to retreat as we closed in, but when one fled, two more arrived to replace them.

Ava and Evelyn were fighting back-to-back, but they were being corralled by five cloaked beings. I moved to help them, but I was cut off by a familiar sight.

Ruby.

I remembered her from my house in Montana. Her sage eyes flickered with evil as her dark, russet hair floated around her shoulders. "Hello, Andie."

I'd thought Beatrix had killed her before, but apparently, I'd thought wrong.

"Moira doesn't want you alive anymore," Ruby taunted. "This should be fun."

A stream of charcoal-colored energy exited her raised palm and aimed right for my chest. She smirked at me as if she had me right where she wanted me, but I quickly proved her wrong.

I dropped to the ground, avoiding the hit, and got back up. With both hands turned out, I focused on Ruby's power.

My anger rose while I pictured my house and everything inside it destroyed. She'd ruined nearly everything I'd owned. Taken precious memories from me that I'd shared with my mother. Shattered items that couldn't be replaced.

Wrath took over rationale, and I stalked forward. My dark-blue magic wrapped around her form, pinning her arms to her side.

She cackled in my face once I'd gotten closer. "Did you really think it would be that easy?" Then she broke free of my hold and slammed dark energy to my chest.

I stumbled back and bent forward.

I sensed Foster's concern, but I softly shook my head. *Let me do this.*

He stayed where he was, minding his own opponents while I lured Ruby in. Though, I could still tell his concentration was split.

Ruby grabbed my ponytail and jerked me upright. "I'm going to enjoy this."

I whimpered under her hold, but the sound was only a decoy. She was hurting me, but not enough to stop my next movement.

Before her dark magic could wrap completely around my arms, I jerked my hand forward and gripped her throat tightly. "You shouldn't have fucked with my house."

Fury fueled my every thought.

I'd already lost so much and while I'd gained a lot since returning to the coven, nobody had the right to take the memories that had been so precious to me.

This bitch was going to pay.

My fingers squeezed her neck until she began to choke,

then I unleashed my syphon energy, pulling whatever power she had and claiming it as my own.

The magic was sour as I absorbed it, but I ignored the bitterness and did exactly what I hadn't intended to.

I sucked the life from the witch in front of me.

Andie, Foster's voice snapped inside my head.

My eyes flicked to his wolf. *What?*

Don't do this, he begged, and I didn't understand why he would say such a thing.

Some of the others here, fighting on Moira's behalf, might have been innocent and deserved a second chance, but this bitch had taken joy in what she'd done. I'd seen it on her face that day in my house.

Ruby was evil, through and through.

It's her dark magic making you think that, Foster pleaded with me.

A part of me knew he was right, but the larger bits didn't give a damn.

At least, not until a lighter energy caressed my spine and traveled straight to my heart.

My hand released the now-unconscious Ruby, and she dropped to the ground with an audible yet satisfying thud.

Beatrix grabbed my shoulder when she stepped next to me. "We have plenty of ways to torture her. Let's not make things easy by giving her death."

The glint in her eyes had a smirk growing on my face. "Thanks for the assist."

Foster had been right. While my fury was my own, Ruby's dark magic had twisted my thoughts to murder.

Beatrix's silver energy wrapped around Ruby, and then the evil witch disappeared.

"Where did you send her?" I asked Beatrix quickly while Foster and Yury gave us a brief moment of reprieve from the battle.

"To a confinement cell buried deep under the coven." The glee in her voice was equal parts impressive and frightening.

Charlie had been right about Beatrix having one of the containment pods hidden, and I couldn't have been happier.

"That's where I'm sending each of them after they've been taught a lesson or two," Beatrix added as we both dodged a purple orb of magic that must have missed its target from somewhere up ahead. "So if you notice very few of the cloaked bodies on the ground, don't worry. We're not completely having our asses handed to us right now."

Well, that was good to know, but now wasn't the time to celebrate.

"We need to find Moira," I said as the four of us fought side by side.

A scorch of blackness cut through my bicep, and I howled in pain before Beatrix could respond.

She pushed me down, and the next blow hit her right in the chest. My eyes widened in disbelief when she dropped next to me, unmoving.

I scrambled to help her, but Yury shoved me out of the way, then created a barrier over Beatrix and himself. "Get to the house. The witch you hunt is there."

Blood splattered over my chest, and I threw my arms up defensively, but Elias already had things handled.

The warlock who had gotten me and then Beatrix hung limply between Elias's snarling jowls. The wolf had grabbed the attacker by the neck and was flinging the body left and right until he seemed satisfied that no more life was left within the dark magic user who wasn't smart enough to know when to back down.

Elias dropped the corpse, and my attention went back to Beatrix's prone form. I was torn between leaving her without knowing if she was okay and finding Moira so we could finish this. She'd just saved my life. Leaving Yury to care for her on his own felt…wrong.

Foster's wolf head nudged against my arm, just under where the black scorch mark still was. It was growing by the second as inky lines extended from the original wound.

I placed a glowing, blue hand over the mark and closed my eyes briefly. More bitterness coated my insides, and when I was done, there was still a laceration over my skin, but nothing was spreading anymore.

Fae were flying above us, dodging streams of darker-colored magic. Loud bangs echoed all around us as the battle raged on. People roared and screamed. Bodies—good and bad—fell and rose and fell again.

My heart felt battered as I sat there, taking in the scene of destruction around us. I let out my own roar just before I slammed my hands to the crumbling dirt beneath me.

Power leaked out of me, moving through the dead ground and striking each dark spot the energy came in contact with.

Bodies jumped toward me, but I was locked into my position, unable to call my magic back to me. I just wanted the fight to be over.

Lashes of power struck my back. Claws tore into my skin. Screams ripped from my throat. But still, I couldn't stop what I was doing. The give and take of magic warred inside me.

I was taking down dark witches and warlocks left and right, but so many of them had switched to attack me that I was surrounded and losing by the second.

Andie! Foster thundered inside my head, and I heard Elias's wrathful howl bellow into the skies above.

I tried to call back to him, but my strength was waning by the second. I knew I should have stopped, but I couldn't, knowing that I was giving the others who had come with us the upper hand with my distraction.

My eyes fluttered closed as the magic inside me shuttered. I was ready to give one last blast through the earth when teal energy covered me, its icy coolness sizzling over my heated skin before hands jerked my body from the dark magic and claws that had been trying to stop me.

My body hung limply in the unknown person's grasp, and I tried to see who had me, but I was distracted by watching Foster shift back to two feet, running along the same path I was being taken.

Seconds—or maybe minutes—later, I was set onto the ground, farther from the fighting than I wanted to be.

Lucinda's iridescent hair cascaded over me while she bent over my body. There was a crease between her eyes, then she punched me right between my boobs.

I sucked in a breath as electricity zipped through my blood and bones, tickling along my cooling skin. My chest heaved, and she grinned. "There you are."

Finn and Foster appeared next to us, and my mate had his arms around me within the blink of an eye.

He was vibrating with fear and wrath. "I thought..."

Words weren't necessary for me to understand what he'd "thought."

"I'm okay now," I promised, returning his embrace. "I just let my ire get the best of me."

Lucinda shook her head. "No, you let it get the best of all those bastards fighting against us." She pointed toward the fight still going on behind us. "You more than leveled the playing field with that little trick."

Good. That had been what I'd hoped for, but between seeing Ruby and watching Beatrix fall, I wasn't sure I had been thinking straight.

Hell, I wasn't even sure how I'd done what I had, but I'd learned to trust my instincts.

Yury and a finally conscious Beatrix materialized next to us, and I gently pushed Foster back, while keeping him at my side, so I could get a good look at her.

With narrowed eyes, she glared at the house behind us,

acting and sounding just fine. "She's in there. Let's go finish this."

Yury reached a hand to Foster. "Thanks for killing that piece of shit."

My mate grunted in reply, seeming to be unable to gain control over his emotions just yet.

Finn grabbed Lucinda's hand, their differing wings brushing against each other. "We should get back out there."

I met Lucinda's stare. "Thanks for the assist out there."

She waved a hand, shrugging me off. "That's why we're all here. Good luck in there."

With that, the two fae pushed off into the air again, returning to the fight.

The four of us turned for the seemingly desolate and crumbling brick structure.

It was time to end this nightmare.

31

FOSTER

Beatrix busted open the steel door we'd found on the side of the house and entered first, much to Yury's dismay. Andie and I followed after them, and I tried to calm my breathing.

Seeing my mate attacked by a horde of supernaturals had nearly rendered me useless. My wolf had tried to intercept, but we hadn't been quick enough, and for a brief moment, I'd thought we'd been about to lose her.

Nothing had ever pierced my soul so harshly.

Shaking off the terror was harder than I wanted to admit, but our job here wasn't done. We had to find Moira and stop this madness from happening again.

We also needed to destroy Andie's necklace.

My wolf had reminded me of that as we'd entered the rundown home.

Spiderwebs covered each of the open rafters above us, along with the chandelier that no longer sparkled under the moonlight creeping in through the dusty windows.

A staircase was up ahead with wooden steps, many of which were either broken or missing completely.

Andie stayed at my side. When we were at the base of the

stairs, she paused and took a deep inhale. "Moira isn't up there."

All eyes stared at my mate, waiting for her to elaborate.

Her hands vibrated with energy at her sides, then she finally looked at me. "She's downstairs, and she has my magic pulsing through her."

"Shit," Beatrix muttered. She straightened. "But you have more of it. We should still be fine."

Yury glanced around the open room, then nodded. "She will be like bug to squash."

A small part of me wanted to laugh at the seriousness of his very Russian accent, but I wasn't capable of finding true humor in anything at the moment.

I grabbed Andie's hand as she took a step forward, heading toward a dark hallway. "Where are you going?"

"I'm following the trail of my energy," she said, as if it was the most obvious thing.

My gaze cut to Yury and Beatrix, then back to Andie. "With just the four of us?"

She nodded, her shoulders straightening in determination while she loosened her grip on my hand. "We can't wait and risk her fleeing."

Fuck. I hated this. I hated that I'd just failed to keep my mate safe and now we were walking into a situation that would likely be far worse than what we'd just faced.

But what I hated even more was the thought of crushing Andie by attempting to force her to stay back, by not believing that she could do what she felt she could.

Defeat Moira.

A good mate considers all scenarios. Just like when you forced her to stop healing the other witches, you may not be wrong to stop her now, my wolf said stoically.

Even though his thoughts aligned with what I wanted to believe, I knew he was wrong.

I knew that, yes, in certain circumstances, I needed to step in. But as I looked at Andie now, her body thrumming stronger than a live wire even though she'd just expunged way too much power, I knew deep down that she didn't need me to hold her back. Not today.

If I attempted to, I'd only be making a selfish choice. That wasn't the kind of mate I wanted to be for her. She deserved better. She deserved someone who stood by her side and supported her at every turn. Not one who abused the bond to control her actions when they did or didn't suit him.

I pulled Andie into my arms once more, holding her tightly against me and giving the tether between us a chance to strengthen from our contact.

A humming pulsed between us, and I pressed my lips to hers, closing my eyes. *Whatever happens, I'll be right by your side.*

She kissed me back, and her hands gripped my tattered shirt. *I love you.*

More than the stars above, I replied fervently.

We parted, and I knew my choice had been the right one.

Andie could do this, and I would help her. Whatever happened next, this was how it was supposed to go. This was why I'd been sent to find her all those months ago.

Now you're thinking like a true mate and alpha, my wolf said with pride.

I'd known for years that I'd failed to give him the life he needed as a wolf, but he'd stuck by me, remaining positive and insistent that there was more waiting for us in this world.

That was more than I'd deserved, but I was never more thankful for him than I was as we traversed the dark, cold, and quiet house, searching for a witch who needed to die.

Andie's hand raised, and she moved next to Beatrix. I stayed just to her right, close but not overbearing.

"Do you feel that?" Andie asked with a whisper.

Beatrix took a deep inhale, her chest expanding fully. "Left."

Andie nodded, and on we went. Every minute or so, we'd stop and the two of them would do the same thing until we finally found a steel door that crackled with energy.

Black tendrils of magic wrapped around the handle, then spread across the rusting surface. Beatrix took a step closer, then glanced up at Yury. "Your turn, big guy. Prove to me why it's a good idea to keep you around."

"Like saving your life wasn't enough." He sneered at her, but there was a brightness in his eyes that softened the glare. While they maintained eye contact, Yury lifted his right arm up and out, blasting blinding power into the door like it was a natural occurrence for him.

The inky energy around the frame fizzled, then disappeared altogether.

Yury crossed his arms and his upper lip lifted only minutely. "Your turn."

She rolled her eyes, then turned for the door. Her fingers twisted and curled around each other as magic bloomed between her palms. The energy slowly trickled out and wrapped around the handle, turning it with what seemed like effortless grace.

The door creaked open, and all four of us were pushed back with the force of dark energy rushing up. I sucked in a breath, then regretted the action when my lungs burned as if I were inhaling smoke from a raging fire.

Andie was first to recover and put up a shield around us that rose over our heads and wrapped around our bodies until the opaque energy slithered beneath our feet.

Beatrix shuddered. "I don't know what kind of fucked-up shit she's been dumb enough to get involved in, but whatever it is, there's no coming back from that kind of darkness."

Andie's face fell. I knew she had been sympathizing with Moira, regardless of everything that had happened, but if this woman had to die, it was the witch's own damn fault.

Plus, it wasn't like Moira would surrender. Whatever

happened once we got to the bottom of these stairs, it would be in self-defense.

Yury moved until he was blocking the way and his glower deepened. "We stay together. Do not spread out or she can pick us off."

Nobody argued with him before he turned to face the darkness looming below. Beatrix moved to his side, and I stuck by Andie, her shield still bubbling around all of us.

The first step past the threshold sent stabbing pains up my calves, but they were nothing I couldn't ignore after a second.

My wolf snarled inside my head. The suffocating magic was boxing us in as we went farther, regardless of Andie's assistance, but there was no going back.

Just as Yury moved to turn the corner, Andie surprised us all by pushing him back and stepping ahead of us.

She'd managed to hide her intentions from me, but I should have known she'd try to do something on her own first.

The three of us quickly caught up to my mate, then paused at the sight before us.

Moira, who had been calm and sleek when we'd last seen her, was standing with her arms and legs spread out, guarding a door that pulsed with even more darkness than the one we'd just come through.

Her eyes were bright and manic as they darted between us. "You can't have him," she hissed.

Him? What the hell did she think we were here for?

Andie took a tentative step forward. This time, I didn't hesitate to grab the back of her shirt, but she'd been prepared for that, and my grip missed as she jumped even closer to Moira.

Not yet, she snapped inside my mind.

At least back up some, I growled in return.

She didn't listen. Instead, my stubborn mate moved another foot closer to the psycho witch.

Between the shadows twisting around Moira, I finally noticed Andie's necklace. The previously white, shimmering stone had several cracks in it and rose away from Moira's chest, the silver chain visibly shaking in the process.

"We're not here for him, Moira," Andie said calmly.

The dark witch sneered. "Yes, you are. They said you'd come for my Malcom, but I won't let you take him. I've fought too hard to keep him safe. I've sacrificed everything!"

Her voice was frantic, and her eyes never stayed in one spot for long. There was no talking sense into this woman. Andie needed to move her ass out of the way.

I glanced at Yury and he turned my way. I held up three fingers, hoping he'd understand it was a countdown. One that would lead to me pulling Andie back and him blasting Moira.

His stiff nod was the only answer I got as I lowered one finger and then took a step forward. Another finger, another step. With a deep breath, I dropped my arm and wrapped my hands around Andie's waist.

Her energy shocked the shit out of me, but I ignored the agony and brought us both to the floor. Beatrix yelled something that sounded like "Stop," but it was too late.

Yury hit Moira with a truckload of magic and sent her slamming back against the door she'd been guarding. The energy bounced back, and while I saw Moira's eyes flutter closed, the power wasn't stopping with her.

Fire crawled over my skin, or at least that was what it felt like, and I lost hold of Andie as she rolled next to me, groaning and trying to get onto her hands and knees.

"Andie," I called, but she didn't respond. Not even when I used our telepathy.

Wolf? I tried next.

He was just as silent as my mate.

Fuck. What had we done?

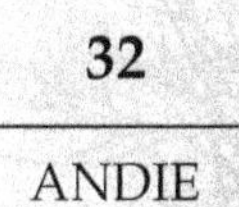

32

ANDIE

Ire and anguish took their turns assaulting my senses as I recovered from Yury's idiotic move. Apparently, I should have been clearer with Foster as to why I'd been moving closer to Moira. It hadn't been because I'd had a death wish. It had been because I could sense the mixed spell behind her.

Whatever she'd done to block our access to her soulmate wasn't working like it should have and any other magic being added to the mess wasn't going to be helpful, but I couldn't risk syphoning the power without taking on the potency of the dark energy surrounding Moira.

I might have battled the black magic before without thinking twice, but I wasn't an idiot. Whatever Moira had turned into wasn't something I wanted any part of.

Foster tried reaching out to me, but our connection was fuzzy at best, thanks to the cocktail of power still swarming within the room.

Beatrix's fingers brushed mine, and our combined magic sparked a light within my core. I forced my gaze up until I could see her eyes. Her face was tense, but she was okay for the most part, and she seemed just as annoyed as I was at the men for getting in our way.

I inched my hand forward until it was pressing over hers evenly. Our shared coven energy moved between us in a way I'd never experienced before. I knew by being part of her coven that she benefited from my magic, but I hadn't truly thought about how that worked before.

Now, it was reigniting our core powers and saving our asses.

Beatrix and I were the first to stand, but Yury wasn't far behind us.

He pointed at Beatrix. "You lied."

"No, I omitted." She lifted her chin defiantly.

I wasn't sure what they were talking about and didn't get the chance to ask because Yury clearly hadn't learned his lesson.

The big ogre charged forward with murder in his dark eyes. That wasn't happening. Not now. Not when Moira wasn't a threat to us.

Magic shot from my hand, wrapping around his arms, then moving down to his legs. He was so distracted by his own emotions that he didn't notice I had him until it was too late, and he went crashing back to the ground like a falling tree.

His resounding roar was cut off when Beatrix snapped her fingers, silencing him with her own power.

"If you'd stop for two damn seconds, you'd see what we already did, you stubborn...man," Beatrix huffed.

I had a feeling she hadn't been about to say "man," but whatever growing emotions I was sure she was feeling toward the gruff sorcerer likely lightened the verbal blow.

Yury got himself up, wiped a hand over his mouth, and then lifted a hand toward Moira. Just when I thought he was going to blast her, he closed his eyes and settled his shaking form.

While he finally listened to Beatrix, I turned back for Foster, who was still on the ground. He wasn't meant to handle magic like the rest of us. I pressed my hand between his shoulder blades. He was vibrating with energy that didn't belong to him, so I syphoned the foreign powers from his body until he began to move on his own.

I helped him up and wrapped an arm around his waist until he shook out his hands. "What the hell was that?"

"A broken spell that couldn't tolerate any other energy getting near it without exploding in our faces," I explained, trying to keep the blame out of my tone. I knew he'd meant well and had only been concerned for my safety.

He chest heaved, and self-loathing radiated from him through our bond. "I almost got you killed."

"That's not what we need to focus on now," I said, then I turned around, pulling Foster with me so that my touch didn't lift from him. He needed the strength of our bond to fully recover from that blow.

Yury stepped toward Beatrix, his face unreadable until his hands grasped both of her cheeks and he kissed the hell out of her.

My eyes widened, and I was one second from turning the other way before Beatrix punched him in the stomach. "Not in front of the kids."

Regardless of the shitty situation we were literally standing in the middle of, I snorted and shook my head.

"You stunning sorceress," he muttered. "Why have you hid that from me?"

Even Foster's mouth flinched upward. *I'd wondered if she was keeping something like that from us.*

I think her secrets are what keep her alive.

Beatrix sighed and ignored his passionately spoken words. "Just open the door, and maybe I'll forgive you for being an idiot."

Moira was still on the ground behind us, and I looked up at Foster. "Help me move her?"

He nodded without having to think twice, but before we could reach for the prone witch, Yury already had the door open, and Beatrix let out a string of colorful words.

We each turned around to see what was going on and found the double wooden doors parted with sparks of magic flickering around the edges. Beyond that were two stone beds in a dungeon-like room.

Stepping forward, I noticed there were no windows, only concrete floors and walls plus the two white marble beds.

No, that wasn't marble… That was moonstone.

The reflecting colors in the stone swirled with natural magic, and I was drawn forward, but Foster placed a gentle hand on my shoulder. "Care to share your intentions this time?"

I didn't know how to answer him, because I hadn't meant to take those steps.

Beatrix glanced briefly at me. "Moira must have been told moonstone would reverse whatever she'd done, but I think she misunderstood whatever message she received."

Together, Beatrix and Yury moved toward the two bodies.

I did the same with Foster at my side. My eyes were first drawn to a young woman who looked like a much-younger version of Moira, given their matching ebony hair and sharp facial structures, making me believe she was the sister we'd heard of before.

She was wearing a soft-white dress that ended at her boney knees, and the sleeves were so long, they covered her hands. Her face was hollow, and I wondered how long she'd gone without nutrients.

The man next to her was in far better shape. His cheeks were full while his chest rose and fell with a steady rhythm. His soft black pants and white T-shirt also filled out better.

"Is she keeping them alive?" I asked with something resembling disgust as I pointed to the frail young woman.

Beatrix's hands hovered over the two bodies, then she nodded. "Seems like it."

"Cut the connection," Foster said, but even I knew that wasn't the best idea.

"The woman could die," Beatrix replied, her voice quiet as she concentrated. "She might be giving her energy to him, but whatever ties them together is also keeping her breathing. At least for now."

I glanced up at Foster, wanting him to know exactly what I thought might be best. "I could heal the man and it would allow us to cut the connection between the two of them."

His head shook, and a pained expression deepened between his brows. "You don't know what Moira has already put inside him."

I focused on the bond between us, sending all my love through it. "I won't continue if there's anything there that can hurt me. I promise."

Foster dropped his chin with a grumble. I knew he hated not being the one to save the day, but this had never been his fight.

This was mine, and I needed to finish it.

His hands slowly slid up my sides, and he nodded brusquely. "I'll be right beside you."

With his agreement, I glanced back at Beatrix. "Do you see any reason why I shouldn't help him?"

She shook her head, then stepped closer. "You've handled worse, but we're both here for you."

Without waiting for anyone to change their mind or anything else to go wrong, I moved next to the stone platform and pressed my hand over the man's chest.

Iciness sliced through my palm, but I kept my pressure steady. There was dark energy swirling inside him just like there had been with Benjamin and James, but Beatrix was wrong. This was worse than it had been with either of them.

Worse because I sensed so much agony coming from this man. He'd been trapped like this for who-knew-how-long, suffering from the darkness with no way out.

As my energy began to spread over him, he groaned and made a choking sound. His eyes fluttered, and I flinched back. Having him wake so soon wasn't at all what I'd expected.

Just as I was about to ask Beatrix if I should stop, a flash of energy blasted around us. The explosion took out both Beatrix and Foster in one go. Yury was already on the defense, but Moira was prepared for that.

She had a translucent, grey shield in front of her and waggled a finger. "I don't think so."

"Protect them, Yury," I hissed. "It's not you three she wants. It's me."

He grumbled something I didn't bother paying attention to. All I cared about was that he moved Foster and Beatrix behind the stones and created a shield around them while I moved closer to Moira.

"You should have killed me while you had the chance," she taunted, then she launched herself at me.

I was ready for her and shoved my palm out, hitting her in the stomach as she came down on top of me.

We tumbled to the floor and my shoulder slammed into the hard floor with a crack.

Her hands reached for my throat, but I kicked her off me and rolled to get on my feet. Before I could, she grabbed my ankle. "You're not going anywhere."

"Wasn't planning on it." I grunted, trying to break free from her hold. "I can help him if you'd stop trying to kill me."

She sneered. "No. It's my job to save him."

Stupid, twisted witch.

Fine. If she wasn't going to listen, then I was going to knock her ass out.

I gathered as much energy as I could in the short second I had before she jerked me toward her again. Once she was above me, I aimed the dark-blue stream of magic at Moira's chest and wrapped my legs around her waist so that she couldn't easily get away from me.

She screeched from the touch of my light energy, just as I'd assumed she would. Her skin crackled like she'd been electrocuted, and she clawed at me with her nails until I finally released her.

When I expected her to back away and recover, she instead lifted her foot up and kicked me in the ribs while I was getting to my feet.

I fell back to the hard ground with a groan, but her hit wasn't enough to keep me down. Not when people I loved were at risk of getting hurt if I failed.

There was a warmth in my chest, and I rose from the ground, my speed increasing and my senses unlike anything they'd ever been.

I could see Moira's dark energy shimmering around her, smell the sour taste of her tainted magic, and hear the rapid beat of her heart.

I had no clue where these new senses had come from, but with the extra energy boost, I launched myself at Moira for hopefully the last time.

Our arms tangled as we fought each other for control. I was trying to play nice, but as her skin grew so cold that it began to burn mine, I realized maybe *nice* wasn't going to keep the people I loved alive.

Moira's hands wrapped around my throat. "You were my last chance, and you ruined *everything*!"

I didn't have a clue as to what she was talking about, but this level of insanity wasn't good.

Her dark magic seeped from her skin and headed straight

for my chest while I tried to muster up my own energy, but whatever she was doing to me was suppressing my normal senses.

Syphoning from the inkiness coming from her was the last thing I wanted, but as she stared down at me with soulless, black eyes, I knew there was no getting out of this the easy way.

I let my eyelids flutter closed and relaxed my muscles, trying to prepare for the onslaught of power I didn't want.

She shook me hard, rattling my bones. "Is the last Bishop witch really that weak?"

I reached up and wrapped my fingers around her forearms. "No, I'm just smarter than you are."

Before I grew too weak, I began syphoning the life from Moira, starting with her chest and working my way to her core.

She was fighting back stronger than I'd expected her to, but I wasn't giving up. I wouldn't let Moira hurt another person I cared about.

If she wouldn't concede, it was time for her to die…no matter the cost.

My insides rattled, and I wanted to vomit from the dark energy filling my core and taking away the normal lightness I felt inside me.

Moira still leaned over me, her eyes narrowing. "What are you doing?"

She still didn't know. She didn't understand that I wasn't just the last Bishop witch.

Ignoring her, I continued my efforts, tugging her magic toward me even as my heart began to slow down and my vision faltered.

"Andie!" Foster roared from somewhere behind us.

At least I knew he was alive.

He raced toward us, but the power pulsing from Moira

and me forced my mate back. He wouldn't be able to touch us while we were locked in this power struggle.

Please, stop whatever you're doing, his voice begged in my mind. *We'll find another way to stop her.*

I'd never heard Foster plead before. Not like that. Not with such a sense of loss in his voice.

I'm sorry, I muttered in reply.

Moira was struggling above me. I nearly had her, but she had me, too. I couldn't kill her without destroying myself in the process.

I heard more yelling. Finally, Moira realized she wasn't going to win against me. She tried pulling away, but my syphon power had dug its way deep into her core. There was no breaking the connection, even if she managed to inch back.

"I'm going to kill you," she hissed.

I opened my mouth to reply, but the only sound that left my lips was the screech of agony as every facet of my body turned to fire.

33

FOSTER

The life I'd never thought I would have flashed before my eyes. One minute, I thought Andie was going to sacrifice herself to end Moira all on her own, but then everything changed.

My mate wasn't in control. Blinding light burned through both her and the dark witch. I didn't know who had done what, but all I knew was that I wanted to be dead.

I fell to my knees, helpless, and held my head between my hands. *Andie, come back to me,* I pleaded to the bond I could feel fading away with every passing second.

She couldn't have been gone. This wasn't how things were supposed to end.

No. I wouldn't accept that.

I couldn't.

With wrath fueling my movements, I got back to my feet and made it two steps before a large hand wrapped around my shoulder.

"Wait," Yury grunted.

I swirled around, my fist raised, but the look of defeat in his dark eyes made me pause, because it reminded me of how I felt in the moment. "Beatrix?"

She wasn't standing next to him, and I couldn't see behind the stone tables where we'd been. When he shook his head…I didn't know how I felt.

We couldn't have lost them both.

"I'm going to kill her," I snarled, ripping out of his hold and taking another step toward the dimming light.

The sorcerer grabbed me again. "I said, *wait*. I've done the only thing that can be done. The rest is up to Andie now."

My lip lifted. "What the fuck does that mean?"

"It means if you interfere, it might be *you* who kills your mate," he spat. "Now, I'm going back to mine."

He walked away, and I was tempted not to trust him, but as the power around Andie and Moira began to cease, I saw their two prone forms lying next to each other and realized that they weren't fighting anymore.

Whatever Yury had done, he'd better pray it brought my Andie back to me. If I lost her, even he wouldn't survive my wrath.

My gaze was frozen on Andie's chest, watching for any sign of movement as I waited for the burning magic to fully dissipate.

With each minute that passed, my heart further shattered. Each step forward that I took had my body quivering with equal parts ire and anguish. Each breath that I took scorched my insides.

Andie remained still, her pink hair tangled around her pale face and her hands laying limp at her sides.

The harder I stared, the more my eyes burned. I begged every god and higher power that I could think of to bring my mate back to me. Even if I didn't deserve her, *she* deserved better than this.

Andie had only ever wanted to help people, and this wasn't how she was supposed to go—and not now. Not when I'd only just found her.

Yury's spell finally ceased, but as I got closer to Andie, Moira moaned painfully. That bitch was still alive?

Not fucking possible.

She reached for my mate, but my foot met her ribs with a swift kick. "Don't you fucking touch her."

Moira's body thudded against the hard wall, and I stepped forward to choke the life from her myself, but a whimper had me on the ground before my next breath.

My hands cupped Andie's cheek. "Baby, please wake up. Please come back to me."

I moved one hand over her heart and calmed my nerves enough to listen to her body.

The heartbeat was faint, but there *was* one and that was all that mattered.

Knowing that our bond would only help strengthen Andie, I leaned forward and pressed my lips to her skin, starting with her forehead, then her cheeks and everywhere in between until her whimpers turned to groans.

"Come on, Andie," I implored. "Open those beautiful eyes for me."

She moved her head to the side, and her lashes fluttered several times before her eyelids finally lifted.

My body felt like it had caved in on itself with relief. I carefully gathered her into my arms and rocked her against my chest. Tears fell down my cheeks, and I probably held her too tightly, but she didn't say anything and I couldn't find the will to let go.

The longer we sat there, the more our bond grew. I could feel her confusion and pain, but it wasn't until she pushed against my shoulders that I finally released my hold.

"Is she dead?" Andie asked with a frown.

I sneered. "If she's not, she will be soon."

Andie tried to get up on her own, but I grabbed under her arms and held her against my side. When we stood, she gasped. I'd momentarily forgotten about Beatrix until then.

Andie fought my grip around her, trying to get to Beatrix, but there was nothing my mate could do. Not in her current state, and especially not if Yury had already given up.

He kneeled over his soulmate, holding both of her hands with his lips pressed against them and his eyes closed.

They may not have known each other more than a couple of days, but I still almost thought I felt his pain, and I knew there was nothing we could do to help him now.

Andie bent down next to Beatrix, and I stayed right next to her. If she tried to do anything to sacrifice herself again, I'd run from this place with my mate in my arms without a second thought.

Her eyes moved over Beatrix's still body. The elder witch's face was slack, and she seemed at peace for the first time since I'd met her. She'd always carried too much responsibility on her shoulders, much like my mate seemed to be doing now.

Andie began to shake and sob next to me, then her head leaned forward until she was resting against Beatrix's stomach. "I'm so sorry. I never… You weren't supposed to… Damn it."

Andie choked harder on her words, and I felt my own emotions rising for Beatrix.

I glanced at Yury. He was still frozen there next to her, holding her hands and unmoving. I attempted to reach out to him, but when my hand moved closer, power radiated from his skin.

I lifted Andie back and she fought against me.

"Look at him," I said. "What is he doing?"

My mate stopped struggling and paused. Her eyes briefly closed, and she sucked in a breath. "He's keeping her alive. She's… She's not gone." Andie's bright eyes met mine. "Help me. Please."

The hope she emanated nearly broke me because I wasn't sure she was right, but for my mate's sake, I wanted her words to be true.

"What can I do?" I asked softly.

"Hold me so that I can draw energy from you," she said. She quieted before adding softly, "And don't ask me not to do this because you know if this were me, Beatrix would give everything she had to save me and you'd let her."

Fuck.

My eyes hardened. "You better take every bit of whatever you need from me. If you don't, I will follow you into the afterlife, Andie Bishop. I won't stay here without you."

Our bond flared and pulsed with life and love and assurance.

"I promise this isn't our end." Her words were confident, but my stomach still churned.

She'd better be fucking right.

Andie pressed her hand over Beatrix's chest, careful to avoid Yury's energy. While she did that, I wrapped my arms under hers until my fingers curved up and over her shoulders, then my forehead pressed against her spine.

That was probably more contact than my mate needed, but I wasn't leaving anything to chance.

It wasn't even a second later that I felt the tug on my strength.

The action made me search for my wolf again. He hadn't returned to my mind since the initial blast, and I hoped Andie taking from me wouldn't make anything harder on him.

There was no sign of his energy inside me, but the hollowness I'd felt without him last time wasn't there, so I tried not to consider his absence a problem. Not when Andie needed all of my focus to ensure she remained okay.

My attention moved back to the people in front of me. A dark-blue glow grew around Beatrix, and Andie's body shook with focused effort under me. The tightness in my chest was making it harder to breathe and only intensified when Andie began to go slack against me.

Don't overdo it, I warned her.

She didn't respond, but I felt her pull harder on me and did my best to keep the ache that was building inside my chest to myself.

Another minute ticked by, and sweat pooled at the base of my neck while my arms began to shake around Andie. I was ready to finally ask her to stop when Yury suddenly roared, scaring the hell out of both of us.

I fell backward with Andie on top of me, and by the time we got back to our knees, Yury was kneeling over Beatrix. They were cocooned in some sort of barrier.

"What the... No!" Charlie cried from behind us.

Mack grabbed onto her and pulled her against his chest while I helped Andie stand.

Both of our friends looked beat to hell, with bloodstains on their torn shirts and fresh wounds on their bodies, but none of that seemed to register with Charlie.

Not as she sobbed for the woman still lying on the floor.

Andie stumbled toward her, and Charlie stepped away from Mack. The two best friends fell into each other's arms, barely managing to hold each other up as they cried together.

Fuck. If there were ever a time for Yury to prove how powerful he was, it was now.

Mack stood next to me with a heavy sigh. "What happened?"

I nodded angrily at Moira, who was still unconscious in the corner. "She happened. What about out there?"

"The dark energy pulsing from this place stopped, and half of the witches and warlocks fighting against us fled. The other half just dropped to the ground with relief. The fight's over."

Mack's words should have given me some sort of gratitude, but I could still see Moira lying there with life in her body. I didn't know how many people had died out there because of her, but I knew there was one in here who might already be gone. That was enough to have me stepping forward.

I moved silently and with intent. I should have done this earlier, but Andie's needs had taken precedence. She had Charlie now, and I wouldn't be stopped.

Bending to the floor, I picked Moira up by her neck and pressed her against the wall. Her feet dangled loosely above the concrete. Her face was slack, just like Beatrix's had been, but there were no feelings inside me toward this woman.

I didn't hate her, pity her, or anything. I just needed her to cease to exist.

My fingers tightened around her neck, and her body jerked in my hold, but her eyes remained closed.

Something stirred in my chest. Maybe my wolf. Maybe something else. I didn't know, but I wasn't stopping to figure it out until I heard this witch's heart stop.

"Are you sure, man?" Mack asked from behind me.

I didn't bother to answer him. I was more than sure about what I was doing.

Moira's body jerked again, but she remained unconscious. A pity, because she deserved to feel the pain of her lungs as I cut off the air to them, but still, I wasn't waiting for her to wake.

The strength of my hold increased, and the stone behind her began to crack while I pushed harder. "Fucking die," I muttered.

Just as the words left my mouth, a zap of power hit my spine. My muscles seized, and I lost my hold on the witch.

She dropped to the ground once again, and I slowly turned around as I regained control of my extremities. Pure, unfiltered rage flowed through me, but as I charged forward, Andie cut me off.

"Stop." Her hand went up. "She might deserve to die, but he probably has no idea what's going on."

I didn't fucking care. *He* was mated to that dark witch. We didn't need him causing problems.

Moira's soulmate was trying to sit up from the table, and Andie went to him without a single protection up around her.

My forward momentum returned, and I pulled her back. "What are you doing?"

Her eyes glared at me, and power flowed between us. "I'm finding out what the hell is going on here."

Charlie was already at the side of the woman we assumed was Moira's sister and Andie jerked out of my hold.

She bent down at eye level with the warlock. "What's your name?"

"Malcom," he murmured. "I tried to stop her. She…can be…saved."

I scoffed. "Like hell that's happening."

Andie moved so that she was blocking Malcom from my view. "What happened here, Malcom?"

I threw my hands in the air and moved to step away. I could finish the job while they were having their little chat.

Don't you kill her before I get what I want to know out of him, Andie demanded through our mental link.

Why not?

Because if she's dead, we don't know what that will do to him, and I'm not leaving here without knowing why the hell my life was turned upside down.

She made a fair point, and I fucking hated it.

I hated that there seemed to be nothing I could do in the moment to channel my anger.

"Fuck!" I paced toward the door before turning around and crossing my arms while I leaned against the wall farthest from Moira and closest to Andie in case she needed me.

Mack joined me, nodding at Yury, who was still on the ground with Beatrix and enclosed in a magical shield. "What happened?"

My jaw ground. If I wasn't allowed to do anything, I really wasn't in the mood for talking.

"Everything went to shit." I growled.

He took that as answer enough as we listened to Andie and Malcom speak.

"I was locked into a magic contract when she found me," he said gruffly. "She tried to make a deal with a dark witch to get me out, but that only made things worse. Moira was tricked, and I became sick."

He coughed and groaned as if he was in pain. Andie's hand flinched like she was going to console him, then thought better of it.

Malcom continued. "Moira went too far trying to fix me. I begged her to stop, but she wouldn't listen. When she sacrificed her sister to keep me alive, I knew there was no stopping her, so I did my best to minimize the damage as time passed."

Andie's head tilted. "How, if you were unconscious and tied to this bed?"

"I wasn't the whole time," he admitted. "I woke a few times a month for short periods. Each time, I'd ask her about what she'd been up to. Some things I had to ignore because I couldn't do anything about them, but other times, I did my best to fix things before they got too far out of hand. Like when she told me she was going to take you to heal me after she learned who you were, but I convinced her your necklace was all we needed."

He paused, coughing and struggling to breathe before continuing. "Moira listened for a while. Then she attacked the pack. She tried not to tell me about the people she took and planned to torture as a way to hurt you all, but I forced her hand. After I found out, I told her I'd break the connection to her sister if she hurt any of them and that they needed to be returned. I don't know how long that took, but she promised she would and the next time I woke, I knew she wasn't lying when she said it was done."

Well, shit.

That, I hadn't expected to hear.

Mack stiffened next to me, and we both continued to listen.

Malcom coughed again. "I begged Moira to kill me and move on, but she wouldn't. I was tempted to break the connection with her sister as I'd threatened before, but I was afraid that would kill Tessa, too."

Andie's hand covered his forearm. "It's okay, Malcom. We're going to find a way to fix this."

Yeah, by killing Moira, I thought, but I must have thought the words too hard because Andie turned back to shake her head at me.

She got up after that and went to Yury. He was still at Beatrix's side, and when Andie reached her hand inside the barrier around them, my heart nearly stopped, but nothing harmed her. I watched her dark-blue energy flow toward Beatrix's chest.

Yury remained unmoving, as did Beatrix. I wasn't sure why they were still trying, but I hoped Andie knew what she was doing.

Charlie came over and joined Andie, doing the same thing. They kneeled next to each other with one hand in the barrier, giving more than they likely should have.

I stepped forward, but Mack stopped me. "I wouldn't do anything to piss them off right now."

I shrugged him off. "I'm not. I'm going to help my mate."

He frowned but let me go. I quickly closed the distance between Andie and me, so I could place my hand on her back.

She immediately began pulling from me, and the weird sensation in my chest occurred again.

Wolf? I called, but there was still no response.

Just when I was about ready to pull back instead of continuing to further risk his spirit, Andie grasped her chest and fell back into me.

Her breath was ragged, but her eyes were open and she was staring up at me with a smile on her face.

"What the hell was that?" I demanded, helping her back up.

"A gift."

When she said nothing else, I was tempted to shake the answer out of her, but then Beatrix woke up and my wolf returned at the same time.

He howled in my head, but the sound was joyful instead of sorrowful. *Everything is going to be okay, Foster. I promise.*

I hadn't been missing his optimism, but I was at least thankful to feel him again.

Andie and Charlie were backing up as Yury stood with Beatrix at his side. Her face was pale, and her arms visibly shook, but she was aware, which was a lot more than I'd thought would happen.

She turned to Malcom with the help of Yury. "We can't let Moira remain as she is, even if we can heal you."

He lowered his head. "I know. I've known that for some time now."

"But we can give the two of you a different chance at life," Beatrix added.

My head jerked up as I held Andie to me. "What the hell does that mean?"

"It means that if Malcom gives me permission, I will take his magic and give Tessa back hers so she can wake up and receive her sister's magic when I take that as well," Beatrix said. Her voice was gravelly, but she kept her head high.

Malcom gaped. "You'd make us human?"

I snarled. That wasn't good enough for me.

Andie turned and looked up at me. "We are not Moira. We

never will be. Taking away her magic will be punishment enough."

My head shook roughly. "No. I don't agree."

But we must, my wolf said. *This is the way it has to be if you want Andie to move on from this day.*

Did you know that before now? I snapped.

He sighed. *No, but I wasn't just gone when I was missing from your mind. I was with our creator, and I know now. Trust Andie and Beatrix.*

Fuck. I did trust them, but I was so filled with rage…I didn't know how I was supposed to just ignore everything that had happened. How was it okay that Moira was going to be living with her soulmate for however many human years they had? Why did she get her happy ending after all that she had done?

Andie's hand pressed against my chest, and she smiled softly up at me. "Don't let her control your emotions. Don't give her that power. Let's finish this and be done. She doesn't have to be dead for us to win. I think that was what Reah was trying to tell me before we left."

Where was my fucking sign that everything was going to be okay?

I tried to minimize my feelings, because Andie didn't deserve them. I just didn't fucking understand how everyone could just suddenly be okay with everything that had happened over the last few months.

Warmth filled my chest, and my wolf's energy expanded through my body, filling every inch of me.

Do you feel that? he asked, but he didn't wait for my response. *That is our creator's power. She trusted us with this path. She had faith we could handle what was needed. Let's show her she was right and that we deserve the gifts she has bestowed upon us.*

What fucking gifts? I yelled. *Besides Andie making it through this, everything has gone to shit.*

Andie is the greatest of them all, but she is not the only one, he said. *We have our new pack and the coven, and because of those two things, Andie has received the wolf spirit. Just as Holden thought. She's going to need us to accept this day as it is so that nothing will stand in the way of your love.*

My eyes focused on Andie, who was still staring up at me, waiting patiently for me to get my shit together.

I closed my eyes briefly and tried to accept my wolf's words as truth. Tried to focus on the Moon Goddess's energy that I could feel pulsing from our connection.

We're going to be okay, Andie's voice echoed through my mind, and our bond filled my senses, making me shudder from the sheer overwhelmingness of everything.

Andie held on to me while I took the time I needed to calm down, to trust what they were both saying and admit that death wasn't always the answer. That killing Moira wouldn't change what had happened in the past.

I wasn't completely okay with everything, but when I finally reopened my eyes and saw Andie's face, I remembered that no matter what, as long as I had her at my side, nothing else should have the power to control me.

We were together, and that was never going to change.

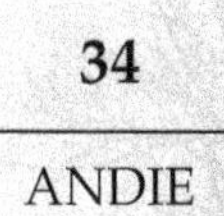

34

ANDIE

Malcom easily agreed to Beatrix's proposal, and by the time Foster was calm again, she had already taken all of his magic and healed the sickness that the dark energy had caused him.

He smiled widely and thanked her a dozen times as she finished.

Charlie helped with healing Moira's sister, whose name we learned was Tessa. She woke up, already having been mentally aware of everything that had happened, and cried against Malcom once the focus turned to Moira.

Beatrix, Charlie, and I stepped up to finish the job together, knowing none of us were strong enough to complete the task on our own, but Yury moved into our path.

"This witch doesn't deserve your kindness." His arms crossed, and he glowered at each of us.

Beatrix pushed forward and placed her hand over his chest. "No, but we are better than her and we're going to continue to be better."

They had a short stare-down, and I knew Foster would appreciate that he wasn't the only one in disagreement with us.

"Should we wake her first?" Charlie asked, brushing back her golden hair.

Beatrix shook her head. "Not worth the risk. We might be better than her, but if she says one more stupid thing, I'm not above punching her in the face."

I smirked. She was serious, and I didn't blame her.

"Let's just get this done," I said, then I nodded for Tessa to come closer.

Malcom helped her stand just a foot away from us while Charlie and I placed a hand on Beatrix's shoulders. With our combined coven magic, Beatrix got right to work, but breaking through the darkness Moira still held inside her wasn't easy.

The energy burned all three of us as we fought against it, channeling the power out of Moira and confining the inkiness into its own little cocoon until we were done stripping Moira of magic.

Beatrix pushed harder and finally was able to begin the transfer of energy from Moira to Tessa. The teal color flowed from Moira's chest and straight to Tessa, whose skin began to glow the moment the magic made contact with her.

Within minutes, the job was done. We stepped back and let Malcom go to Moira.

I went straight into Foster's waiting arms while watching Charlie do the same with Mack. Though, before I could think too much on their connection, a new one of my own flared to life.

Luna chose well for my host, a soft, feminine voice said in my mind.

I wasn't sure if I was supposed to say "thank you," but I did anyway.

Tend to your mate, she replied quietly. *We'll have our time soon.*

When I did as she said, Foster's brows were pinched. "What was that?"

I grinned widely. "My wolf. The gift I mentioned before."

He didn't seem as shocked as I'd expected him to be. "Did you know?" I asked.

"Elias might have mentioned something, but I was a little too furious in the moment to celebrate," he said quietly. Then he pulled me flush against him. "Celebrating is something I hope we can do as soon as we leave this God-awful place."

I glanced behind us. "Seems we're about done here." Then I frowned. "Unless there's still fighting happening outside."

Charlie stepped closer with Mack still by her side. "No. That's why we came to find you."

I fought back against the sorrow that filled me when I knew the question that I needed to ask next. "How…bad is it out there?"

Her eyes flicked up to Mack then back to me. Her stance stiffened. "Not good, but it could have been worse. The fae made all the difference and Cait with her glowing purple wolf was something else to see."

I tried to be thankful for the small wins, but then Mack and Foster shared a dark look that told me the losses were going to hurt for a while.

Moira was finally awake, and she was crying in Malcom's arms. "I'm so sorry," she repeated several times over.

Tessa glanced at the rest of us before meeting Beatrix's stare. "I know you have no reason to trust me, but I'd like to find them somewhere to start over if you'd be okay with that."

Beatrix tapped her foot and crossed her arms. "Only if I can send a witch with you. I also want their memories wiped once you get your goodbyes in."

The sister sighed and nodded. "Understandable. Thank you for this mercy."

Beatrix's nod was stiff, then she turned to the rest of us. "How about we go check on everyone else and find a volunteer to go with these three?"

"Wait," Foster said, "we need to destroy the necklace. Moira corrupted its purpose."

I'd forgotten all about my moonstone that still hung from Moira's neck. I stepped forward to take it back, but Tessa cut me off and removed the silver chain herself, wincing as she did.

"Be careful with that," she said before dropping it into Beatrix's open palm.

Yury created a shield around the stone and Beatrix raised her other hand, but I stopped her. "I'd like to do it."

She raised a brow, then conceded, handing the necklace to me. Tears pricked in my eyes as I said a silent goodbye to the gift from my aunt. The one that had changed everything in my life.

Yury's shield still remained, and I lifted my right hand while drawing on my core energy—the deeper parts that weren't as easy to access and had helped me bring Beatrix to life…or consciousness.

Foster's warmth covered my back as he stood behind me, holding my shoulders and offering his silent support.

With a heavy breath, I sent a surge of power forward and out of my palm right into the center of the teardrop-shaped moonstone. The white parts had already begun to turn grey, and when my dark-blue magic pierced its surface, the smooth rock cracked and vibrated within my hand.

Seconds ticked by, then shards of the necklace tried to go flying through the room, but Yury's barrier kept that from happening.

I pulled my magic back and when the shield fell, there were only small chunks of the stone left and nothing magical about them any longer.

Foster grabbed my hand and took the remnants from me. "You did what you had to."

My head nodded, but knowing that didn't lessen the ache that was beginning to grow inside my chest.

Beatrix shuddered and grimaced. "Let's get out of here."

Even though I was ready to be home, I wasn't ready to see the aftermath of the battle, but I also knew there was no avoiding it. If we were going to move forward with our lives and make these last few months mean something, then we had to face the consequences head-on.

Slowly, we all left the room huddled in our groups of two with Tessa, Moira, and Malcom in the middle.

We might have made them human and let Tessa keep her family magic, but that didn't mean we trusted them.

Empathetic, not idiotic.

There was a fine line between the two, but I was certain we hadn't crossed to the wrong side.

Foster's head leaned against mine once we were outside. I felt his strength fill me as the sight before us began to register with not only my mind, but my heart.

Bodies lay on the scorched ground and people hovered over them, weeping for their lost loved ones. Hooded witches and warlocks stood helpless as they stared around them.

At least until they saw Moira walking with us.

Everyone froze and Evelyn appeared in front of us, holding a glowing hand inches from Moira's neck. "Why isn't she dead?"

"Because that is not how this story ends," Beatrix said loudly. "If anyone has a problem with that, you're welcome to come speak with me."

Gasps and murmurs sounded throughout the gathering crowd. Seconds ticked by, and I thought nobody was going to say anything, but then one of the hooded witches dropped her cloak, stepping forward in jean shorts and a white tank top.

Her blonde hair was cut short like a pixie's and her blue eyes held dark circles beneath them. "Do you have any idea what she did to us? What she threatened and tortured us with to make us do things we never wanted to do?"

Beatrix stiffened. "No, I don't and I'm sorry that you went through whatever you did, but I assure you, Moira has been dealt with, and she won't ever hurt anyone again."

The woman pointed at Beatrix and sneered. "Your assurances don't mean dick. That witch should have her head taken off."

Cheers from the others rose from the gathering crowd, and I glanced back at Tessa, who was standing defensively in front of her sister and brother-in-law.

Shit, this wasn't good.

I stepped forward and met the glare of the woman speaking. "I can relate to how you're feeling. Moira hunted me for months. She destroyed parts of my life that I can never get back. But the woman behind me? That isn't the witch who ruled over you." I turned and pointed briefly. "Focus for a moment and you'll see she no longer has any magic. She is weak and defenseless. If we killed her now, we'd be no better than she is. Is that what you want?"

The woman's square chin trembled. "I want to sleep without nightmares of her torture and threats."

"And with time, I'm sure you will," I said softly, "but murder isn't going to bring you closer to that. Let Moira serve out her days as a human with no magic and no memory this world exists. You can move on with your own life. Find the happiness you want and focus on that."

The tension pressing in around us didn't seem to lessen, but there were no other outbursts and I hoped that was enough for now.

Beatrix stepped to my side. "We will offer homes to anyone who needs one. We intend to create communities where you can be safe among the supernaturals. I promise you, positive change is coming and we will all heal from this together."

It was weird to hear Beatrix speak so passionately, but that was what everyone needed, and I was glad she could see that as well.

Foster squeezed my hand. "You handled that much better than I did, and I'm sorry I couldn't understand your reasoning sooner."

I rested my palm over his heart and smiled up at him. "I knew you would in time. Just like the rest of these people will, too."

Evelyn approached us, looking at Beatrix. "How do you want to clean this up now?"

"Make sure the invite I just made is extended again to anyone who has been under Moira's rule and doesn't know where to go," she said. "Then we will gather our fallen, we celebrate their lives and their sacrifices today, and tomorrow, we will deal with those captured and begin rebuilding our world into something newer and better than what we have always known." Beatrix looked up at Yury, and the tiredness in her eyes finally began to show.

He wrapped both arms around her, holding her up as I imagined he would continue to do for many years to come— even while they drove each other crazy.

Evelyn nodded and turned to go do just as I assumed Beatrix had asked her to. Mirra and Vi joined us next.

Mirra bowed briefly before Beatrix. "You handled today differently than I would have, but I think the results will have lasting effects, ones that will help pave the way for the supernatural world you envision."

Beatrix smirked. "I sure hope so, because if I was nice to all these people for no reason, I won't be happy about it."

I chuckled to myself and leaned against Foster's shoulder. Some things would never change.

Mirra nodded and glanced at Vi, who tilted her head once. "Would you mind if we escorted Moira to her new home?"

Having someone I didn't know do this job wasn't ideal,

but Beatrix didn't seem to mind, given that she nodded, then explained what she wanted.

"They can pick the city and state, but their memories of the magical world, including Tessa, will need to be taken from their minds. Give them something to remember that is lackluster and let them figure the rest out. Her life is the only gift they'll receive."

I could feel Foster's glee at that small win through our bond, and honestly, I felt the same way. A punishment more than losing her magic was perfectly okay with me.

Beatrix whirled around and pointed at Tessa. "If you interfere in this process whatsoever, if you go back to your sister and tell her of this world, you will not be met with the same mercy we have shown here today. Do you understand?"

Yury bristled before the young witch could answer. "We cannot trust that." He then sidestepped his soulmate and pressed a hand over Tessa's head. "After her memories are changed, if you speak to your sister of our world or of this time, we will know and you will suffer immense pain until you bring yourself to us to admit your betrayal."

When he released her, a spark of white energy flickered between her forehead and his palm. Tessa winced and rubbed the spot where he'd just touched. "You could have warned me first."

He smirked. "What fun is that?"

He and Beatrix really were perfect for each other.

Mirra and Vi took off with Moira, Malcom, and Tessa. Once they disappeared, I hoped like hell that we never saw the latter three again in any capacity.

"We're going to see how we can help Holden," Mack said with an arm still around Charlie.

She met my stare with agony in her eyes, and I didn't miss the quiver in her lips that she fought against. I wanted to go to her, but before I could, Lucinda and Finn joined us and Mack was already pulling her away.

I'd see my best friend again just as soon as we all made it home.

Finn had a limp in his left leg, and Lucinda's shoulders were leaning crooked when they stopped next to us, but all in all, they seemed to have fared well.

Finn reached over to shake Foster's hand. "It was great to meet you both," he said, then he surprised me when he reached to embrace me. "Lucinda doesn't do hugs, but this is from her."

I chuckled against his shoulder and winked at her when she rolled her eyes. "I appreciate it."

When we pulled apart, Foster tugged me back to his side. Possessive bastard, but I loved it, so I didn't say anything.

"What will you guys do now?" Foster asked him.

Finn glanced at Lucinda and smiled. "Now, we're going to go back home and hopefully relax for longer than a day, but knowing my Lucy, she'll find some sort of trouble for us to be a part of." He leaned closer and fake-whispered. "She likes to pretend she hates people, but she secretly loves helping them."

Lucinda scoffed and pushed him away from us. "Only because I get to kill evil bastards like we did today." Then she pointed at me and stepped closer. Her finger roamed over my chest. "I knew you were different when I met you, and I didn't think I was going to like that, but you're not so bad, Bishop Witch."

Warmth filled me. Making new friends wasn't something I had ever been great at while growing up and, even with Lucinda's brash personality, I knew after today, she was going to be someone we could count on for years to come.

"Same to you." I reached my hand out to squeeze her elbow.

She looked down, stiffened slightly, then shrugged. "We're going now before this gets awkward." Then she nodded at

Yury. "What're your plans, Hulk? You know I'll have to answer a million questions when we're back."

I glanced back, and my heart swelled. Yury had Beatrix in his arms still and was shaking his head. "I don't answer to you or that king. I will be back when I want to be."

In other words, the sorcerer was here to stay, and I couldn't wait to be witness to the bickering between him and Beatrix that I knew would last a lifetime.

Lucinda smirked at me. "Have fun with that."

"I'm sure I will." I grinned in return, giving the new soulmates one more look.

The fae huffed. "Shit. You will. I'm going to have to visit. You can't have all the enjoyment."

Foster surprised me by his next words. "You're both welcome anytime." He paused and locked stares with Lucinda. "Thank you for saving her when I couldn't."

My chest tightened at the thick emotions in his deep tone.

Getting buried by all of those witches and warlocks seemed like so long ago, but in reality, it had been maybe an hour ago.

She nodded stiffly. "Right. Well, we'll see you guys around."

With one last wave goodbye, Lucinda and Finn flew into the sky before shimmering out of sight.

My eyes searched around and found the vampires gathering a few of their injured with a witch helping by keeping a portal open to a house I didn't recognize but assumed was their local nest.

Amersyn stood with her shoulders straight and jaw tight as she watched Maciah and Zeke transport people through. Rachel moved to her side, wiping a tear from a cheek, and whispered something I couldn't hear before they hugged.

I wanted to say goodbye to them, but we'd have another chance to talk. For now, they could have the time they needed to heal from whatever losses they'd endured today.

Roman and Cait made their way to us with another wolf I didn't recognize. He was tall with a big beard and auburn hair. He had scorch marks on both arms and another on his forehead.

Beatrix stepped forward and put her hand out. "Would you like some help, Vaughn?"

He nodded but kept his eyes down.

My gaze went to Cait, who had tears in her eyes. I opened my arms, and she went right into them. "It's going to be okay," she murmured over my shoulder, but I knew she was talking to herself instead of me.

Damn it. I wished we'd been out here longer to help. I had no idea how many people in total had been lost, but it seemed as if there'd been more than I could imagine.

"I'm really sorry, Cait," I whispered in return.

Her hold on me tightened. "You have nothing to be sorry for. We did what was needed, and everyone who showed up here knew the risks. I even had my Luna Marked power back to help, which saved more than a few lives, but that doesn't make the hurt any easier. At least, not today."

When she finished speaking, she pulled back and I grabbed her hands. "We'll visit soon, okay?"

She forced a small smile to her face and blinked her glossy eyes. "I'm going to hold you to that."

Roman and Foster had their own goodbyes, and then Beatrix was done with the wolf I assumed was from their pack.

"We need to get back to our packs," Roman said, "but don't hesitate to call if anything else comes up."

Foster shook his hand once more. "And you do the same."

I hugged Cait once more and then they headed to an open portal with hunched shoulders and heads down.

I glanced up at Foster, my throat aching from the heavy emotions. "This isn't going to be easy to come back from."

He shook his head and offered me a small smile. "But we're all going to be stronger because of it."

My head leaned against Foster's chest, and he wrapped his arms around me. We were surrounded by destruction and heartbreak, but he was right.

We'd come together to stop not just Moira, but dozens of others who'd thought they'd had the right to take what wasn't theirs. We'd proven that the races could work together, and we were one step closer to peace.

One step closer to our happily-ever-after.

EPILOGUE

ANDIE

One Year Later

Waking up in not only a new bed, but a new room and house wasn't as hard as I'd expected it to be. Especially not when I opened my eyes and saw the love of my life lying next to me with a smile on his face.

"Good morning, my beautiful alpha female," Foster murmured as he stroked my cheek.

I adjusted my pillow and moved closer to him until our noses were nearly touching. "Good morning, my sexy alpha."

His forehead pressed against mine, and he closed his eyes. "It's weird to know I'm responsible for this pack now. I thought I knew what to expect, but nothing is like it was before."

Last night, Foster had officially been given control over the pack and Holden was now retired while Piper was leading the pack of wolves in the city, as previously planned.

Though, with the growing community next door, it wasn't as stressful of a job as it once had been for Holden.

I smiled softly at my perfect mate. "That's because this is

different, but there's nothing wrong with that, so don't overthink this. Just keep doing everything you have been these last six months. The pack trusts you, and you've already been doing a great job."

He sighed and nodded, then rolled over. I tried to pull him back, but he was insistent on reaching for something.

Foster came back to me with a little velvet black box in hand and a slight blush to his cheeks. "I wanted to give this to you last night, but given how long the celebrations lasted and what happened once we got home…"

I chuckled and raised a brow. "You mean when I jumped you and forced you to our bedroom?"

"I wouldn't use the word 'forced,' but yes." He winked, then lifted the box between us, his voice turning serious. "You had to lose so much to get to this point in our life and while I know you're happy now, I wanted to give a little piece back to you."

He cracked open the lid of the box, and all the air left my lungs while tears filled my eyes. I had to blink several times to make sure I was really seeing what I thought I was. When that didn't work, I sat up in bed and took the box from him.

The tip of my finger traced over the shimmering, white stone set in an intricate white gold band. "Is this…?"

He nodded. "It's a piece from the necklace. I asked Beatrix if I could keep a piece and have it turned into this ring. When she said *yes*, I picked the biggest stone from the shards and had it made. This is my gift to you for accepting me and this pack and moving here."

My arms wrapped around his neck, and I held on tightly, sobbing over his shoulder. "A gift wasn't necessary, but I will cherish this for the rest of our lives. Thank you so much."

I pulled back and he took the box from me, grabbing the ring and then my left hand. Casually, he slid the band onto my ring finger.

Most supernaturals didn't get married or wear rings since

being bonded was so much more than human traditions, but as Foster slid that ring into place, I couldn't lie.

My heart felt like it was going to explode with emotions, and I was torn between weeping like a baby and jumping on him like I had last night when we'd barely made it into our room.

I love you now and I'll love you forever, his voice whispered across my mind.

I closed my eyes and leaned into him. *You are more than I ever could have dreamt of.*

His lips found mine, and my fingers reached up to grab the back of his neck, but instead of holding him to me, I felt him flinch beneath my touch.

"What is it?" I asked softly.

His responding growl was full of annoyance. "Mack needs help. One of the pups can't shift back on his own."

"Go. We have the rest of our lives to devour each other," I said, pushing him back before he thought to ignore his beta.

Foster glowered. "I don't know how long I'll be."

"Then I'll pop over to Charlie's or help Patsy or anyone else I find." I smiled and slid out of bed. "The pack has been my home for months, even if we didn't officially move in until yesterday."

He grumbled on his way to the bathroom, and I grinned, throwing myself back onto the bed. We might have interruptions every day, for as long as Foster wished to lead the pack, but I already knew this was where we were meant to be.

An hour later, I was sitting with Charlie on her front porch at the pack while we watched Gemma run after her son Bryson with the biggest of smiles on her face.

"I'm glad you're finally here," Charlie whined, then she

nodded at our friend. "I've been spending too much time alone with them."

I raised a brow and laughed. "And why is that suddenly a bad thing?"

"Because Bryson is too damn cute with his soft dark curly hair, chubby cheeks, and those honey eyes... Seriously, it's just too much." She huffed and crossed her arms.

"Aw, am I going to be an auntie soon?" I teased.

She rolled her eyes and groaned. "If Mack had anything to say about it, yes, probably."

"But Mack doesn't?" I questioned, trying and failing to keep the amusement out of my voice.

Charlie glared at me. "Oh my God, you're just as bad as that damn mate of mine. I've barely had a year with him. I'm not ready to share. Is that so bad?"

I reached for her hand. "Of course not, and I feel the same way. Just enjoy Bryson and don't overthink anything. You'll be a mom whenever you're supposed to be."

That didn't mean it would be when she wanted it to be, but I didn't need to tell her that. What was most important was that she was happy and she had Mack.

Their bond had started to slowly form before we'd defeated Moira. An interesting twist that had confused many of us, but according to Beatrix and what she'd gleaned from our ancestors, some bonds weren't meant to be before their time.

Once the first community had been opened at our coven, it seemed supernaturals all over had the same gift as Charlie and Mack bestowed upon them.

Bonds began popping up left and right between mixed races, which made forming the communities even easier than Beatrix had predicted.

The coven-turned-community was growing every passing week, and there was another one starting in Northern

California, along with one in almost every state within the U.S.

We'd put our people on the path, and they'd run in the right direction with everything. The council and their hunters hadn't been a problem since we'd disbanded them, either. At least, not ones that we couldn't handle. Plus, it helped that a lot of people already knew of Maciah and Amersyn and their nest.

Apparently, nobody wanted them to come hunting for them, and that was even more impactful than the council had been. Our friends didn't hide who they were.

Bryson squealed, distracting my thoughts, and I laughed when I realized Gemma was now on the ground with the toddler playing drums over her ass.

She blew blonde hair out of her face, her light-brown eyes looking over at us. "A little help?"

Charlie was first up and swooped Bryson into her arms. The glow around her told me all I needed to know.

My best friend was ready for a family. She just needed to admit that little fact to herself.

Bryson pointed a pudgy, little finger at me. "Woo-woo!"

Gemma and Charlie both grinned while I sighed. I wasn't supposed to bring my wolf spirit out for just any reason, but this little boy loved the hell out of her for some reason.

Excuse me? the spirit said pointedly.

Oh, you know what I mean, I replied quickly. *Unless you know something we don't, you're the only wolf he's obsessed with.*

She paused briefly before speaking. *I know lots of things you don't.*

Instead of elaborating, the dark-blue wolf spirit leapt from my chest, and I wobbled but stayed on my feet. A challenging task that had taken me months to conquer, but passing out every time she wanted to run with Elias wasn't my idea of a good time.

Charlie let a wiggly Bryson down, and he quickly chased

after his "woo-woo," as he called the wolf spirit. She dimmed her glow and trotted just ahead of Bryson, playing tag just like he loved.

Gemma and Charlie joined me, and I wrapped an arm around each of them, smiling like a fool. "Life is good."

They each rested their heads against me. "Hell yes, it is," Charlie agreed.

I caught Gemma's other hand moving to her stomach. "It's about to be doubly good."

I gasped and grinned impossibly wider.

The path here might not have been an easy one, but damn if I wouldn't walk it again just to have all of this.

* * *

Five years later

VACATION... I HADN'T THOUGHT THAT WAS SOMETHING WE'D truly ever get, and maybe this wasn't really one, but I was trying to think of our time away from the pack as the getaway we'd been dying to take for months.

Though it wasn't the private retreat we'd envisioned, being in East Texas was perfect for us.

"Momma, come see Daddy!" Aspie called from across Cait's yard, where we were currently all gathered.

Cait's hand rose over her mouth, and she nearly choked. "Oh, that little girl is lucky her daddy loves her."

My eyes finally registered what my daughter had done, and I couldn't stop from laughing my ass off as I made my way toward them.

Aspie, our three-year-old daughter—named Aspen after my mother, but her nickname "Aspie" had stuck—stood behind Foster, who was seated on the grass. She had his hair done in what I assumed were supposed to be braids. Instead, they looked like knots he might not be able to get untangled…

"Oh, baby girl," I cooed. "Daddy looks so handsome."

He glared at me but stayed silent.

She beamed up at me with dimples on her rosy cheeks and strawberry-blonde curls bouncing around her shoulders. "He purdy."

"Why yes, he is," I said. "Why don't you go play with Dawsyn, River, and Brixley?"

Her bright-blue eyes lit up and she nodded. "Yes, Momma."

I watched with a bright smile on my face as she ran sideways to join the other kids, who were playing with Embry—Cait's best friend in Texas—and her mate Mateo, along with Vaughn and his mate Kelly.

We weren't sure if Aspie had a wolf or not, but time would tell. Either way, we'd love her with our whole hearts and knew she was going to be special in her own ways, whether she turned out to be a witch, a wolf, or something else entirely.

Cait and Roman's daughter Dawsyn was leading the pack of kids, a role she took seriously as the oldest, while Vaughn and Kelly's son River seemed to be having a blast showing rollie pollies to his parents.

Charlie and Mack's daughter Brixley was the youngest of the pack at only one, but she did her best to act just like the big kids did, even if she couldn't use her words the same.

Foster moved off the grass and stood next to me with his arm around my waist. "If I have to cut my hair, we're trading her in for a new model."

I smacked his chest playfully. "You know you wouldn't last a day without Aspie."

His grimace turned into a grin. "Maybe not, but still. The kid needs to start playing with your hair instead of mine."

Yeah, that was never going to happen. Cait had already warned me of the time she'd had to cut hers thanks to Dawsyn. I preemptively negotiated with Aspen to make sure that didn't happen to me. Bribes might have even been involved.

"Where are all my evil babies?" Beatrix's voice sounded gleefully behind us.

Foster and I turned to see her and Yury coming through a portal together. He'd been holding her hand until she'd seen all the kids and they'd gone running toward her.

Not many adults could stand Beatrix on a good day, but these four kids? I didn't know what had happened to the old witch, but as soon as the babies had been born, it was like she'd flipped a switch and become the world's best grandmother overnight.

The kids started begging for magical animals—which were thankfully just an illusion—from their favorite GiGi, and she, and even Yury, happily obliged.

As Foster attempted to tame his knotted pigtails, we walked back to sit with our friends. Cait and Roman had turned the backside of their pack house into the perfect place for gatherings, with tables and outdoor couches spread out, along with playsets for the kids.

We had all decided to gather when Cait and Roman had told us they'd had something to talk about, but so far, they'd said nothing about what that might be.

Cait, Roman, Embry, Mateo, Vaughn, Kelly, the pack beta Sam, and her new mate Jackson, were already seated together when Charlie, Mack, Foster, and I joined them.

"So, is the gathering for wolf packs or something for all the races?" Foster asked once I was settled in his lap.

Roman shrugged. "I called Maciah, but he said they were on an important hunt and to fill him in later. Since this may not really affect them, I didn't press the issue."

"What about Lucinda?" Charlie asked. We'd both become close with the snarky fae during her visits to L.A. and kept trying to convince her and Finn to move back, but we hadn't quite succeeded. Though, I hoped that would change soon.

Cait grinned and let out a soft chuckle. "Lucy told me to fuck off when I told her we didn't actually have a problem she could fight her way out of. Then she said she and Finn would be by later, but to start without them."

"Sounds about right," Foster muttered from behind me. He tolerated the snarky fae a lot better these days, but she still wasn't his favorite person, even after she'd saved my life.

I glanced back at Beatrix and Yury. "Do we need them?"

"No, they already know." Cait made an *oops* face. "We needed a babysitter, and they love her."

The shifter wasn't wrong.

"So spill it," Vaughn said with an arm around Kelly.

I knew Roman and Cait were close to them, but I hadn't been around them much over the years. Though, the packs were getting better about gathering more often, thanks to the insistence of Perry's mate Silvie all those years ago.

Cait smiled widely at Roman and nodded at him. He leaned forward and rested his forearms on his knees before speaking.

"We think the kids are going to need somewhere to intermingle with the other races once they're older," he began, but I cut him off.

"Like boarding school?" I gaped. There was no way I was sending my baby girl to be raised by other people just to increase her social skills.

He shook his head. "No, not at all. More like college. They'd be grown, but this would allow them to get out into the world while still being in a safe, supernatural environment. We saw the positive effects of the communities when bonds began surfacing. Now that we know how common mixed-race connections are, we were thinking our next step after the communities are mostly finished should be colleges."

Well, that didn't actually sound terrible.

"Like, with lecturers?" Sam asked with a raised brow that lifted her nearly white hair out of her blue eyes. "What would the kids learn?"

The more people spoke and asked questions, the more I could see the benefits of this. Especially for teenagers like my cousin Benjamin who'd had a tough time over the last few years. He yearned for more than the community he'd grown up in, but it was all he'd ever known. Not knowing where to go when he knew he felt so strongly about getting away was a shitty thing to watch him go through.

Thankfully, he'd made some new friends as our community grew, which had helped not only him, but his mom Reah. She was once again a participating member within the community. Seeing her grow stronger within herself every day was something I enjoyed.

Cait leaned forward, her smile growing as she answered Sam's previous question. "As much as they can or are interested in. Some can go just meet others and experience life outside of their communities. Some might want to learn how to become one of the enforcers and take defensive classes. Others could be interested in deepening their magic. Whatever it is, we'd try to offer it."

Sam glanced over at Jackson. "We could have fun with that, mate. What do you think?"

He scratched the short, golden curls on his head and shrugged. "Whatever you want, babe."

She turned back to Cait. "Count us in as long as the pack can spare us. I'd love to teach defensive classes to some kids."

After the few encounters I'd had with the small shifter, I'd learned she was all bite and very little talk. I wasn't sure she was the best choice for a teacher because of that, but maybe that was more the parent in me thinking.

Roman raised his hands as more of us started chatting about the possibilities. "While we're glad you don't hate the idea, we're getting ahead of ourselves. Let's get the communities stabilized first and then circle back to this. But as long as we have your support, we'll be searching for locations that could be used and putting more information in writing."

"Well, if all you were looking for was our approval, then you have it, along with our support," Vaughn said with a wide smile. "Now, let's get that barbeque going. I'm starving."

Kelly shook her head and sighed, but love for her mate still emanated from her eyes.

Foster pressed his lips to my temple, and a shiver ran down my spine when his contentment spread through our bond.

More than five years later and he still took my breath away.

Looking around at our friends who were more like family, I leaned back against his chest and let out a happy sigh.

The road to this point hadn't been easy, but we'd made it through together. More importantly, I knew that whatever came next, good or bad, we'd face that together, too.

My head turned to Foster as the chatter started up again and before the kids could come toddling back to us. I pressed my lips to his and smiled, letting our foreheads rest together. "I love you."

His chest rumbled, and his palms pressed in on my sides. "I love you and this life you've given us."

My mate liked to believe I was responsible for bringing all of us together, but I didn't think so. I briefly glanced up at the sky and knew we were all destined to find our way to each other, thanks to a certain Moon Goddess and whatever friends she had up there.

I laced one of my hands through his and grinned. *Aspie has her GiGi and lots of aunts and uncles around. I bet she wouldn't miss us if we disappeared for a bit.*

His eager growl echoed through my mind. *Maybe we could give her that little brother she's been asking for.*

Just when I thought my heart couldn't get any fuller...

Follow my lead, I said giddily.

I'll follow you anywhere, Mate.

Keep reading to find out what to expect next for Mystics and Mayhem! Also, join my reader group for exclusive teasers and other fun updates!

AFTERWORD

First, let me just say…WOW!! Four series in this world already. I knew I wanted to get here some day, but I wasn't sure that would ever happen. As of now, we're going to call these first four "Phase One" of the Mystics and Mayhem world. A phase that is now complete! **insert all the happy dancing**

If you haven't read the other books in this world, here is the recommended reading order: Broken Court(Lucinda and Finn), Luna Marked(Cait and Roman), Scorned by Blood(Amersyn and Maciah), then Fated to the Wolf(Foster and Andie).

You've just gotten to know the other leading characters in this last book, but besides a confirmation that they end up together, there are no other spoilers you need to worry about between series.

Now, for Phase Two. That is coming sometime next year. There will be another wolf shifter trilogy and this one will feature Dawsyn, Cait and Roman's daughter who you just saw in the epilogue. She will be grown, in her 20s, and off on her own, experiencing the supernatural world for herself.

I hope you're excited to see this world continuing! I'm not

positive what future books look like, but this next series will be the only one that has a child of past main characters as the lead.

I have plenty of other ideas. Though, the rest is up to you! Your continued support guides my decisions heavily and I can't wait to share what's to come.

Thank you again for reading and for supporting my dreams!

STAY IN TOUCH

Find Heather on Facebook:
Reader Group:
Want to talk all things books and get updates before anyone else? Come hang with me in my reader group!
Heather Renee's Book Warriors

Author Page:
Teaser and big updates are also posted here!
Heather Renee Author

Newsletter:
I send this out sporadically. Don't worry. You won't ever be spammed by me and you get a couple goodies when you sign up!
http://smarturl.it/HeatherReneeNL

ALSO BY HEATHER RENEE

Fated to the Wolf (A Mystics and Mayhem Series)

A complete New Adult Witch and Wolf series (dual POV) featuring an abandoned witch, a rogue wolf, and their broken bond.

Scorned by Blood (A Mystics and Mayhem Series)

A New Adult Vampire series featuring a supernatural hunter and the sexy vampire bound to protect her no matter the cost.

Luna Marked (A Mystics and Mayhem Series)

A complete New Adult wolf shifter series (dual POV) featuring a strong-willed leading lady and a patient, yet fierce alpha male.

Broken Court (A Mystics and Mayhem Series)

A complete New Adult Urban Fantasy series featuring an unconventional and anti-heroine leading lady, a broody love interest, and a fae kingdom with a vile king.

Royal Fae Guardians

A complete Young Adult Urban Fantasy series featuring fae, magic users, a sweet romance, along with snark and humor.

Shadow Veil Academy

A complete Upper Young Adult Urban Fantasy Academy series featuring shifters, elves, witches, and more.

Elite Supernatural Trackers

A complete New Adult Urban Fantasy series featuring witches, demons, a smart-mouthed female lead, alpha males, and a snarky fairy sidekick.

Raven Point Pack Series

A complete Upper Young Adult Paranormal Romance series featuring wolves, witches, vengeance, and fated mates.

Blood of the Sea Series

A complete Young Adult Paranormal Romance series featuring

vampires, open seas adventures, and the occasional pirate.

Standalone

Marked Paradox - A complete Young Adult Fantasy fae story about a realm divided and one fae to bring them back together.

ABOUT THE AUTHOR

Heather Renee is a USA Today Bestselling author who lives in Oregon. She writes Paranormal Romance and Urban Fantasy novels with a mixture of romance, humor, and sass. Her love of reading eventually led to her passion of writing and giving the gift of escapism.

When Heather's not writing, she's spending time with her loving husband and beautiful daughter, going on their own adventures. She loves to hear from her fans, so visit her website: www.HeatherReneeAuthor.com and check out the Contact Me page for ways to connect.